The Heat Is On

"Who's the dead guy?"

"Antonio Marcotti. He owns Bella Luna, the Italian restaurant on Lakeshore Drive."

"How'd he die?"

"He was stabbed. Repeatedly."

"Crime of passion." He looked at her when he came to a stop sign. "Were you passionate about the guy?"

"Me? No way. I was mad at him because he tried to stiff me with a high-priced dish, but not mad enough to kill him."

"No hanky-panky going on the side?"

"Ugh. No." She shuddered at the thought.

"Okay. I'd advise you to stick to the facts next time you're being interviewed, and don't offer anything extra. Got it?" He pulled up in front of the office.

"Next time?"

"Oh yeah. They're not finished with you, not if they're checking your clothes for traces of blood or anything else that might prove you did it."

D0468945

TOASTING UP TROUBLE

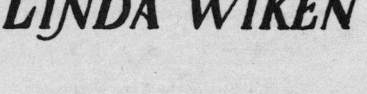

LINDA WIKEN

BERKLEY PRIME CRIME, NEW YORK

BERKLEY
PRIME
CRIME

An imprint of Penguin Random House LLC
375 Hudson Street, New York, New York 10014

TOASTING UP TROUBLE

A Berkley Prime Crime Book / published by arrangement with the author

ISBN: 9780425278215

PUBLISHING HISTORY
Berkley Prime Crime mass-market edition / July 2016

PRINTED IN THE UNITED STATES OF AMERICA

10 9 8 7 6 5 4 3 2 1

Cover illustration by Anne Wertheim.
Cover design by Katie Anderson.
Interior text design by Laura K. Corless.

Penguin
Random
House

To Mom and Dad—
Tack för allt!
I miss you.

Acknowledgments

Starting a brand-new series is both exciting and daunting. What makes the journey such a delight are the many who join in along the way.

I'm very touched to have the support of my sister, Lee McNeilly, who doles up equal amounts of encouragement and comments as my first reader. My long-time partner in crime, first as co-owners of a mystery bookstore, and now as a fellow writer and inspiration, Mary Jane Maffini, aka Victoria Abbott, is never too busy to read my words and tactfully steer me on the right path. Thanks, also to the amazing group of friends who were there from the beginning, my critiquing group, The Ladies' Killing Circle: Joan Boswell, Vicki Cameron, Barbara Fradkin, Mary Jane Maffini, Sue Pike, and the late Audrey Jessup.

I couldn't ask for a more terrific team at Berkley Prime Crime—my delightful editor, Kate Seaver, and Katherine Pelz, assistant editor; the eagle-eyed copyeditor; the very creative artist who does my cover work; and, the extremely energetic publicist, Danielle Dill.

My agent, Kim Lionetti from BookEnds Literary Agency, is one very savvy person who provides guidance, nurturing, and some killer titles. Thanks, as always, Kim!

Thanks also to the booksellers, librarians, reviewers, bloggers, and readers who make this all worthwhile.

I'd also like to acknowledge the cooking wizardry of Nigella Lawson, whose cookbook *nigellissima* is the basis for the very first Dinner Club Mystery. The ideas are all hers; the tweaking is all mine. What fun it's been eating my way through this menu.

And, an apology to the friendly folks in Burlington, Vermont, where the series is set. I so enjoy my visits both in person and in writing. However, you may be puzzled. I've taken liberties with the geography and inserted the scenic village of Half Moon Bay at your Northern edges. It is fictitious, and I hope you will welcome the locale and its food loving, sleuthing characters.

CHAPTER 1

"You know, it doesn't count if you eat a truffle on a Friday. Calorie-wise, that is. Especially if it's the first Friday of the month."

J.J. Tanner grinned at her friend and colleague, Skye Drake, then popped the chili dark chocolate truffle into her mouth. She closed her eyes as she chewed and finished it off with a long sigh. "What about eating two truffles?"

"Don't push it," Skye answered, laughing. "So tell me, what do you think? Aren't they to die for?"

"Oh yeah. I'd go for it, Skye. I think we could work these into any event, and I like the idea that we'd be the exclusive distributor for the truffles. And maybe as part of this new venture, she'll keep us in our own personal supply."

Skye slid out from behind her desk at Make It Happen, the event-planning business she owned, and struck a goddess pose. "You think this body needs any more calories?" She looked down at herself and smirked. "Not likely. You, on the other hand, my slender young nymph, are welcome to my share if this comes to pass."

"Young," J.J. sniffed. "I do recall us being classmates at Champlain College, and it wasn't yesterday, you know. Are you finding it more difficult to remember things these days?" She flashed a grin. "Anyway, happy to help, as always. So this means the corporate bash is wrapped up?"

"As ready to go as it will be. Saturday night is my big event, and I'll be very relieved when it's over. It doesn't matter how many years I've worked as an event planner—I always hold my breath until cleanup begins. How is your Italian princess party coming along?" Skye hefted a hip and sat on the edge of her desk and folded her arms across her chest. She wore her long blonde hair up in a chignon on days when she had meetings with clients. Today had been one of those days.

J.J. sighed. "I'm excited about it. The Italian part of the theme is a done deal. After all, what else would it be when the sweet twenty-one-year-old-to-be is of Italian heritage? And I think the 'princess' is delighted with my suggestion of making it an Italian Designer Delight. Everyone invited is being asked to carry or wear in some manner an Italian designer item. Angelica Portovino wants to be a fashion designer herself, you know. She's a very fashion-conscious gal, even though her purchases are far out of line with most twenty-one-year-olds I know. But with a wealthy Italian dad who's made it big in technology, the sky's the limit, so to speak."

"You've been waiting to use that one, haven't you?"

"Absolutely. Seriously, it will all come together once I have the replacement caterer and menu wrapped up."

"Who's at the top of your list?"

"Someone in my book club suggested Antonio Marcotti. She was at an event he catered last year, and she's eaten at his restaurant several times since then. She says the guy's a marvel with food. Italian, of course."

"Is he the one who owns the place on Lakeshore Drive?"

"Yup. Bella Luna. I was pleased that he did agree to take on the job when I phoned him earlier this week. It's such short notice, but when I'd filled him in on the theme, along with a couple of food requests from the client and the budget, he said it all sounded fine. Actually, I think the name of the client was the major selling point. We have a meeting on Monday afternoon to go over the menu."

"Sounds like a good fit. And talk about lucky. Think about it: if the original caterer had been even one week later in giving notice, you might have been up that proverbial creek without a paddle."

"Don't I know it." J.J. looked at the clock that hung above the credenza that doubled as a coffee station. She started to tidy her desk. "I really can't believe Marcotti is able to fit this event in at such short notice. I take that as a good omen."

"And what about your own personal food dilemma?"

"Ah, you mean the one where I have to come up with a cookbook and then choose an entrée from it, and, furthermore, actually prepare it for the Culinary Capers? My second hosting of the dinner club?"

"That would be the one."

"I don't have anything in mind yet, but I'm on it."

"I wouldn't be a good friend if I didn't point out that it's been nearly a week since the last dinner-club evening. That's right, isn't it? One week on Sunday?" Skye peered over the red frames of her reading glasses.

"Are you enjoying this inquisition?"

Skye smiled. "Yes, I am. Thanks for asking."

"I have had other things on my mind—namely work, boss. But it won't be a problem. Tomorrow morning we're all meeting at Beth's coffee shop, and I'll announce the name of the cookbook, hence the need to hit the bookstore tonight. That'll still give everyone two weeks to go out and buy the book, or borrow it, and come up with a dish to go along with the entrée I choose. I'm sort of leaning toward Italian."

"Hmm, wonder where that comes from?"

"You're right. I think I'm on a roll. I'm even dreaming in Italian these days. In fact, I may just ask Antonio Marcotti for a few suggestions. However, it still remains that the major problem with choosing the main course is the part about having to cook it myself."

"Oh, come on, now. You pulled off the last dinner you hosted, didn't you? Everyone loved the whatchamacallit you made."

J.J. sighed. "You can't go too wrong with chicken jambalaya. There was a reason I chose a Southern cookbook, you know. But I do think my period of grace is coming to an end. I've been a member of Culinary Capers for six months now. I really need to come up with something a bit more complicated, or I could lose my spot. And I'm trying. How does this sound—al dente or al forno, sautéed or seared? Don't I sound like I know what I'm talking about?"

Skye gave her a thumbs-up.

J.J. sat back and laughed. "Wow, who'd have thought I'd actually be contemplating making an elaborate meal?"

"Could have knocked me over with a feather when you said you were joining the dinner club," Skye answered with mock sincerity.

J.J. threw the small stuffed beaver, the revered mascot from their college days that sat on her desk for just such moments, at Skye. "Thanks for the support."

"You're welcome, and remember who you bring the leftovers to." Skye waited a beat before continuing. "By the way, since the princess party is still two weeks away, are you able to meet with a new client tomorrow?"

J.J. paused in the middle of corralling her hair in a ponytail. She knew it was seriously time for a haircut but, wouldn't you know it, the week she'd planned it, her hair had fallen just right, in soft curls well below her shoulders. And even the bangs had behaved. Now, if only it could be that agreeable the rest of the month. She picked a long dark brown hair off her white cashmere top. "Business is really picking up these days. That's two new clients this week, right? Which one is mine?"

Skye walked back around her desk and scrolled down her computer screen before answering. "Her name is Olivia Barker and she's the communications person for Kirking Manufacturing. They're planning, to quote her, "a very special retirement party" in I think she said five months."

"I love a client with a long timeline. It sounds like fun. Who's on your list? And I hope it's a long way off also. I know you have that fund-raiser coming up next month."

"Don't remind me."

"Still having problems with the chairperson?"

"She is a diva in her own mind. Very much the reason I prefer dealing with the male gender."

"So that's why I get Ms. Barker," J.J. shot back, smiling all the while.

Skye shrugged. "You might get lucky. She may be a gem."

"Perhaps. Or I may need to do a little polishing along with the planning. Is there anything I can help you with?"

The phone rang before Skye had a chance to reply. She shook her head in answer while picking up the receiver. J.J. watched her old friend and, more recently, her boss as she wound a thick strand of blonde hair that had escaped its bonds around her finger. *She's tired.* It had been a long week, what with the current client list and the new ones being added, as well as trying to come up with ideas that would revamp their website. They weren't yet at the stage where they had too many clients.

J.J. could help with the former but not the latter, although she loved tossing out ideas. That's the part she loved the most about being an event planner—not the final product, but the process of creating it. She smiled as she checked her e-mail for a final time that day. She was lucky to have landed on her feet, in such good company and in such a beautiful place. Half Moon Bay in Burlington, Vermont, skirting Lake Champlain. She truly was one lucky gal.

CHAPTER 2

"Let's see . . . Canadian, French, Greek. Here we go, Italian," J.J. said softly to herself as she walked along the cookbook aisle at Book Titles, the newly renovated independent bookstore on her route home after work. She needed that cookbook tonight.

She scanned the titles and authors and pulled out the ones that looked of interest to flip through. She liked looking at the pictures. That was her downfall. While she loved the whole idea of cooking elaborate meals, her forte was in the reading of cookbooks. She had an entire four shelves reserved for those books, part of a large bookcase that ran the length of one wall in her apartment. But only cookbooks with large and colorful photos of the dishes. She'd buy them according to the themes and photos, then look through them over and over, enjoying a vicarious thrill seeing someone else's labor right there in bright colors.

And although her friend Evan Thornton had persuaded her to join the Culinary Capers dinner club, she secretly believed she would never have caved if it hadn't been for this one weakness. The one obsession that cost her money but was not a vice. Cookbooks. Okay, she admitted to herself, buying mysteries was another passion that fell into the same category. But now she could really indulge in cookbooks without a twinge of guilt.

She grinned as she started flipping through the pages of *nigellissima* by Nigella Lawson. Great photos, easy-to-read recipes—although she had no idea how complicated they might be—and, best of all, Italian food. She quickly scanned the rest of the cookbook section and then made her way to the checkout clutching her prize. It would be an Italian night at casa Tanner.

She drove home quickly, unlocked the door to her apartment, and slid through before Indie, her two-year-old Bengal cat, could dash out into the hallway. That had happened on more than one occasion, resulting in a test of wills: one demanding to be outside and on the prowl; the other insisting that Indie was an indoor cat. She'd compromised by setting up a portion of her large wraparound balcony as a cat playground complete with a large patch of real grass. Of course, the mesh blocking the sides and top were what gave J.J. peace of mind, while Indie didn't seem to mind too much, except when trying to catch a bird midflight.

She checked her phone messages—a reminder her car needed servicing, a hang-up, and the chance to win a fabulous vacation, all of which she deleted—and then dished out some canned food for Indie and tossed a green salad for herself.

As she ate, she eyed her briefcase on the floor by the kitchen counter. No, she wouldn't go over that budget tonight. She didn't even know why she'd brought it home. She'd made herself a promise when she left her old life behind—no more late nights working on a project. Her own life was as important as her job. She would be kinder to herself.

She found herself thinking back to her days as an account planner with the high-profile advertising agency McCracken and Watts in Montpelier, Vermont. Just before she got bogged down once again in thoughts about Patrick Jenner, her ex-fiancé, she shook her head and reached over to pull her new cookbook out of its bag. She ran her hand gently over the cover before opening it. She had to admit, she was a cookbook junkie. She loved the colors, the travelogues that accompanied her favorites from overseas, and the feeling that she actually knew her food.

She did realize, though, that loving cookbooks did not a good cook make. Oh what she'd give for osmosis. She sighed and finished eating her salad. She couldn't wait to share *nigellissima* with the others in the club. But that would have to wait for their planning session.

J.J. sipped her espresso while watching the dwindling lineup of people ordering their coffee and, hopefully for Beth's bottom line, something sweet to go with it. Beth Brickner kept smiling, although J.J. bet her feet hurt by now. It was eleven A.M. and the Cups 'n' Roses coffee bar had opened at seven. J.J. knew that Beth tended the front counter with the help of one barista for the first couple of hours. After that, the part-timers started their shifts but Beth held her ground at the cash. She enjoyed the customers, as she'd once said.

As if she realized she was being watched, Beth looked over and smiled, transforming her sixty-four-year-old face to about twenty years younger, J.J. thought, and she smiled in return. Her attention shifted to the front door and the two people walking through it. Connor Mac and Alison Manovich, two more of the Culinary Capers members. When Evan Thornton arrived, Beth would slip away from her duties and join the other members.

After collecting his usual mochachino, Connor slid in beside

J.J. in the group's regular booth, which formed a semicircle in the right corner of the shop, with most of it facing the street. It was J.J.'s favorite spot, and it allowed her to watch the passersby and, admittedly, led to distractions at times, especially when the discussion focused on cooking techniques.

"You're looking great, J.J.," Connor said, reaching over to squeeze her hand. "I've been meaning to call you, but the week just slipped by. Are you free for dinner tonight?" He ran his right hand across the slight growth of beard on his chin.

J.J. gave about two seconds' thought to playing hard to get. After all, Connor was gorgeous and was probably used to women falling all over him. And what self-respecting single gal would admit to being available at the last minute on a Saturday night? But she felt comfortable with Connor, and she knew that after about six months of dating, this was as exciting as it would get between them. That was okay. She was all for friendship. Dinner would be good, and she said so.

"Great. I'll pick you up at six? Thought we'd try that new spot downtown, the Hidden Keg." He leaned closer and lowered his voice. "In fact, I second-guessed you and already made reservations. Hope you don't take that the wrong way."

J.J. shrugged. "Of course not. They'd be easy enough to cancel if I said no and you couldn't find another date." She was teasing him and he knew it.

"Okay. See this spot over here on the bench?" He pointed beside him and slid over the few inches. "I know my place."

"And I know my place is in this chair," Alison said, setting her plate with two sour cream twists down beside her mug of regular coffee. "Hey, Connor, J.J. How's it going?"

"Good, although hectic," J.J. answered first. "What about you, Alison? Keeping the bad guys in their places?"

Alison sighed, took a long sip, and sat back in the chair. She looked like a teenager when she went casual, like the jeans and T-shirt with the hoodie over top that she was wearing today. Fortunately, her police uniform seemed to add several years, along with that necessary air of authority, when she was working. "Tell me about it. For a small village, Half Moon Bay does have more than its share of loonies, I sometimes think."

"As long as they're not dangerous, too," Connor muttered.

"No, they're usually not. They seem to leave their weapons behind. Or they're saving them for downtown Burlington. Thankfully."

J.J. hadn't noticed Evan enter until he slid in beside her on the other side, placing a medium cappuccino in front of her. "Beth says this'll save you having to get up and fetch your own. She'll be right over. Howdy, all."

"Wow, Evan. Is that a swath of gray I spy in your hair?" Alison asked playfully.

Evan ran his right hand lightly over the spot in his short red hair. "It is. Do you think it makes me look worldlier?"

Alison took a closer look. "Not really, sorry."

"All right, how about more scholarly? I'll settle for that."

"Oh, definitely," Alison agreed and took a quick sip that almost covered her grin.

"Huh."

"Well, I think it makes you look worldly, scholarly, and older, which translates into trustworthy, even with all those freckles," Beth chimed in, taking the empty chair beside Alison. She missed Evan's grimace but knew that would be his response. "Keep it, Evan. It really looks good, whatever the adjective."

Evan smiled. "Why, thank you, Beth, arbiter of good taste."

"Oh boy. Before we get carried away with the niceties, what have you got for us, J.J.? At what level have you set the bar?" Alison asked.

J.J. looked around the table, a big smile on her face. "All right, here goes: I'd like to introduce you to Nigella Lawson." She flipped over the cookbook she'd had sitting on the table in front of her, and balanced it upright. "*Nigellissima* is my choice for the next Culinary Capers dinner."

She glanced around from one to another, hoping to see her own excitement mirrored in each of the faces. Okay, that might have been asking too much. No one ever leaped up for joy right at the reveal. She started flipping through the pages. "Great photos, aren't they? I'll pass it around and you can all have a more thorough look. I bought it just last night, so I haven't had time to really read it through carefully, but I might go with the beef pizzaiola. So, if I do the meat dish, we need a pasta to start with, followed by my pièce de résistance—I know I'm mixing my countries here—and then two side dishes, and a dessert."

Beth looked at the index in the back of the book, running her finger slowly down the names of the dishes. "This looks like it could be fun."

She passed it to Alison, who did the same. After it had made its way around the table, J.J. leaned forward, crossing her arms on the table. Her desire that they should all buy into this choice had intensified as the others had checked it out. "So, what say you? Is it a go?"

Connor laughed. "You are into this one, aren't you? As I remember, last time you winced and shrugged your way through our checking out the book."

J.J. sighed. "You're right. Last time I just chose something I thought would be doable. This time, I was enthralled looking through the cookbook, and I'm hoping that will translate into a delectable meal."

"Well, if that's the vibe you're getting, then I'd say we should all be on board," Evan said. "I vote yes." He looked around the table, and the others nodded their agreement. "There. A done deal, J.J."

"Great. I hope you don't mind that this book is at the upper end of the price range we'd set."

Alison finished her cappuccino before speaking. "I'll probably just borrow it from the library again. But I'm happy to try out a side dish."

"Dibs on dessert," Beth added.

"Guess I'll take the other side dish and we'll confer, Alison," Connor said. "What does that leave for Evan?"

"That would be the pasta," J.J. pointed out.

Evan thought about it for less than a minute. His eyes lit up as he announced, "I've been thinking lately about buying a pasta machine to make my own fresh pasta. This is the kick in the pants I need to do just that. Besides, Michael can't object to the expense if it's for the dinner club." He grinned.

"I can't picture Michael objecting to anything you decide to do." Beth had taken on that motherly tone she sometimes used with Evan. J.J. wondered if he noticed it. But if he did, he never let on. Or maybe he enjoyed it.

Even though Beth was at least two decades older than the others—retired now for five years from being a high school music teacher, and owner of the Cup 'n' Roses for two years— the difference in ages wasn't a big deal.

"That's great. So, *nigellissima* it is, and we feast on these wonderful recipes at my place in three weeks."

Heaven help me.

CHAPTER 3

J.J. glanced at the large circular wooden clock that hung on the wall above the water cooler. The morning seemed to be dragging—not unusual for a Monday, she admitted. She was about to make that comment to Skye yet again when the phone rang. Skye grabbed it.

J.J. waited a few beats to make sure the call wasn't for her and then reached for her own phone. She'd left a message for her new client, Olivia Barker, the previous Friday but hadn't heard back yet. She knew the signs of a busy client, but she did need to start the flow of information if this event was to be successful. Great timing. Barker took her call, and after half an hour J.J. hung up and eyed the several pages of notes she'd made, eager to get to the planning. Fortunately, it wasn't a rush job, not with five months until the event, because she had to focus on the event earmarked next on her calendar.

She called up the Portovino file on her computer. She

wanted to take another look at what she'd budgeted for the catering for IDD, or the Italian Designer Do as she thought of the Portovino birthday party.

She gave her notes a final perusal before printing them out and tucking them into a folder to take along to the meeting she had arranged with the new and last-minute caterer, Antonio Marcotti, for two thirty P.M. She just hoped he'd respected the budget when coming up with a menu for the affair. She knew that Marcotti's prices could be in the high range, but she did have that budget as the bottom line. However, she also realized that a really outstanding food experience was worth the price. But what if the price was outside the budget?

J.J. checked her watch, her right hand ready to push open one of the double glass doors. She took a quick look down at the short green leather jacket she'd chosen to go with her long black-and-white jersey blouse, black skinny pants, and open-toed black leather booties. She felt confident. She *was* confident. Time to make it happen. *Bella Luna, la cucina italiana* was etched on both doors along with bunches of grapes hanging from a grape vine. She was right on time. Hopefully, Chef Antonio Marcotti had indeed made himself available, as promised.

The lunch-hour crowds were thinning out, and only two tables had diners finishing what looked to be desserts.

She waited a few minutes at the hostess desk close to the front door, and when no one appeared, she made her way toward the kitchen, at the far end of the room. She stopped about two feet away when the swinging doors flew open and a tall dark-haired beauty pushed through with a tray of two espresso cups and a small bowl of flaked chocolate.

"No one is allowed in the kitchen," she said, sailing past

J.J. After depositing the espressos, she returned to J.J. and asked, "What can I do for you?"

"I'm here to see Mr. Marcotti. I'm J.J. Tanner. We have an appointment at two thirty . . ." She peered at the woman's nametag and added, "Lucy."

"I will tell Chef Marcotti that you are here." She disappeared through the door.

J.J. picked up a menu from a stack perched on the end of the bar that spanned the length of the remaining wall. She sat on a bar stool and scanned the items. Gnocco frito or Tuscan spiced crisp dumplings. Nodini or warm bread knots, olive oil, rosemary, garlic, and sea salt. Olive calde or warm marinated olives. Her mouth was watering already. She stopped herself from turning to the dessert page, knowing all would be lost at that point.

The doors flew open again, and this time it was a swarthy-skinned man in a white chef's tunic, top buttons undone to allow the flap to lie against the right side. Touches of gray highlighted the black hair that curled out around the edges of the jacket and his chef's hat. *The complete picture*, J.J. thought, then stood and held out her hand. "Good to see you, Chef Marcotti. Thank you for taking the time to meet in person." She realized he was a fraction shorter than her five foot six.

Marcotti gave her hand a quick, firm shake. "Signorina Tanner, please join me for an espresso." It was a rhetorical question as he led the way to a table for four in a corner far from the customers. As soon as they were seated, Lucy appeared with their espressos, a tiny dish of flaked chocolate with a tiny silver spoon, and a plate of chocolate-dipped biscotti. She also handed Marcotti a small pile of papers and, after eyeing J.J. thoroughly, left them alone.

Marcotti took his time stirring a small spoonful of chocolate shavings into his espresso, appreciating the fragrance, and then taking a sip. He then waited for J.J. to do the same before starting to speak.

He shoved the papers toward her. "Let us get right down to business. I am a busy man and cannot take too much time away from the kitchen. This is the menu I've proposed for the Portovino party, along with the cost of each item. If you'd like to take a few minutes to read it all over, and if there are any questions . . ." He let the suggestion trail off.

J.J. went through the menu carefully, noting that he'd included all the items the client had asked for, along with some others that made up a well-balanced menu. She stopped at one item, especially when she noted the cost.

"I'm not sure we can include the funghi, Chef Marcotti. I don't really think we need it, do you? There's a wonderful variety already, and it really is more than the budget can afford." She had been firm on the exact amount of the budget.

Marcotti leaned back in his chair and folded his arms across his chest. "Funghi. Do you know what it is? It is seasonal mushrooms, sautéed to perfection with mascarpone, gorgonzola, and a touch of marjoram. Sensational. Perfect for an event such as this. The guests will love it and so will Signor Portovino, of that I am certain. It is my specialty, my signature dish. It must be included. You will have to adjust your budget in some other area."

J.J. bit her tongue, holding back the retort that begged to escape her lips. She took another sip of espresso, buying time to come up with a tactful response to the imperious person across from her.

"I can appreciate the quality of your special dish, Chef, but I really cannot afford it. There's nothing I can adjust at this point. I will certainly keep it in mind for some future event, though. It does sound delicious." She hoped her smiled looked sincerely apologetic.

He scowled. "Ms. Tanner, you are the one who came to me, begging me to help, and on such short notice. You should have come to me in the first place, you know."

She almost expected him to shake his finger at her, but he continued without any added gestures, except to cross his arms in a confrontational pose.

"You asked for my advice. I give it to you. You do not take it. That is not a good working relationship. I have not worked with your company before, and it's only because I know of your client that I have agreed to do this. I am very much in demand, you know. I have adjusted my schedule to meet with you. Now, in return, I ask that you adjust your budget."

J.J. tried counting to ten. She would not let her one-quarter Irish temper on her mother's side get the better of her. "I will have to get back to you on that, Chef Marcotti." *With the same answer.* Time to deflect. "I see you have a Venetian stew on your menu, and I was wondering: what ingredients do you use in it?" She'd spotted the same dish in *nigellissima* and had briefly thought about trying it, until she'd noticed the long list of ingredients, most of which she'd never heard of.

Marcotti tilted his head and looked at her for a few seconds before answering. "Why do you want to know? Are you planning on attempting to make it?"

A small laugh escaped J.J.'s lips. "No, it's just that it sounds tantalizing. Believe me, I'm not a very good cook. But I do belong to a dinner club, the Culinary Capers. And I'm the host next month. I'm doing an Italian theme. Can you recommend where I should shop for ingredients?"

"Now you want my help with your little cooking adventure? You really are too much, Ms. Tanner." He stood up. "I will expect to hear back from you in two days at the latest. I cannot hold a spot on my schedule for you if you cannot agree to my requests. And just remember, a Marcotti event is one that will be remembered."

He turned on his heel and marched back into the kitchen, leaving J.J. to stare openmouthed. She felt the heat rising on her face. She looked around to see if anyone had heard. She felt mortified along with being plenty angry. So he hadn't appreciated her attempt to steer the conversation to what she thought would be safer ground.

She looked at the door through which he'd disappeared and then down at the plate and chose the largest biscotti. She ate it slowly, finishing the espresso, which was now cold, and tried to look tranquil. After blotting her lips on the white linen serviette, she gathered the papers into her briefcase and left with as much dignity as she could muster.

The practiced feeling of calm had left her by the time she reached the office. She marched over to her desk, dropped the briefcase on the floor—forgetting how much she'd paid for it—and started pacing until Skye eventually finished her call and hung up the phone.

"What?" Skye asked.

"That overbearing, officious jerk."

"Not the best of meetings, I take it."

"Do you know what he said?" And J.J. proceeded with a detailed rendering of the encounter.

"Huh."

"His requests." J.J. almost spat out the words; she was still angry. "His arrogant demands. I—we—have a client. Marcotti is also working for that client." J.J. finally sat down. "What would you have done?"

Skye shrugged. "I'm not sure. I probably would have handled it much the same, although I think I'd have fewer facial expressions."

"What do you mean?"

"Oh, you know. I love playing poker with you. Everyone does. Your face reveals your inner thoughts, and I'm sure this Chef Marcotti got an eyeful even if your words were chosen with care. Oh, well. Tell me about the budget. How much over would this dish make it, and is there really no way to juggle it again?"

J.J. pulled out the page with the offending item on it and walked it over to Skye. "Guess which one it is."

"Ouch. I'm guessing it's the funghi at fifty-five dollars a pop. Man, that would add up to almost a quarter of the food budget. What would he suggest you cut out? The decorations?"

"Probably. I've kept the costs reasonable in other areas, knowing we'd have to splurge a bit on the food. And although Mr. Portovino is loaded, he's not a spendthrift. He has made that clear."

"So, what are you thinking of doing?"

"I'll wait a couple of days and then phone Marcotti. My answer, unless I can figure out a way to include this, will be a resounding no."

Skye walked over and gave her a quick hug. "It's your show. Your budget. Your decision. He will just have to accept that."

CHAPTER 4

The next morning, J.J. kept looking at the clock on the wall behind the head of the gorgeous blonde gazing at her computer at the reception desk of Portovino Technologies. J.J. didn't like to be kept waiting, but what could she do? This was Lorenzo Portovino, president and CEO of the largest high-tech business in Vermont. It was his timetable. She was doing this job for him. She must work on her lack of patience, she thought. Maybe some yoga classes?

Finally, almost twenty minutes later, another equally stunning blonde called her name from an open doorway. She held out her hand for a brief shake. "I'm Jasmine, Mr. Portovino's assistant. So nice to meet you after all our telephone calls."

She smiled, but J.J. didn't get the feeling there was much warmth behind it. Ms. Efficiency. She motioned and J.J. followed her down a short hall where she knocked on a door and opened it at the summons to come in.

J.J. stood in silence for a moment, taking in the mixture of

sleek modern furniture and total masculine presence. Portovino looked up from his desk and motioned for J.J. to sit down
across from him. Certain she wouldn't be able to escape out
of it gracefully, especially in the black pencil skirt she'd chosen
to wear, she sank into the comfort of a black leather chair. Her
power suit. She'd thought she'd need it, but she hoped she
wouldn't regret it. For now, she'd enjoy the moment.

"Sorry to keep you waiting, Ms. Tanner." He waved his
elegant hand in the direction of the phone. "Even with all our
amazing electronics, one cannot avoid using the telephone
and that, as you probably know, can make it difficult to attend
to matters quickly." He chuckled. "I think that sometimes,
rather than saving us time, e-mail can lead to wasting more
time when people actually talk to another human being. They
are so desperate for conversation, you know."

Portovino gave a quick nod, although J.J. hadn't said a
thing. "Now, you already have all the information you need
for the upcoming party to celebrate the twenty-first birthday
of my Angelica. I just wanted to meet with you one last time
to make certain everything we initially spoke about is on track.
I do have faith in your company since, as you know, I'm going
on the recommendation of my good friend Jonathan Porter.
But I do like to assure myself." He sat in silence for a few
moments, studying her. J.J. tilted her chin up slightly, kept a
pleasant look on her face, and tried not to squirm under the
scrutiny. This had been the routine at their previous meeting,
too. Finally, he said, "*Buono.* Now, please bring me up to date."

"I'm happy to. As you know, I've met with your daughter
and she's delighted with the Italian designer theme. I understand she's going to college next year to study fashion design,
so it seemed appropriate." She paused to see if there would
be a comment. He merely nodded.

"The decorations, as requested, will be discreet but very
much in keeping with the theme. We'll have several panels

of Italian street scenes installed on various walls in the dining room, which will be free of furniture to use for dancing. Out on the patio there will be frescoes of the Italian countryside—vineyards and villas."

"Yes, yes. This all sounds very tasteful, and I leave that in your hands. You've met with Angelica, and I trust that will be the basis of everything. You have the music, the caterer, sufficient staff?"

"All is under control," J.J. said, hoping he wouldn't ask for specifics. She had the feeling that, although he wanted to know she knew her instructions, he didn't really have the time to go into details. That was part of the reason all communications up to this point had been handled by his assistant over the phone.

She was right. Portovino stood and extended his hand across the desk. "Good. Now, please feel free to contact my personal assistant, Jasmine, if you have any questions or need anything done."

J.J. got out of the chair as gracefully as she could manage and shook his hand.

As if she'd been summoned, or perhaps had been waiting outside the door, the blonde reappeared. Tall, slender, and blonde, Jasmine was probably a fashion model on the side, thought J.J. She motioned for J.J. to follow her.

"Thank you, Mr. Portovino," J.J. said. "It will be an evening to remember, I assure you."

J.J. stood outside the office building enjoying the sun breaking through the clouds that had hung low all morning. The beacon of light illuminated the large wooden house number sign done in folk-art style, which seemed to be a good omen. In fact, the entire front façade of the place put its best foot forward in the welcoming glow.

Office building was really a misnomer. In fact, the

two-story white clapboard house with pale blue trim, built in the 1920s as a post office, had also seen life as a private home and now provided space for three businesses. The entire building was owned by Evan Thornton. He used the main floor for his interior design business, Design Delights. The staircase divided his business into its two halves—the design offices on the right and the showroom on the left.

The upper floor had also been divided in half. To the right it housed Make It Happen, which was owned by Skye with J.J. as her one full-time staffer. The other half was leased to attorney Tansy Paine, someone, J.J. realized on first meeting her, that she'd never want to face in a courtroom.

Evan had appeared on the front porch, which wrapped around both sides of the house, while J.J. daydreamed. He waited for her to reach him before starting in with the questions.

"So tell me, how did your meeting with Antonio Marcotti go? That was today, wasn't it?" Evan had his hands in the pockets of his cream-colored chinos, and he leaned casually against the post. He wore a beige V-neck pullover with black triangles on it over a white shirt, and he'd pushed the sleeves of both up to his elbows. His sense of style usually drew eyes away from the fact that he was on the rotund side and his face hadn't lost its boyish cute looks. His red hair was so short on the sides and back that it looked more like fuzz, but the top sported a variety of lengths, all standing at attention and tinted a darker shade. Except for the now infamous gray patch.

J.J. could tell he was trying to look disinterested, though not too successfully. She sighed. "That was yesterday afternoon, and let's just say, it was not a mutual attraction."

He grimaced. "I'm sorry to hear that. Just watch your every step with him."

"What do you mean?"

Evan looked to be making a decision. "Let's just say he's an aggressive businessman." He shook his head. "He has ideas of his own and has to be charmed into realizing how wrong some of them are. You wouldn't believe all the drama we went through in redecorating his restaurant a couple of years ago." Evan started waving his hands around. "First it was leather for the bar, the base of the bar that is, the countertop was always to be quartz. Then he had second thoughts and wanted granite. Let's just say, my choice was the better one. Then, Marcotti totally pooh-poohed my suggestion of flannel suede for the upholstered chairs, demanding silk, which not only is subject to staining more easily but also costs more, too."

J.J. tried to remember what the chairs had looked like, wondering who had won that one. She re-focused on Evan's recital of tribulations.

"He was paying me big bucks but he had a mind of his own, and we clashed on many an occasion."

"So in the long run, who won?"

"It was probably a draw. He eventually saw the light on many things, especially the upholstery, while I agreed to rejig the budget—several times. I hope it all goes more smoothly for you." Evan sighed. "But he is a master in the kitchen, and I managed to put on a few pounds over those months. Much to Michael's chagrin. He's been trying to put me on a diet ever since."

J.J. leaned against the other side of the pole. "Well, Marcotti is doing the budget dance with me, too, but it's not my budget and I don't really have any wiggle room. Any suggestions on how to handle him?"

"First, get everything in writing. And then flattery, my pet. Every great artist loves to bathe in flattery. Just rave on about his dishes and lather it on heavily about how no one but him will do for this event. I'm sure that will do the trick."

"Hmmm. As much as that goes against my grain, I'll give it a try. I guess I should eat there first, or he may know I'm trying to pull a fast one."

She eyed Evan, a speculative look on her face. "Are you free for dinner at Bella Luna tonight, so I won't stand out being there all by myself? I'd hate to get cornered by Marcotti and have to talk to him. Not until we've settled things."

Evan hesitated. "Uh, I'm not really sure. I . . . Maybe another time."

"Please. Michael is welcome, also."

Evan shifted from one foot to the other. "Well, yeah, okay. If it's that important to you."

J.J. grinned. "Yes! That would be great. Thank you so much. Shall we meet there? I'll make reservations for six thirty."

Evan nodded.

J.J. gave him a quick kiss on the cheek. "You're a doll. See you then."

She almost skipped up the stairs to the office. She'd show Antonio Marcotti who was boss. Or at least, who had the final say on the budget.

CHAPTER 5

J.J. glanced around at the other tables in Bella Luna. It looked entirely different by night, with candles and dimmed lighting, and already almost three-quarters of the room was filled. Evan had just ordered the wine, an Italian nero d'Avolo, and was studying the antipasti section of the menu. Michael seemed a little preoccupied, or so J.J. thought. She hoped he wasn't annoyed at her for instigating the evening. He was such the opposite of Evan, with premature gray hair that looked a little shaggy around the ears, black-framed glasses, and a pipe sticking out of the breast pocket of his brown leather jacket, although she'd never seen him smoke it.

J.J. thought about her own outfit, a long-sleeved black-and-white wrap dress with tooled black leather booties that had taken her all of two seconds to decide on, and wondered what it might say about her.

"I read about the new picnic area for the Laurel Grove Arboretum in the newspaper this morning, Michael," J.J.

said, hoping to get him talking. Besides that, she loved hearing about his work as a landscape architect. Like with her cookbooks, it was seeing the project that interested her the most. She'd never make it as a gardener. "Wasn't that the design you worked on?"

Michael looked a bit startled, like he'd been elsewhere, which was probably true about his mind, anyway. "I read that also. As usual, they got it wrong. At least the bit about the footpath over the creek."

Evan excused himself and headed toward the restrooms. Michael watched him go and then leaned forward a bit. "I was wondering if this was such a good idea, coming here tonight."

J.J. felt startled. "Why wouldn't it be? Did Evan tell you about my meeting with Marcotti? Do you think I should just back off?"

"Your meeting? No. He hasn't said anything about it. I'm referring to the last time Evan and Marcotti met. Has he not told you?"

J.J. shrugged. "Not specifically. He did warn me that Marcotti can be a hard person to deal with, but he advised me to blitz the chef with praise in order to reach my end result."

Michael snorted. "I imagine he's succeeded in blocking it out, as he usually does with anything that's upsetting in his life." He shook his head, but he had a slight smile on his face. J.J. knew he was in his early forties, but at the moment, he looked about eleven. She often thought there was a lot more to Michael Cole than met the eye, and even though she'd often been over to their house, J.J. felt she didn't really know him very well.

"They had a major blowout," Michael went on. "Evan had a heck of a time getting paid, and each time he approached Marcotti, it got more vicious. Evan finally threatened to take him to small claims court. In fact, he'd started the process when Marcotti sent a check to him by courier. Shortly after, some rumors about Evan and his business started surfacing.

Of course, there's no real way to tie them to Marcotti. But he'd always threatened some such action if Evan didn't back off. We haven't been here since, although we used to dine here frequently."

Michael glanced around the room and J.J. did the same, wondering if Marcotti might get wind of their presence and come storming out of the kitchen. *That's fanciful*, thought J.J. *We're paying customers, and I'm certain Marcotti wouldn't want his other customers to know something like an unpaid bill—his own—was the source of bad blood.* She took a deep breath and tried to calm her fears. She stared at Evan as he made his way back to the table. Why hadn't he told her this part? And why had he agreed to come tonight? Oh, right. She'd begged him.

The server appeared with the wine and three glasses, and they went through the ritual of Michael sampling the first glass poured. Evan ordered a dish of prosciutto and pear along with some artichoke dip for them to share, then took a small taste of his wine. He gave an appreciative sigh and then lifted his glass in a toast.

"To J.J. We wish you much success with this event. I think being associated with Portovino Technologies could lead to many more events in your career."

J.J. clinked her glass with the other two and laughed. "Always the businessman at heart, Evan. You're probably right, though. I'm having fun working with his daughter right now. She's not the princessy type at all. Really levelheaded and knows what she wants, and she's also got an eye for fashion. She's even been giving me some pointers."

"And what could a twenty-one-year-old possibly teach you, my dear?"

"Leggings versus tights; Manolo Blahnik versus Jimmy Choo." J.J. stuck her right foot out from under the table, showing off her new booties.

Evan leaned over for a look. "Impressive. To me, those say *single, successful career woman who is no pushover.* I think you'd better wear them for the duration of this job."

"I know you've had some unpleasant dealings with Marcotti, Evan."

His eyes narrowed, Evan looked at Michael. Then he shrugged. "That's true. It's in the past and something I don't like to think about. I do still recommend the man's food, though. It is truly the food of the gods."

J.J. sat back in her chair. "I'll have to remember to read between the lines with you." She turned to Michael. "Is there anything else about Evan I should know?"

"He does have good taste," Michael admitted, "but not always good judgment." He looked pointedly in the direction of the kitchen door.

J.J. turned around, then quickly turned back at the sight of Marcotti stepping into the dining area. "What is he doing? Did he see us? Is he headed over here?" she asked Michael while making note that Evan had suddenly buried his head in the menu.

Michael chuckled. "You're both safe. He has his back to us and is receiving compliments, no doubt, from the table next to the door. Now, if he doesn't swan around the room in search of more accolades, you should be all right."

J.J. took a quick sip of her wine and also turned her attention to the menu. Nobody spoke until Michael gave the all clear. "I can see this was an excellent idea, coming here for a restful meal. He's gone back inside and let's hope he'll stay there."

The server came and took their orders, and only then did Evan come up for breath. "The food will be worth this discomfort. Believe me."

J.J. leaned over and touched his arm. "I believe you and will continue to do so in the future. No worries."

Michael shook his head and dipped a piece of Italian flat

bread in the olive oil–and–balsamic mixture left by the server.

Over dinner, they discussed everything from politics to Oprah to new movies in town. That's one thing J.J. particularly enjoyed about the couple: they were never at a loss for topics, and it was easy to linger over meals for hours of enjoyable conversation. By the time their checks arrived—J.J. had insisted on paying for them all but the guys wouldn't let her—she felt more relaxed than she had in days.

"I've really enjoyed tonight," she said as they stood to leave.

Evan kissed her on both cheeks, as did Michael, who said, "I think you should try Rocco G's for some help with your upcoming feast. Have you ever been there?"

"That's the bistro on Claymore Street that has a small shopping area tucked into the back? I've ducked in for an espresso from time to time but not really looked around."

"Rocco Gates is the owner, another Italian. I think you'll find him a lot more pleasant to deal with, and I know he'll be happy to give you advice on cooking."

J.J. thanked him and left the restaurant feeling she could conquer the world, or at least one dinner party.

CHAPTER 6

Friday morning, the day before the big event, dawned sunny with the promise of mild temperatures. The forecast for Saturday was even better, much to J.J.'s relief. She took a final look in the hall mirror and grabbed her briefcase after shrugging into her lightweight jacket. Penance for overindulging the previous evening when she'd attended the monthly meeting of another book club she belonged to, which always meant lots of chocolate desserts, was walking to work. However, on the beautiful spring day that awaited her outdoors, it was more like a treat. And if she gave it some thought, ten blocks wasn't that much of a hardship, she had to admit.

She had her hand on the door handle when Indie came bounding down the hallway and tried to edge between her and the door.

J.J. bent over and scooped him up with one hand, carrying him into the living room and depositing him on the back of the periwinkle blue loveseat in front of the window. "You enjoy the scenery from this spot, Indie. I'll take you out on a leash later today. I promise."

She hurried back to the door and let herself out, checking to make certain he hadn't squeezed through unseen. One of the reasons she'd chosen a Bengal cat was the breed's inquisitiveness and energy. Served her right!

The smell of bacon sifted under the door of the apartment next door. She hadn't seen her neighbor, Ness Harper, in a few days but knew he was in town from the assorted cooking odors that wafted along the hallway. A retired police officer and a bit of a recluse, he once explained to her that he'd become a fanatic about cooking in recent years. In fact, he'd appeared at her door the odd time with offerings of new dishes he'd tried. He'd had to admit to forgetting to halve the recipes and ending up cooking more than one person could eat, even with a day or so of leftovers. She'd tasted potential that first time and was always happy to oblige.

J.J. ran lightly down the stairs and out the front door, pausing to take a deep breath and just enjoy being out in the morning sun. She ramped up to a good pace once she'd reached the intersection of Bryden, her street, and Gabor Avenue, one of the main roads leading to the lakeside, where she turned left. Half Moon Bay, a suburb of Burlington, Vermont, was labeled a village and hugged the north end of Lake Champlain. It boasted its own four-block boardwalk and narrow sandy beaches and an assortment of stores and services that stretched three blocks.

At the far end of Lakeshore Drive, which skirted the bay, was the turnoff to the gated community of Forest Grove, the location of the Portovino estate. There were five similar large estates of an acre or more hugging the shoreline with equally magnificent houses set back and comprising the moneyed area of the village.

J.J. smiled at the sight of the lake getting ever closer. She never tired of the water and, in fact, had her own favorite spot near the south end of the boardwalk where it blended into a treed area. Several small clearings overlooking the lake were woven into the wilderness pathway that continued where the boardwalk ended. She paused for a final look at the view before turning left on Erin Street, one street past where her office was located. She stopped in at Cups 'n' Roses and got her usual latte to go. She debated waiting around for a quick chat with Beth, but eyeing the line, decided that work would be the more practical choice.

It had been an easy decision, and a wise one, for J.J. to make the move to Half Moon Bay when things had gone awry in Montpelier. A chance meeting with her old college classmate, Skye Drake, had led to a job offer in Skye's relatively new business, Make It Happen, and the rest, as they say, was history.

Climbing the stairs to the office, she itemized what had to be done today, the day before the big birthday bash. She couldn't believe how time had flown by. She'd certainly been kept busy keeping on top of all the details for the birthday, and most of it had gone smoothly. Of course, and she felt her shoulders tense as she thought of it, the hardheaded Antonio Marcotti had continued to present a challenge. In fact, it hadn't been until last Friday that he'd finally agreed to follow J.J.'s menu. She couldn't believe it had happened at long last.

She unlocked the office door. Skye had taken the day off. She'd driven to New York City the day before to pick up her dentist boyfriend, Nick Owens, on his return from a visit to his ailing mom in Ottawa. They had planned a leisurely drive back today, and J.J. didn't expect to hear from her until Monday morning.

She went through her morning routine of answering phone calls and e-mail before getting on with the most pressing business. For today, that was going over, yet again, the last-minute details for the birthday party. She wanted everything to be memorable for Angelica Portovino. She needed to connect with the small decorating company she'd hired. They should be ready to start at eight the next morning to hang the tasteful wall panels and string up the tiny white lights around the large stone patio.

Next on her list: checking in with the security company that would also be in charge of the valet service. She'd already spoken to the deejay, someone whom Connor had recommended, the day before and he'd assured her all was ready for the outdoor patio. A call to the managers of the string quartet planned for the buffet area and the live rock band for later in the evening confirmed that all was on track. And, of course, she'd need to connect once again with Marcotti. If she was lucky, he'd be busy and she could double check the time frame with his assistant.

By the time she'd cleared her list, the remaining coffee in her cup was cold and someone was knocking on the door. Before she could call out, the door was pushed open.

"J.J., sweetie, I need to talk to you." Tansy Paine didn't wait for an answer before scuttling over to drop into the white leather swivel chair across from J.J.'s desk. Her spiky red hair and the fact that she was always in motion at top speed made J.J. think of a deranged elf on the loose. Despite the fact that she must be on the late side of forty.

"Okay. What's on your mind, Tansy?" She hoped it wasn't the matter about Tansy wanting to talk Evan into paying to have both their offices painted. Tansy usually got what she wanted, although this time Evan had stood his ground, pointing out it had been only one year since the last time.

"I want you to talk to Evan. About the paint job. He always listens to you. In fact, if he didn't already have a partner and if his tastes were a little different, I'd bet he'd be making a play for you. Now, don't argue with me. Not about Evan and not about the paint." She paused to glance around the room. "This is such a bland color. Really. You'd think a happening business like this one would want vibrant tones to communicate to clients just how vital you are."

J.J. inwardly cringed at the pun although she knew Tansy hadn't done it on purpose. J.J. couldn't think of a thing to say. She tried changing the subject.

"I heard you won that big fraud case earlier this week."

"Yes, I did." Tansy seemed obviously pleased. "Now, back to the paint. I've written him a letter outlining all the reasons we need this done and done now. I'll drop it off on my way out to lunch and let him have the weekend to think about it. If he talks to you, I want you to back me on this, you hear?"

"I do hear you," J.J. answered. *But I won't back you.* She respected Evan's right to make his own decisions about his building.

"Good. I've given myself the rest of the day off, celebrating the win. The court case win, I mean, although I'm sure it's just a matter of time with Evan." Tansy paused at the door. "Good luck yourself. I guess the Portovino party is up next. I know that's your first big social event. I hear it's the talk of the social circuit."

"Thanks, Tansy," J.J. said as the door closed. Just what she wanted to hear. More pressure.

J.J. used her lunch break to walk the three blocks to Rocco G's on Claymore Street. She needed to put aside the Portovino project for a short period of time and clear her head, knowing that after lunch she'd be fueled to go over everything yet again.

The next Culinary Capers meal was also looming, and she hadn't really given it much thought. She'd checked to make sure she had the list of ingredients for the pizzaiola with her. She'd toyed with the idea of doing a test run of the dish, particularly since she'd decided to substitute turkey for beef, but decided that would take part of the excitement out of it. So for now, she was contenting herself with making sure she had everything in hand and, possibly, getting some cooking tips from Rocco Gates himself.

Since Michael had first suggested the place, J.J. had gone about finding out all she could about it. The website served up some interesting information: the business was celebrating its tenth year in the area, was owned by Rocco Gates, contained a store stocking ingredients from Italy as well as more local items, and offered cooking workshops. It was too late to take one of those, but J.J. filed the information away for future reference.

Rocco G's also provided a small bistro that served lunches and, on weekends, an early brunch. She'd never eaten there and, wanting to be loyal to Beth, had only stopped in once or twice for an espresso. But it was time for more.

She pushed open the bright blue wooden door and delighted to the sound of the tinkle of a single bell. An older man looked up from the newspaper he had spread on the counter in front of him.

"Welcome, *signorina*. What may I help you with?" He straightened to his full height, which brought him eye level with J.J.'s five foot six. His curly black hair was salted with strands of gray, and his blue eyes twinkled.

"I'm hoping you're Rocco Gates." J.J. stuck out her hand. "I'm J.J. Tanner."

Rocco shook her hand and held it for a few extra moments. "A pleasure, Ms. Tanner. I am Rocco and at your service. What can I do for you?"

J.J. already liked the guy. "I belong to a dinner club called the Culinary Capers and the only problem is, I'm really a terrible cook. My next turn to host, and cook the main entrée, is coming up in a week and I've decided to do an Italian evening."

"Excellent choice."

J.J. smiled. *Good start.* "So, the way it works is we choose a cookbook and then everyone has to make something from it for the dinner. I've decided on *nigellissima* by Nigella Lawson and I've chosen to make beef pizzaiola. Here's the recipe." She handed him what she'd printed out. "I'd like your advice on the ingredients and also maybe a substitute for the anchovy fillets."

He looked it over. "Hm. I've seen this cookbook. Italian-inspired, I think it said. This is fairly straightforward. You've decided on turkey cutlets rather than the beef or veal escalopes suggested in the recipe, I see."

J.J. nodded.

"And, forgive my asking, but you're allowed to make changes to the recipe?"

"We can and often do, although this is my first time trying anything so daring. Last month's dinner was beef, so I thought at the last minute to change it up. Do you think it will work? The turkey, I mean."

He nodded. "It should be fine. Quite a different texture and a more subtle flavor, of course, but it should be a pleasing taste. All right. I will show you a garlic-infused olive oil I think will work well with the rest of the ingredients. I also have the capers and black olives, cured in oil. They are both imported and of the highest quality."

She followed him to the store shelves. She gazed in awe at the huge selection of olive oils in their own casks. She hadn't realized that there was such a variety in basic oils and those with the addition of herbs and other flavors. He offered her tastes of two of them.

"Wow, the garlic really comes through in the second

one," J.J. agreed. "Which do you think would work the best?"

"I'd say the first one. If we substitute miso for the anchovy— I see you have it crossed out—the rest of the flavors will still be blended."

In no time at all there was a small pile of items on the counter. Rocco had been thorough in explaining his reasons for choosing each, and J.J. felt like she'd just had a private lesson.

"This is great. I so appreciate it, Rocco," she said, smiling as she pulled out her credit card. She glanced as the door flew open and a young harried-looking woman rushed in. Strands of hair had escaped the ponytail holding them and her jacket was half-off. She stopped abruptly when she noticed J.J. and Rocco.

"I'm really sorry I'm late, Rocco. I had car trouble again," she said, her voice quavering.

Rocco swept a hand through the air. "It's a no big problem, Zoe. Come, meet a new friend." He turned to J.J. "This is Zoe, my very capable and as you can see, conscientious noon-hour helper."

"Nice to meet you," J.J. said.

Zoe smiled and nodded then rushed into the kitchen.

Rocco smiled as he shook his head. "The young. Always in such a hurry, especially the mama of twin boys. Now, will you permit me to offer you an espresso before you leave?"

"I'd like that." She also wanted a grilled chicken and avocado wrap she'd spied but thought that would be awkward, since he'd offered her an espresso. She had a veggie protein bar stashed in her desk drawer, which she'd eat when she got back to the office.

She thought about Rocco on her walk back. He'd seemed like a really nice guy, kind and helpful, not like the other Italian she was dealing with at the moment. So that was a bonus. And, he'd given her some very good suggestions, which in theory should make her feel more confident about her cooking for the next Culinary Capers dinner.

And all those bottles of olive oil lining the wall. She might just have found something new to obsess about. She'd ended up buying a second, different bottle for use at home just because she'd been so intrigued.

She'd be sure to visit again soon and hopefully leave with lots more cooking tips and, yes, olive oil. Once the princess party was a wrap this weekend.

Then her life would be back to normal.

CHAPTER 7

J.J. was dressed and ready to go before her alarm clock went off the morning of the birthday party. She'd spent a fitful night, awakening several times to lie motionless worrying about the event. She resorted to using concealer to mask the dark shadows under her eyes. She gave herself one last critical look in the mirror. Her bouncy long hair was under control, held back and in place with an elastic. Her black short-sleeved cotton blouse and black jeans looked like she meant business. She'd allow enough time to come home for a couple of hours before the event for a quick rest and to transform herself into a socially acceptable attendee.

She forced herself to slowly eat a bowl of granola while Indie sat on the crossword puzzle on the table and watched. It was his favorite spot every morning, even though she never shared with him. His bowl sat freshly filled and would stay that way until she'd finished eating, at which time, Indie would leap down and eat his own food. It never varied. She was happy for the routine in her somewhat chaotic life.

She rinsed her dish in the sink and grabbed the binder with all her notes in it. She wasn't trusting anything to memory today. She doubled checked to make sure she had everything she needed and then quickly ran over the timeline for what remained to be done. She'd made copies of the information she needed from the large white binder in the office. She also had a paper copy of vital phone numbers, even though most were already keyed into her smartphone, and a list of possible backups in case of an emergency. Event Planning 101 basics.

After a final look in the hall mirror, she took a deep breath, grabbed her car keys, and walked out the door.

"Watch yourself, missy, or you'll end up wearing clothes of many colors," her neighbor, Ness Harper, grumbled as J.J. almost bumped into him. She'd been trying to zip closed her purse while walking down the hall. Obviously not a smart idea.

"Oops. Sorry, Ness. I should pay attention to where I'm walking."

"Humph. Lucky that I saw you. Where are you going in such a hurry on a Saturday morning? Haven't you heard of a day off?" He put his garbage bag on the ground and ran a hand through the unkempt strands of his gray hair.

"I have a big event happening tonight, a twenty-first birthday party for Lorenzo Portovino's daughter, and I need to get over there to make sure the setup and everything runs smoothly."

"The Portovino estate. Hmm, that's the big time." He paused and looked like he was about to say something, then gave his head a small shake. He grabbed his garbage bag again and headed to the back stairs, saying over his shoulder, "Good luck, missy."

"Thanks." J.J. watched him until he reached the emergency exit door and then hurried to the front stairwell. By the time she was in her car, she was running through her mental checklist.

The gates to the estate were closed, but J.J. could see the large cube truck from Festive Rentals parked at the end of the long driveway. She leaned out her window and pushed the button on the intercom. After she gave her name, the gates were opened and she drove slowly, enjoying the view.

The two-story stone-and-wood house seemed to go on forever, but she'd realized the first time she'd visited that that illusion came from the large six-car garage set very closely to the far end of the house. Even without it, the mansion commanded the center spot on the property, with a winding driveway arcing in front and outdoor guest parking beyond the garage. She drove to that area and left her new green Mitsubishi Mirage parked just to the left of the building. It looked good there. But later, she'd park behind the house.

The front door was opened by the butler. J.J. had been surprised the first time this had happened. Butlers were not in her purview but Angelica had explained, as if it was of no importance, that there had always been a butler in the Portovino household.

J.J. walked into the large open foyer as Angelica ran down the circular staircase toward her. She looked more like an excited eleven-year-old than someone celebrating twenty-one years. Her curly long dark hair framed an oval face with large brown eyes. J.J. admired the metallic leggings and multicolored long T-shirt she'd chosen, which were so perfect to her slender body. Not many could pull off that look. Well, maybe at twenty-one they could.

"I'm so excited. I don't think I can make it through the day without bursting."

J.J. laughed and grabbed hold of Angelica's hands. "Then it's a good thing you'll be off in the city for most of the day with your friends. What time is your hair appointment?"

"We're doing the full spa thing first—mani-pedi, massage, lunch, and then hair. There are six of us and we'll all come back here to get dressed. Do you think that making a grand entrance at nine thirty would be tasteful?"

J.J. laughed. "I think nine thirty will be perfect."

Angelica pulled her iPhone from her pocket and checked for a text. "OMG, they're on their way. Papa has hired a limo for us and it's just done its last pickup. They'll all be arriving here to stash their overnight bags. I've got to get moving." She started toward the stairs, then stopped on the bottom one, turning back to J.J.

"Thank you so much, J.J. I know it's going to be perfect."

Here's hoping.

CHAPTER 8

The extra tables and chairs was the only delivery arriving on time. The deejay showed up half an hour late to set up his equipment, the flowers were next to arrive, and then the decorations were an hour late, but fortunately it didn't take that long to attach them to the walls and, in some places, the ceiling. So the team she'd hired were finished on time. The catering truck arrived an hour late, and J.J. was just about to call Antonio Marcotti when she saw a black truck pull around to the back of the house, followed by a black Cadillac Escalade, obviously driven by the boss. Sweeping past her and talking loudly to his crew, Marcotti didn't give her a chance to comment. She backed out of the kitchen, closed her eyes, and took a deep breath. It was all coming together. It would be fine. That would be her mantra for the next ten hours or so.

And before she knew it, the time had arrived to head home for that badly needed break. She tried napping, but when that didn't work, she contented herself with lying on the bed with slices of cucumber on her closed eyelids and Indie perched, kneading, on top of her, and tried to clear her mind of all thoughts. After about twenty minutes, she gave up and went in search of food. A quick protein-filled snack to keep up her energy would have to do. She found that eating a heavy meal made her sluggish when she needed to be alert. She grabbed a few individually wrapped Ghirardelli dark chocolate squares in case she needed to stoke her fires during the long evening ahead.

J.J. took a final look in the full-length mirror in the corner of her bedroom. She'd decided to wear her sleeveless black crepe wrap dress, plain but striking, an easy choice, since she felt her most confident in it and was certain she'd need an extra dose of confidence tonight. She'd bought the dress when she'd still been working at the ad agency and had to attend numerous clients' social events. The image that looked back at her said *confident, in charge, and ready to kick ass.* She smiled, admitting to being a tad over dramatic.

Watching closely, Indie lay on the bed, curled up against the two throw pillows with quilted covers, their bottom halves covered in fur. "What do you think? Will this do?" J.J. asked and took the fact that Indie decided to lick his lips as an approval. Of course, he then proceeded to lick many others parts of his body, too. She shrugged and gave him a quick pat on the head.

She grabbed her critical list, which had the evening's schedule on it, along with her contact list, stuffed them back into the binder, and grabbed her large black satin hobo bag. The satin was a concession to the elegance of the evening, the size a necessity in her line of work. It held a four-inch-by-four-inch plastic container with everything from safety pins to Scotch tape to pens, scissors, and a screwdriver. One never knew.

She drove through the front gate, wide open this time, and

parked her car around back near the kitchen door at precisely six P.M. The invitation stated the event would start at eight. Again, the butler seemed to be waiting in anticipation of her arrival and opened the door before she could ring the bell.

She wandered through the rooms, taking it all in, and then went through a second time with a more microscopic gaze. In the living room, she decided a vase of white and purple orchids would look better on a side table rather than on the grand piano, and out on the patio she checked to make sure there were no burned-out bulbs in the strings of tiny white lights that encircled the space.

When she entered the dining room, where the large formal dining table had been removed and buffet tables set up in the center, she ran into a woman dressed in a black skirt and blouse with the Bella Luna logo on the front left side.

"I'm Mr. Marcotti's assistant, Kim Schaffer." She held out her hand and J.J. shook it.

"J.J. Tanner. Nice to finally meet you in person. This looks fabulous, Kim," J.J. said, walking the length of one side.

Kim allowed a small smile. "Yes. Chef Marcotti is always very particular about how his food is displayed. If you'll excuse me, I have a lot to oversee in the kitchen, but please let me know if you have any questions."

"I will, and thank you for all your help and fielding my phone calls."

She'd found dealing with Kim to be the total opposite of dealing with her boss. Nothing flamboyant. No dramatic displays. Just a cool, almost dispassionate discussion of the details. That was fine with J.J. She felt she could count on Kim.

By the time she'd checked on everything, she noticed it was just before eight. She saw Lorenzo Portovino enter the foyer and look around. He gave her a quick salute of approval and went back into his study. She heard some girlish squeals from above and watched as Angelica and her friends came quickly down the stairs. She hoped none would trip with the combination of heels and dress lengths.

"It's so amazing, J.J.," Angelica said. "What do you think of my dress?" She did a dramatic twirl and her long chiffon skirt swirled around her in a mass of blues, mauves, and pinks. The sleeveless bodice had plenty of bling, set off dramatically by a wide black sash. "It's my own design. Do you like it?"

"It's breathtaking. In fact, you all look quite glam."

"Just the effect I was going for."

All the girls began talking at once and then screeched as the doorbell rang.

"We'll make our grand entrance later," Angelica called out as they retreated back upstairs.

The butler waited until they'd disappeared and then opened the door. An early guest had arrived. J.J. disappeared into the library and let herself out onto the patio. She needed a quiet moment before everything exploded into action. It was quite easy to picture living in such a fantasy house, especially with the magic she'd helped to create. She heard the string quartet tuning in the background and took a deep breath before opening the doors into the living room.

The next time she looked at her watch, it was eleven thirty, time for the late-night buffet to be laid out. She took a few minutes to watch the dancing and spotted Angelica, long skirts hiked up, shimmying with a dark-haired young man— her prince, J.J. suspected from the looks on their faces.

There were a few people standing in groups in the dining room, small plates in one hand, juggling drinks with the other. She made her way over to the table and ran her eyes along it. Two large tiered stainless serving dishes held place of honor at each end. She wondered what was in them and then felt a hot spot in the pit of her stomach. She walked slowly over to the closest one and cautiously lifted the lid.

Funghi.

She caught herself before crying out. That double-crossing Marcotti. She'd told him they couldn't afford it. Several times. It wasn't on the finalized menu that they had agreed upon. But, she realized, Marcotti was playing by his own rules. She carefully placed the lid back on and took a deep breath before heading into the kitchen.

Marcotti was nowhere to be found, and Kim quickly made herself scarce by ducking outside. J.J. realized there was little she could do about it at the moment but promised herself she'd deal with Marcotti before the night was over.

CHAPTER 9

J.J. looked at her watch a second time just to be certain. Two A.M. She let out a deep breath and took a final look around at the foyer. All the guests had left. The entertainers, too. Angelica had kissed J.J. on each cheek and given her a big hug before wandering up to her bedroom, girlfriends in tow. Even Lorenzo Portovino had shaken her hand and said how pleased he was with everything. Time for J.J. to head home for a few hours of sleep before coming back to supervise the removal of the decorations. She hoped to have it done before the family arose and had arranged for a cleanup crew to arrive at eight.

Now, to deal with Antonio Marcotti. She'd checked on the progress in packing up the kitchen and waited until only a few of his staff were still around. As they all headed out the back door, J.J. caught up with Marcotti and asked for a few moments of his time.

He made a big show of looking at this watch and started to follow the others. She trailed him but then blocked his access to his black Cadillac Escalade. The three remaining staff, including Kim, hustled themselves over to the black catering truck and left without a backward glance.

"I'm very upset with you, Chef Marcotti."

"How could you be upset? You heard the praises for my food. I made this event a success for you. You have nothing to be upset about." He made a gesture with his free hand, shooing her aside and opened his car door.

"I'll agree it was all very delicious. But I will not pay for the funghi. It was not what we'd agreed upon. You will have to absorb the cost of the dish."

Marcotti placed his bag of knives on the backseat and closed the door, turning back to her. "Oh, but it is there, right on the contract."

J.J. gasped. "It is not. And if that's so, it was added after the contract was signed."

"That's quite the accusation. Who would believe you? They would say you were trying to cover up your own budgeting error. You are a nobody with a nothing firm. I, on the other hand, have a renowned reputation. You should think very carefully before tossing around any accusations. Now, if you'll be so good as to leave me alone, I'm tired and want to go home."

J.J. clenched her hands at her sides, willing herself not to reach out and do some damage. "I, too, am tired. Too tired to deal with this deceit now, but we will continue this discussion. Believe me, it's not over."

J.J. turned on her heel and stomped with as much dignity as she could muster over to her own car. She slid in and drove off without a backward glance. She couldn't chance the possibility of being overcome by the desire to run him down.

When she reached home she was still seething. She put the kettle on to brew a cup of chamomile tea and ran a hot bath, dropping a handful of lavender Epsom salts into it. Unfortunately, she didn't have her copy of the catering contract at home, but after taking care of the morning cleanup, she planned to drive straight to her office and secure it. Who knew what he might attempt to do with it? She could picture him trying to break into her office, maybe even at this very moment. Should she dash over there? No. He wouldn't do that. He was too sure of himself. He thought she'd kowtow and not put up a fight. Well, she'd show him.

She grabbed her tea and stepped gingerly into the steaming water, sinking down with a sigh. When she felt sufficiently soothed, she dried herself and headed to bed.

She was surprised when the alarm woke her at seven. She was sure she wouldn't be able to get a bit of rest, but she'd underestimated just how tired she had been. She still felt tense, though. She did some stretches to try to work out the kinks in her shoulders, dressed in a comfortable long multi-colored T-shirt and black leggings, fed Indie his usual mix of canned and dry food, then, armed with resolve, headed back to the Portovino estate.

Her first hint that something was wrong came when she rounded the curve leading up to the entry gate. Two Burlington Police cars were parked, one at the side of the main road, almost blocking it. She could see more police cars and a police van farther up the drive, toward the house. Unsure of what to do, she pulled over to the verge.

A police officer got out of his car and walked over to her, indicating that she roll down her window. After asking her name, he asked what she was doing there.

"I'm an event planner from Make It Happen. I was in charge of the birthday party held here last night, and I've come to supervise the cleanup this morning. My crew should be arriving shortly. What's happened?"

"I can't tell you that. Would you please wait in your car? I'll get someone to talk to you."

J.J. did as told, trying to see as much as she could, wondering what was wrong. She dearly hoped it wasn't one of the Portovinos, maybe taken ill overnight. But that wouldn't call for all the police. What if something valuable had been stolen during the party? She checked to see if she had her lists handy. They might want to know whom she'd hired for the evening. After about fifteen minutes of numerous scenarios running through her brain, a man in a brown suit with a police badge hung from his breast pocket approached her car. "Would you step out of your car, Ms. Tanner?"

"What's going on? Has someone been hurt? Has there been a robbery?"

He eyed her a few seconds before answering. "I'm Detective Ozzie Hastings, Burlington Police. There's been a death. A murder, actually."

J.J. gasped and leaned back against the car. "Not one of the family members?"

"No." He took a few moments before continuing. J.J. tried to keep her imagination in check. She concentrated on his wavy blond hair that looked awfully long for a police officer, the obviously rumpled white shirt, and the blue striped tie. And his accent: soothing, one that could lull you into a false sense of all's well. Obviously a Brit of some sort. She wondered how long he'd been in the States. His eyes sat over deep bags even darker than she imagined hers were this morning.

He finally looked up at her. "I understand you were here late last night. What time did you leave?"

"It was shortly after two A.M. I waited until most people had left."

"And you walked out to your car alone?"

"No. I was with the remaining staff who catered the event. Bella Luna. What's happened?"

"Bear with me. Was there anyone still here when you left?"

"Yes, Mr. Marcotti. He was just getting into his car when I drove off."

"And was there anyone else around?"

J.J. shook her head. "Not that I could see. Of course, the butler closed up after us, but he was inside. Mr. Marcotti could tell you better than I if anyone else stayed after I left."

"That won't be possible."

J.J. had that sinking feeling sometimes described on TV mystery shows, one that always lead to the same question and announcement. She had to ask it, though. "Why not?"

"Mr. Marcotti is dead."

It still shocked her to hear it said out loud. "I can't believe it. He can't be. We were speaking just a few hours ago. What happened?"

The detective didn't answer right away. He appeared to be studying her, which made J.J. feel all twitchy. She willed herself to remain outwardly calm.

"I'd like you to go down to the police station at some point today to give a statement about the night's events. Would you do that?"

"Sure, but I'm meeting my crew here to take down all the decorations inside."

"Not now, you aren't." He held up his hand as she opened her mouth to speak.

"We're treating this entire estate as a crime scene until we have a few more answers. The decorations will have to stay."

"Until when?"

"Until I say so."

"What will Mr. Portovino say?"

"This is police business. Does that answer your question?" He stood straight and struck an aggressive pose.

She nodded. "All right, I get the message. But you will let me know as soon as it's possible?"

He grunted as he turned away and strode toward the house.

CHAPTER 10

The next morning, J.J. went through it all again, this time for Skye's benefit.

"Oh man, that's so terrible," Skye moaned and sat back in her chair. "He's dead. You're a suspect. And we're left with an incredibly high bill to pay, what with his conniving last-minute addition. I know"—she held up her hand—"I shouldn't be so crass and uncaring. But it is all part and parcel. How are you holding up?"

"Well, I was feeling fine. But what do you mean, I'm a suspect?"

"It stands to reason. It sounds like you were the last one to talk to him, and you did argue. I think anyone who had anything to do with him later that night could be a suspect. I know you didn't do it, which goes without saying."

"Well, thanks for that. I was a bit shaky yesterday, especially when I went to the police station to give my statement and then sign it. Just being in that building can make you feel guilty. And then later in the day I got the all clear to go back to the estate and remove all the party stuff. The police were still working out in the yard, and I had an escort walk me from my car and back. The same for the cleanup crew. I was lucky they were able to come at a moment's notice. It was really creepy, though."

"I'll bet."

"Oh, and one more thing: I didn't mention the argument." She'd totally forgotten—well, partially forgotten—and then felt she had to hurry up writing the statement for the officer standing at the corner of the desk.

Skye looked at her, head tilted, eyes wide, and an "are you nuts?" expression on her face.

"I will tell them next time. If there is a next time." She crossed her fingers, hoping her involvement with the police had ended.

Skye just shook her head. "Did you talk to Mr. Portovino? I wonder how he's taking it."

"He was there and talked just long enough to mumble something about it being dreadful, but that was about it. His daughter, Angelica, went into hysterics when she heard, apparently. However, the promise of a new car calmed her down. Or so one of the maids told me."

"Huh. Healing powers for sure."

Before J.J. could answer, the office door flew open and two uniformed police officers walked in.

"Ms. Josephine Tanner?" the older one asked, looking from Skye to J.J.

She raised her hand slightly in answer.

"Detective Hastings would like you to accompany us down to the station. He has a few more questions for you."

J.J. gulped and immediately hoped they hadn't noticed. Her hand shook slightly as she reached for her purse. "Of course."

She glanced at Skye and raised her eyebrows. Skye made

the universal "call me" sign. J.J. nodded and followed the officers out the door.

J.J. sat ramrod straight in the wooden chair, staring at the
navy cloth baffle behind Detective Hasting's desk. Although
it was totally blank, she kept hoping something would mate-
rialize to draw her attention away from having to deal with
the fact that she was back at the police station, this time for
a formal interview. She wondered if they used different
terms for suspects as opposed to bystanders.

Eventually, Hastings stopped reading her statement and put
it down on his desk on top of his notebook and several other
loose papers. He sat looking at her in silence for several minutes. She tried returning his stare but then felt her eyes being
pulled back behind him to the baffle. Still nothing showing.

"That appears complete, Ms. Tanner."

She relaxed a little. That voice. She'd always had a thing
about British accents. He sounded like such a Boy Scout. She
wondered if they had those in England. It was a comforting
voice, anyway. Helpful. Reassuring. He crossed his arms on
his desk and leaned forward. She tensed again.

"Now, tell me, what have you left out?"

"What do you mean?" Her heart started pounding, and she
was sure he could see her white Chico's shirt fluttering.

"Well, for starters, the entire part about your argument
with the deceased. Was there anything else?" Hastings leaned
back in his chair and picked up his coffee mug. After taking
a taste, he spit it back into the mug.

J.J. opened her mouth to protest and then closed it again.
What to say?

"What were the two of you arguing about?"

"You mean as we were leaving?"

He frowned, and she was certain he also growled. "Yes."

"Umm, we were discussing the evening's event." *Keep to the facts. Do not ramble on.*

"And did this include the raising of voices?" He picked up a pencil and started lightly tapping the desktop.

"Umm, I might have gotten a bit carried away."

"You were arguing." It was a statement.

J.J. swallowed. "Yes."

"About what?"

"About a dish that Mr. Marcotti had snuck onto the menu after I specifically told him not to do so." J.J. held her breath, wondering what would come next.

"I see. And, why would that lead to you being so angry?"

"I wasn't so angry. All right, I guess I was. It was a very expensive item and the budget was already at its limit. I'd told him that. He chose to ignore it."

Hastings leaned back in his chair, arms folded across his chest. "Just how angry were you?"

J.J. wondered just how much to tell. All of it, she guessed. She took a deep breath. "As I said, I was upset by the additional cost that he'd snuck in there. So, I told him he would have to absorb the cost. And then he threatened that if I followed through on my threat to expose him, he would spread the word that I was totally incompetent."

"He was a powerful man in his industry?"

J.J. nodded. She didn't trust herself to speak. She was reliving the conversation. What a jerk. Not a good thing to voice in the present circumstances.

"So, we'll say that made you extremely angry?" Hastings sounded almost sympathetic, but that could have been the accent.

J.J. nodded again.

"Whoever killed Marcotti was plenty mad at him. There was a lot of rage in the stabbing."

J.J. gasped. "I didn't do it. You have to believe me." She

thought about what he'd said. "He was stabbed? I couldn't. I could never stab somebody. How gruesome."

"Every murder is gruesome, Ms. Tanner. You can go for now. I'm sending an officer with you to collect the clothing you wore Saturday night." He held up his hand to prevent her responding.

But J.J. just stared at him. She couldn't think of a thing to say. She couldn't believe this was happening. To her. To Marcotti. She finally nodded and stood shakily. A female officer appeared and, after getting her instructions, escorted J.J. out the back door, the way she'd come in.

J.J. sat in silence the entire way to her place. When they got in her apartment, the officer followed her to her closet, where J.J. had hung her dress while waiting to take it to the dry cleaners.

"And your shoes?" asked the officer.

J.J. handed them over, and the young woman left. J.J. looked in the bedroom mirror and watched as the tears rolled down her cheeks. After a few minutes, she took a deep breath, wiped her eyes, and said to her image, "Suck it up. You didn't do it and they'll figure it out. You have nothing to worry about."

Indie had wandered in sometime during the process and now wound his sleek body around her legs. She crouched down to pick him up and sat with him in her lap, stroking his back until he finally had enough. She watched as he jumped off her lap and stalked into the kitchen, no doubt needing some sustenance after all that.

Her gaze strayed around the living room. It was her sanctuary, had been her sanctuary ever since she'd fled Montpelier and her disastrous engagement. She'd even decorated the apartment in blues and white, beach colors that were a reminder of childhood and the summers spent on the East Coast at her grandparents' cottage. So much for a haven from the nasties of the world. Not even the entire wall of books, mainly mysteries but also her treasured four shelves of cookbooks, could cheer her up.

She sighed and glanced out the window, groaning when she realized it had started pouring sometime after they'd arrived at her apartment. Ordinarily, she loved the sound and smells of rain; however, right now she was in the mood for neither. She also realized her car was parked in the lot behind the office, so she had two basic options for getting back to the office: by foot or by cab. Her other possibility for a ride was her neighbor, Ness Harper. He might just be home, and better yet, being a retired cop and all, he might be a sounding board for what had just happened. Hopefully, he was home. And hopefully in a good mood.

He answered on the fifth try.

"Yeah?" He opened the door a crack, just enough for J.J. to realize Ness was still in his bathrobe.

"Hi, Ness." She leaned toward the opening, wanting to make sure he saw who it was standing there. "I'm really sorry to bother you but I have a very big favor to ask."

She paused. He said nothing. That didn't surprise her.

"Uh, I need a lift to work."

"Why?"

"It's pouring outside, in case you hadn't noticed."

"My question was why. Where's your car?"

She took a deep breath and hoped to get through the explanation without having to dwell on it, because she was afraid if she did that she'd get the shakes or start crying again. "Uh, a body was found outside the event I organized Saturday night, and the police just had me in at the station to answer some questions. The officers picked me up at work and drove me to the station, then one of them brought me here and took away the clothes I was wearing that night." She sighed and realized her voice was shaking. "And left me here."

Ness Harper opened the door wider and stood blocking

the doorway, arms crossed and legs slightly apart. "And just why do those blockheads think you're a suspect?"

"Because I was the last person to see him?"

"There's gotta be more."

She tilted her chin and straightened up. "And we'd had a rather loud fight outside just before leaving."

He looked at her a few seconds before replying. "Okay. Just give me a minute to throw some duds on. I'll knock on your door." He closed his door in her face.

J.J. went back into her apartment. She was used to the abrupt manner in which Ness dealt with people. They'd shared the elevator one night shortly after she'd moved in, and he'd told her that he'd had his fill of people in his thirty-five years working as a cop. Now all he wanted was to be left alone.

She usually tried to abide by that, although her first invitation to him to share a spaghetti dinner at her place had been snapped up. And since then, he'd had her over for pizza a couple times, and more recently he was trying out new recipes on her. She still respected his privacy and never pried into his life, present or former, but realized he was someone she could count on. As he'd just proven.

It took less than five minutes for him to knock on her door. She grabbed her purse and raincoat, and ended up trailing him down the hall. He didn't speak again until they were out of the parking lot.

"Who's the dead guy?"

"Antonio Marcotti. He owns Bella Luna, the Italian restaurant on Hart Street."

"How'd he die?"

"He was stabbed. Repeatedly."

"Crime of passion." He looked at her when he came to a stop sign. "Were you passionate about the guy?"

"Me? No way. I was mad at him because he tried to stiff me with a high-priced dish, but not mad enough to kill him."

"No hanky-panky going on the side?"

"Ugh. No." She shuddered at the thought.

"Okay. I'd advise you to stick to the facts next time you're being interviewed, and don't offer anything extra. Got it?" He pulled up in front of the office.

"Next time?"

"Oh yeah. They're not finished with you, not if they're checking your clothes for traces of blood or anything else that might prove you did it."

J.J. felt the tears about to fall again. She gave her head a shake. "I am innocent."

"Well, then don't sweat it. If they get it wrong, we'll set it right." He sounded a little less gruff, so J.J. looked over at him. She wanted to give him a hug but thought better of it.

"Thanks, Ness. Thanks for the lift and the advice." She hopped out of the car.

"'snothing." He waited until she'd closed the door, then pulled a U-turn and sped away.

J.J. dashed into the building and watched as Ness's gray Chevy sedan turned the corner, not headed back home, but toward the city. Maybe to the police station?

CHAPTER 11

"Do the police have any ideas or suspects, except for you?" Skye asked after listening to J.J.'s account of her morning.

"They're not really into sharing, Skye."

Skype jumped out of her chair and enfolded J.J. in a hug. "Don't worry. You didn't do it. Who could believe you'd do such a thing? And really, being ticked off with a person, even though he was a slimeball, is hardly a big enough motive to kill that somebody."

J.J. sighed. "That's what I think, but who knows what the police think? Ness Harper said it sounded like a murder committed in passion or something like that."

"Passion? Hm. Was Marcotti playing around on his wife? Maybe coming on to somebody on his staff? Or even bothering a guest?"

J.J. shrugged. "I have no idea. I just know it wasn't me. Now, we'd better give some thought about damage control. Make It Happen wasn't mentioned in the newspaper article this morning, but it's sure to surface soon. And if my name gets mentioned as a 'person of interest' or whatever they call them, it might not be so good for business."

"Now, don't you go worrying about that. We'll just issue a statement, if necessary, keeping it short and sweet. Something to the effect that Mr. Marcotti's catering services were used at an event organized by Make It Happen and our condolences to the widow. Something like that. He was married, I'm assuming?"

"I have no idea. I know nothing about the guy, but I know who would."

"Evan."

"Right." J.J. headed for the door. "I think I'll just go have a chat with Evan and see what I can find out. I also want to get his take on the fast one Marcotti pulled."

J.J. ran down the stairs, although the two-inch heels on her black leather boots made it tricky going. She knocked on the door to Design Delights and walked in without waiting for an answer. Evan Thornton looked up from the newspaper he was reading and stood to walk over to J.J. He looked so solemn that J.J. almost smiled. He hugged her, then settled her in a chair.

"I was just reading about the murder," he said, rushing over to pour her a cup of tea. "That's so dreadful. Absolutely unthinkable. Here, have some of my special chai tea, guaranteed to soothe all irritations, and tell Evan all."

He passed her a cup and sat down with his own, pulling his chair over until they were almost knee to knee.

J.J. took a sip and then told the entire story once again. When she had finished, Evan looked shocked. Then he placed his teacup down carefully on the desk and started pacing.

"I feel so responsible. I knew he could be a bastard in business dealings, but I never ever thought he'd pull a fast one like that on you. Truly, J.J., I should have warned you off when you first mentioned him." Evan looked so distressed that J.J. reached out to touch his arm.

"I believe you, Evan. I'm shocked about what he did to us, of course, but it's now taken second seat to his murder. And what's worse from my perspective is that I'm a suspect."

"No way."

"Yes way. I was the last person to see him. We walked out to our cars at the same time, and we were arguing. I'm sure his staff heard us as they scurried to the van, trying to escape the scene. Probably the butler heard, also. Then next morning, he's found dead in his car. Knifed."

"You wouldn't use a knife."

"Oh, thanks, Evan," J.J. said. "What would I use?"

Evan looked horrified. "I didn't mean it like that. I mean, using a knife is very up close and personal. And it takes a lot of strength, I'd think. You'd really have to hate the guy to do something like that, and I know that lets you out. You'd only just met him. I'm thinking that kind of hate take years to build. Besides, you wouldn't harm a fly."

J.J. raised her eyebrows.

"Okay, a spider maybe, but not a fly."

J.J. started laughing. "Thank you for the testimonial, Evan. But it would be better if you could come up with another suspect. Can you think of anyone who might fit that bill? You worked with him on the restaurant reno for several months. Can you remember anyone, maybe a supplier or a contractor or even one of his staff, who might have a hate on for him?"

Evan sat and thought, finally shaking his head. "There were some encounters of the yelling kind, for sure, but I can't come up with any one single person who seemed that upset. Of course, we had our set-to but that was it. I'll bet it was something personal, like the husband of someone he was sleeping with."

"He was married, wasn't he?"

"Yes, but he was also Antonio Marcotti. He had quite a reputation with the women." Evan went over to pour himself another cup of tea.

"I didn't know that."

"Why would you?" he asked, his back to her. "The food business is a very insular little community. And then there's his Italian connections. I've heard he was a big wheel in that community, too."

"Hm. Do you think his wife," she shrugged, "you know . . ."

He turned around and went back to his desk. "Knew about his affairs or kill him?"

"Either. Both."

"I met Gina Marcotti a couple of times when they were thinking of using my services to decorate their home. She was really into my ideas but totally ignored Marcotti when he was around. So maybe she did know, but I think she just didn't care enough about him to get upset. Which probably means she didn't kill him, either. I understand it's all her money anyway, so I guess she gets to do all the choosing at home. They have quite the palatial digs. But I'd love to get my hands on their color scheme. That's all it would take to give the place some high-class glam."

J.J.'s eyes wandered to the clock on the opposite wall. "Oh man. Look at the time. I feel like I've wasted the entire day. Where did it get to?" She held up her hand. "Don't answer that. I know, unfortunately. Guess I'd better get going. Thanks, Evan."

He nodded. "Keep the faith. They'll catch who did it."

J.J. certainly hoped so. She returned to her office and found a note on her desk from Skye, who was at a meeting downtown with a supplier and would call later.

J.J. looked outside and felt cheered that it had at least stopped raining. It seemed something could go right. She looked at her computer and then out the window again. She knew she wouldn't be able to concentrate on work. Not today. She locked up and headed for home.

Eight o'clock. Less than ten minutes since J.J. had last looked at the wall clock. Time was dragging tonight, and she couldn't seem to concentrate. She'd tried brainstorming some creative ideas for Olivia Barker and the retirement party she was organizing, however that hadn't worked. Next, she'd tried some visualization with the recipe for beef—now turkey—pizzaiola from *nigellissima*. Again, not into focusing. Even the latest mystery by one of her favorite mystery authors, Victoria Abbott, couldn't hold her attention.

She should just admit it and deal with it: she was scared. She was not a murderer, but the butterflies started fluttering in her stomach whenever she thought back to being inter-viewed in the police station. She needed to have faith in the system, but she readily admitted she didn't. Not when it was her reputation—her life—at stake. She needed to talk to someone who knew the ropes. She knew that Alison was on duty, so not her. But Ness Harper was at home. She'd indulged her senses in the aroma of sauerkraut wafting from his apart-ment when she'd walked past the door earlier.

She was just about to open her apartment door when some-one knocked on it. Through the peephole, she spied Ness.

"Wow, talk about the same wavelength," she said, pulling the door open. "I was just coming to see you."

Ness grunted and pushed past her to the living room patio door. "Come here. Turn off the light in here while you're at it."

She did as she was told and peered over his outstretched arm, which held back the drapes a crack. "What am I looking for?"

"What do you see?"

She leaned forward until her forehead touched the windowpane. "Umm, a dark car across the street. A light car on this side of the street. Nobody out walking. Is that it?"

"The dark car. It arrived just as you got home and has been parked there ever since. No one exited it."

She turned to look at him. "I don't get it. Oh, do you think whoever is in that car followed me? I didn't notice it or anyone for that matter."

He grunted. "It means he's good. So you don't recognize the car?"

"No. I don't think so. But it's dark, even with that streetlight close by, and I can't really see it that well from here."

"It could be the police, but I somehow doubt it. There's no reason for them to be following you." Ness headed to the door. "You wait. I'm going to see who it is and what he wants."

J.J. stared at the door from which Ness had just exited for less than a minute, and then she grabbed a sweater and her apartment keys and followed. She'd reached the front sidewalk when she saw Ness strolling along the sidewalk, then in a move she'd never thought him capable of at his age, dash around the car and yank open the driver's door.

"Get out of that car and keep your hands where I can see them." His voice was loud enough for the entire neighborhood to hear.

J.J. went scurrying across the road as a dark-haired male exited the car. He had his hands up in front of him as he turned to face Ness. They were about eye level with each other, but the other guy was definitely younger. J.J. took him to be about her age.

"Just take it easy," the stranger said. "I'm going to reach across with my left hand and remove my ID from inside my jacket. Okay?" He kept his movements slow and his eyes on

Ness as he pulled out and opened his wallet. He held it up for Ness to read.

"Says you're a PI. How do I know that's not fake?" Ness growled.

The stranger sighed. "Look. My name is Ty Devine. I'm fully registered as a private investigator in the state of Vermont. Take a closer look at it. Feel the damned logo. It's raised."

Ness did both, then grunted. "So what are you doing tailing J.J. Tanner?"

J.J. had inched up behind Ness as he was speaking. Without looking at her, he said, "I thought I told you to stay put."

"I want to know, too. Answer the question, please." She realized her voice was shaking and wished she hadn't opened her mouth.

Devine looked from one to the other. "I'm looking into the Antonio Marcotti murder."

J.J. gasped. "But why follow me?"

"Who's your client?" Ness demanded. "And why follow her?"

"You know I can't tell you my client's name, but what I can tell you is I've been involved in this case before the murder. I was in the vicinity the night it happened, and I witnessed Ms. Tanner arguing with Marcotti, get into her vehicle, and leave. Marcotti was still alive at that point."

"What? You saw that?" J.J. said, her voice much stronger and louder. "Why didn't you tell the police? Then they'll know I didn't kill him."

"I did tell the police. It just took me a day or so to do that. I needed to ensure certain things before doing that." He leaned back against his car.

"In other words," Ness said, his voice dripping with sarcasm, "you had to make sure your client was okay with your sharing the fact that you were tailing Marcotti? What's the problem? The wife think her husband was fooling around on her?"

J.J. shot a glance at Ness. "You got that out of what he just told you?"

"What else would it be? You didn't confront Marcotti and kill him yourself, did you?"

Devine started laughing. "Good try. I left right after Ms. Tanner."

"So, you were following her? Does the wife think J.J. here was the mistress?"

"What are you saying?" J.J. shrieked. "You've been following me for a while? You think I had something going on the side with the guy? Are you nuts?"

Ness shushed her, and she realized an older couple walking their schnauzer were suddenly scurrying faster to pass them.

"Let's go inside and finish this conversation," Ness suggested, looking pointedly at Devine.

Devine shrugged. "All right by me." He locked his car and followed them up to Ness's apartment.

Ness pointed to the living room. "Ness Harper's the name. Do you want coffee?"

"No," J.J. said in unison with Devine's "Yes."

Ness shook his head. "Go make yourselves comfortable."

When he joined them with two coffees, J.J. was sitting in a well-worn club chair next to the sliding patio door while Devine had chosen the leather recliner. His chair. Ness glared at him as he handed over the coffee.

"So talk."

Devine took a sip first. Then another. "Let's just say there's been some concern that Marcotti had something going on the side and that a lot of money has been spent on gift items, namely jewelry."

Ness finished off his coffee in two gulps. "Hah. You think J.J. might be the one, and so you're still tailing her, hoping to see when she goes out so you can search her apartment for the stuff."

J.J.'s jaw dropped open. "No way. You were going to break into my place? That's illegal, and what makes you think I was fooling around with Marcotti? Could you not hear us arguing? Is that what lovers do?"

Devine smiled. "Of course they do. Don't try to play innocent."

J.J. jumped up. "I'm not playing. I am innocent." She stopped just short of stamping her foot. That would make her look childish, she knew. "I only met the guy a few weeks ago."

"On March third. You've since been to his restaurant a couple of times."

"He's doing, or rather *did*, a catering job for me. For my client. I needed to confer with him, and then I wanted to taste his food to make sure it was as good as I'd been told."

"You hired him to cater an event and you had no idea what his food tastes like?" Devine sounded like he didn't believe her.

"I went with a recommendation from someone whose judgment I respect," she huffed.

Devine shrugged. "I'm dealing in facts here."

"You are not. You're dealing in suppositions. The fact is, I hired him to cater an event. Next fact: he stiffed me with an unexpected addition to the menu. Next fact: we argued. That's all I had to do with the guy." She sat down abruptly and crossed her arms, then her legs.

Ness looked from J.J.'s angry face to Devine's amused expression. "Let's call it a draw. J.J. was not his mistress, therefore you do not have to follow her any longer. And you certainly don't have to search her place. J.J., you can now relax because the police know you're not the murderer."

"Unless she snuck back there and killed him."

"You didn't follow her all the way home?"

Devine shook his head sheepishly. "I felt confident that's where she was heading and equally confident that nothing else would happen at that hour of the night."

"Shows how wrong you can be," J.J. threw in. "And, just for the record, I did not go back and kill him. I did go home and went to bed. It was almost three A.M. for Pete's sake. I had to get back to the Portovino estate in just a few hours."

Devine stood. "All right, then."

"All right," J.J. answered, standing also.

Ness glanced from one to the other again and then stood. "Glad that's settled. Good night to you both. Don't slam the door on your way out, Devine. J.J., just wait a minute."

Devine nodded at them both and left.

Ness waited a few beats after the door had closed. "I'm not totally sure how much I trust that guy. Be sure to lock up whenever you go out."

"Do you think he's dangerous?" She felt a chill run down her spine.

Ness shook his head. "He won't physically harm you, but he still has a client, and I'd say he's not about to quit."

CHAPTER 12

So what did all that mean? J.J. wondered as she got ready for work the next morning. Ty Devine had told the police that Marcotti had been alive when she'd left, so she was in the clear. But then he had left soon after and hadn't followed her home. So she might not be in the clear if he'd also mentioned that to the police.

But why did he leave if he was supposed to be following Marcotti? Could he be the killer?

Intrigued by the question, she added a long scarf in shades of neutrals to the long-sleeved white blouse and green pants she'd chosen, then stopped abruptly when she checked the mirror. Her pants were green and her jacket was red. She looked like a Christmas tree. Obviously, too much on her mind. And where had those green pants come from anyway? She vaguely remembered buying them on a lark at some point but thought they'd been relegated to the back of the closet. Obviously, they had to be added to the Goodwill bag. These days she started with blacks, adding a bit of color, something different, each day. It made life so much easier to build on black. She was working hard on her time-management skills.

At the office, anxious to talk over the previous evening's events, she waited patiently for Skye to finish a phone call with a client. She glanced down as she sat at her desk, just to make sure she had indeed changed to the black pants. All was good.

Skye hung up the phone and raised her perfectly shaped eyebrows. Even from that distance J.J. could see that Skye had recently been to an esthetician, possibly even that morning.

"What's up?" Skye asked. "Have the police been bothering you again?"

"Not the police," J.J. answered, and then filled her in.

"Wow. Being followed by a mysterious and handsome private eye."

"I did not say he was handsome."

"No, but you blushed when I did." She wiggled her eyebrows. "Anyway, Marcotti sounds like a total creep, cheating on his wife and stiffing colleagues. We got off lightly, I'd say, since he's not able to continue to give us grief."

"Ouch."

"I know that sounds callous, but I didn't know the guy personally and I do know what he did to you. Obviously, there's at least one other person on his list who got shafted by the guy. I'm sure the police have discovered that by now, so I'd say the heat is probably off you." She smiled and cocked her head. "Wouldn't you?"

J.J. sighed. "You're probably right. I don't have time to sit around worrying about this anyway. I have to finish the proposal for Olivia Barker today."

"You do that. It's just what you need to take your mind off this murder business."

J.J. had made it to page three of her proposal when the office door swung open and Tansy Paine marched over to J.J.'s desk, put both hands on it, and leaned toward her. "Do you need a lawyer?"

J.J. moaned. "What? No. What did you hear? I don't think I need a lawyer."

"I think you should have one on speed dial even if you don't need representation at this moment. I'm happy to recommend someone in case you do. I don't do criminal litigation, you know."

Skye stood up. "Thanks, Tansy. J.J. was just getting all mellow and into her work, and you waltz in and bring it all up again."

Tansy stood straight, almost at eye level with Skye's five feet three inches. "It's all over town. Marcotti's murder, that is. And I have it on the best authority that J.J. is a suspect."

"Who said that?" J.J. demanded.

"A friend who shall remain anonymous. She's a good pipeline into the police department." Tansy straightened the hem of her orange jacket, which was just short enough to show off her tiny waist.

"Well, I'm innocent, and I'm pretty sure they realize that by now."

Tansy reached over and patted her arm. "Why, honey, I'm just looking out for your best interests. I'm certain, knowing you, that you wouldn't kill anybody, but the police need to solve this, and from what I hear, they're not racking up a lot of other suspects."

She looked from J.J. to Skye. "I have to get back to my office. Piles of work to tackle. But just remember, I'm right across the hall whenever you need me."

J.J. sat mesmerized watching Tansy glide back the way she'd come, handling her four-inch heels like they were sneakers. Skye sat back down and shook her head.

"She means well. I guess." She looked at the Keurig coffee machine atop the cherry wood buffet that had once resided at her home. The closed doors held a wider variety of options. "I think I'll go get a latte. Can I bring you anything? A latte?"

J.J. nodded. "Yes, thanks."

She just gotten back into the proposal when the door opened again and Evan walked over to where Tansy had been standing.

"I need to talk to you, J.J."

"Sure, Evan." J.J. looked closely at him. His straw-colored V-neck sweater looked wrinkled and didn't present his usual striking effect with the beige shirt that was under it. He mostly went for contrast. "What's up? You're looking weird. No offense."

He sat in the armchair across from her desk. "The police had me in for questioning last night."

"The police? But why? Was it about Antonio Marcotti?"

"That's right." He tugged at his shirt collar as if he were wearing a too-tight tie. "You see, we had a set-to just after I finished the job for him. He took forever to pay me and gave me the runaround whenever I asked. Long story short, I eventually paid, but then the rumors about my work ethic started. I challenged him on it, and he just laughed and said who would ever believe me over him?" Evan slumped back in the chair looking dejected.

"The man just gets viler by the minute. That's much like what happened to me, that last part anyway. But that was a couple of years ago. Surely the police wouldn't think you'd waited this long to kill him."

Evan crossed his arms and stared at the hardwood floor. "I just happened to run into him a couple of days before he died. Michael and I had dinner out, then stopped off for a drink on the way home." He looked at J.J., who nodded for him to go on. "Marcotti happened to be there, too. I mentioned that he'd better treat you fairly, and he took a poke at me."

"He hit you?"

"Yeah. And there were witnesses."

"You didn't hit him back, did you?"

"No. I'm not into that physical stuff. I did say something like he'd better watch his step, though."

J.J. groaned. "Oh no, Evan. Who were the witnesses? Are they reliable? Were they his staff? They could be seen as biased."

"We'd stopped in at the Hutch. You know that's where a lot of the people in the business hang out after they close up shop. Unfortunately, a lot of them knew both of us."

"And you did that for me? I'm feeling bad that it's ended you up in trouble." J.J. went over and gave him a hug.

"It's not your fault. I've been wanting to confront him for a long time." Evan flashed a small smile. "I could never prove he'd bad-mouthed me, but I could head him off this time, or so I thought."

J.J. sat back down and stared at her computer. After a few minutes of silence, she said, "And the police think you killed him because he hit you? That's awfully flimsy."

"I think it is, but as Tansy says, they've got to pin it on someone."

"You've talked to Tansy about this?"

"She waylaid me as soon as I got in this morning."

"That pipeline of hers is very fluid." J.J. thought a moment. "Look, I need to get out of here and clear my head. Why don't we go to lunch?"

Evan shook his head. "Can't. I have a client coming in half an hour. Thanks for the thought, though. So, you really don't think the police are a threat?"

J.J. smiled. "Nah. They've got two of us on the list now, and from what I've been hearing about Marcotti, I'll bet there'll soon be more. Despite what Tansy says." She crossed her fingers anyway.

o   o   o

J.J. finished the proposal at the same time her stomach started alerting her it was time for dinner. She read over the proposal again before e-mailing it to Olivia Barker. Then she printed out a copy and left it to be filed by their part-time office worker, Brittany Stewart, when she was in on Friday after school.

Next on her list was a stop at Rocco G's on her way home for some advice on what vermouth to use for her pizzaiola. With only a few days until the big dinner, she could feel her stress level starting to rise whenever she thought about it.

She found him alone in his shop, staring at the shelves of olive oil to the left of the checkout counter.

"Hi, Rocco. Hope I'm not interrupting. You seem deep in thought."

He turned to face her and smiled, but not before she noticed the worry in his eyes. "J.J., my friend. How nice to see you. And what can I do for you today? Some shopping, some advice, or some espresso? Or maybe all three? Let me fix you an espresso to lay the workday at rest."

"That would be nice. Can you join me?"

"Delighted to." He gave her a small bow and went to tend to the drinks while J.J. settled at a bistro table. She watched the passing traffic on the street until Rocco joined her a few minutes later.

"For *la bella signorina*." Rocco sat across from her and lifted his cup. *"Salute!"*

"Salute!" She sipped and savored. "Mm, this is delicious. There's something about the beans you use—or is it the machine? Or the person making it?"

Rocco chuckled. "Perhaps a combination of the three. Now, what brings you here?"

She took another sip before answering. "I need your advice on vermouth."

"Ah, the big Italian feast is this Sunday, am I right?"

She nodded. "Yes, and I've been so busy at work lately that I haven't given it another thought since we last spoke. Now I'm starting to feel a bit anxious."

"You must not let your mind travel to that place. It will show in your cooking. Have confidence in your ability to do this. I have complete faith in you."

J.J. laughed. *What a delightful man.* "Easier said than done, I'm afraid, although I do appreciate the vote of confidence. I'll need a lot more than that in order to get on track."

"*Si.* It has been a difficult week, has it not? I understand the police were questioning you about Antonio Marcotti's death."

"It's all around the village, isn't it?" J.J. sighed. "Yes, they did but I sort of have an alibi, so I'm hoping they're through with me." She crossed her fingers.

"They may have found another suspect to take your place," Rocco said glumly.

"Who? What have you heard?" Did he know about the police questioning Evan Thornton? She changed her mind about that when she looked at his face. "Not you!"

"Oh yes, me. I spent most of the afternoon at the station answering questions. Being interviewed, they called it. The inquisition, I call it."

"But why? Besides both being in the business, why would they suspect you?"

Rocco finished his espresso and looked at her a few moments before speaking. She felt a slight chill run down her spine. "We were rivals. And, we were sworn enemies. Everyone knows. It was a matter of honor, from the past. However, we both chose to hang on to the past and let it color our dealings in the present. Foolish, when I think of it now. But for all these years, it's been very important to us both."

"May I ask what it was about?"

Rocco shook his head. "Something in the old country, before we came here. We were from the same village, did you know that? Went to school together. We were friends then. And we both immigrated to this country around the same time, but we were no longer friends at that point. A woman . . ." His voice trailed off and he appeared trapped in that past.

J.J. wasn't sure what to say. She waited, turning her gaze once again to the outside.

Finally, Rocco roused himself and sat up straighter. "I did not do it. I am not a murderer. I must make sure the police believe that."

"I know there are at least two other suspects, and from what I understand, he made a lot of enemies. Surely there'll be more names added to that list."

Rocco snorted just as the front door opened. J.J. was astonished to see Ty Devine enter. He looked surprised to see her, then smiled. She couldn't help but notice that the smile reached his eyes, which seemed to twinkle a brighter blue as he got closer.

"Well, well. Tracking down the suspects, Ms. Tanner?"

"What? No. Rocco is helping me with some cooking advice." She glared at Devine, resenting his intrusion, even if he was easy on the eyes.

Devine held out his hand to Rocco and introduced himself. "I hope you don't mind if I ask you a few questions about Antonio Marcotti."

Rocco sighed and pointed to a chair at the next table, which Devine pulled over. "No, I suppose I must get used to this. In fact, J.J. and I were just talking about his untimely death."

J.J. frowned just as Devine looked at her. He smiled, like he'd been right, which annoyed her even more.

"I understand you knew Marcotti for a long time and had some history," Devine stated. "Do you have an alibi?"

"No. I was at home, asleep at the time of his death. Alone except for my cat."

J.J. looked at him. A fellow cat lover. *Nice.*

"Were you able to provide the police with any help in the matter?"

Rocco shrugged. "Not really. They were aware that Marcotti was not an easy man to get along with and I know they were trying to make me lose my temper. But I did not. I would not fall into that trap and appear to be one who flew off the handle easily and maybe committed murder in a fit of rage." He looked pleased with himself, which made J.J. wonder if the police had given Rocco many details about the murder. She hoped so.

"I'm sure the police have a few pages of suspects by now," she offered. "His reputation was well known, apparently."

Devine nodded. "If you were looking for a murderer, where would you go next?" He looked at Rocco.

"You know that he was part owner of the High Time Fitness Center?"

Devine nodded. J.J. leaned forward. It was news to her.

Rocco looked at his hands, folded on the table in front of him, and then up at Devine. "Did you also know that he was having an affair with one of the personal trainers?"

Devine shook his head. "Tell me about it."

"Her name is Candy Fleetwood and she's young enough to be his granddaughter. But he always was a fool when it came to *le signor.* It's a widely known secret in the Italian community. I'm sure even his beautiful but aging wife is also aware of it."

J.J. glanced at Devine, but his face didn't give away a thing. He stood and stuck out his hand. "Thanks for the tip. Nice to meet you, Mr. Gates." He nodded at J.J. and left.

Rocco stood and gathered the cups. He looked out the

window before walking back to the counter. "Perhaps that man will get at the truth."

J.J. took that as her hint to leave. "Let's hope so." She realized when she reached home that she hadn't gotten any advice after all.

Or maybe she had.

CHAPTER 13

J.J. consulted her computer for the address of the High Time Fitness Center before leaving the house on Friday morning. She needed her car for this prework visit and thought over how to handle her questions as she made her way to the parking lot in back of her apartment building. Her once-shiny new Mirage needed a wash, but she didn't know when that would happen. Not with her schedule these days.

By the time she arrived at the center, she'd come up with a plan. She'd ask to talk to Candy Fleetwood about setting up a personal fitness program, and if she wasn't able to slip in the necessary questions about Marcotti, she'd follow through and enroll for the bare minimum program. It would probably even do her some good, she rationalized.

She had to wait twenty minutes for Fleetwood to appear. "I'm sorry about the wait, but I had to finish up with a client. You asked specifically for me. Who recommended me?" Candy looked delighted and not at all suspicious, to J.J.'s relief. Nor in mourning. But as J.J. well knew, looks could be deceiving.

"You know, I can't remember who. It was a few months back. Probably a client. But I'd written down the name of this place and yours, and today's the day I decided I needed to do some work on my body."

Candy grinned. "All over, or are there specific areas you want to focus on?"

J.J. shrugged. "I don't really know. Tell me what you'd suggest, then I'll have something to base a decision on."

"Sure. Come with me."

J.J. took the opportunity to figure out what had attracted Marcotti to Candy as she led the way through double doors, down a hall, and into the gym area. There was the obvious one: her stunning good looks, in a young, blonde cheerleader way. But she also seemed genuine, although it was probably too soon to judge that. As Candy pointed out the various stations, she sounded so bubbly that J.J. felt herself being sucked into the fitness vortex.

"So, what do you think?" Candy asked, as they wound up back at the front reception desk. "Do you want to sign on and start tomorrow?"

J.J. didn't really, but she hadn't found a way to ask her questions, so she agreed.

Candy made a small *yippee* sound, at the same time clapping her hands and bouncing on the spot. "I'm so happy. You'll find it will make such a difference in how you look and in your life. And we'll have so much fun. I'll just go and start working out a program for you. Just sign up with Janice at the front desk and check for an available time, and she'll slot you in. Byee."

Candy squealed again and disappeared back through the doors. J.J., trying not to take offense from the remark about how she looked, pulled out her credit card to pay. By the time she'd booked her appointment for the following Monday morning, she sensed that someone was standing behind her.

She almost knocked Devine over as she abruptly turned. "What are you doing here?"

Looking exasperated, he shook his head. "I don't have to ask why you're here." He grabbed her arm and pulled her toward the front door. They stopped several feet from the receptionist. Still, he kept his voice low, which added a sinister quality to it.

"What are you trying to do? Wreck my investigation? You know what the police will do when they find out you're butting in?"

J.J. pulled her arm out of his grip and turned her back to the receptionist. Who knew if she could read lips? "I've signed up for some sessions with a personal trainer, that's all. I've been thinking about doing it for a long time now. I've wanted to get in shape for a while but never took the first step. There are so many gyms and spas around, you know. Actually hearing a name and a place was the incentive I needed." She bit her tongue to keep from rambling even more.

Ty stepped back and gave her the once-over. "You already look in shape."

J.J. felt her cheeks do a slow glow. She chose to ignore the comment, looking at her watch instead. "Oh, look at that. I have to run. I'm late for work. Byee." She could have kicked herself for that. Obviously, Candy was already having an influence.

She quickly exited before he could say anything else or stop her. She didn't look back until she was in her car, and then she took a deep breath before driving off. She wasn't happy that Ty knew of her plan, but there was nothing she could do at this point.

She would just have to make sure it panned out.

She took the time during the short drive to the office to wonder about Candy's seeming lack of distress. Maybe she and Marcotti weren't having an affair after all. Maybe she'd been in it only for the gifts and was really one cold-hearted femme fatale. Or maybe she didn't know what had happened. But his death had been in the news and surely the staff at the fitness center had been told. He had been their boss, after all. J.J. stowed her thoughts as she pulled into the parking lot behind the office building.

By midafternoon, J.J. had to admit to hunger pangs. She'd skipped lunch. Not a good idea. However, she was having dinner with Connor Mac later. She'd better snack up before going. Nothing worse than pigging out in front of a date.

"Hi. I'm here," Brittany Stewart announced as she pushed open the door to the office.

Skye looked up from her computer. "Great, Brittany. How was your school week?"

"Hi," J.J. threw in.

Brittany shrugged. "It was so cool. I have a hot date tomorrow to go to see Cirque du Soleil. I think it's the first time they're performing in Burlington, and it's so cool that I'm going. Is it all right if I work a bit later tonight and skip tomorrow morning?"

"Sure," Skye agreed. "We've got some snail mail that needs to go out and some filing." She looked over at J.J. "Anything else?"

"Nothing aside from the website update that you were going come in special to do tomorrow. Are you still able to get that done?"

"It's a snap. I can do that with my eyes closed," Brittany bragged. She went right to work, sorting through the paper tasks first. Individual binders were kept for each event, and keeping them up to date was Brittany's job. Also, even though most transactions were handled by e-mail these days,

Skye insisted additional paper backup of everything be filed, just in case.

J.J. watched her for a few minutes. Oh, to be so excited over a date. She wondered what that felt like. It had been a long time. Of course, it was a long time since she'd been a high school senior, too. She was certain Brittany had no shortage of dates. Over the past five months she'd worked for them, she'd seemed more interested in talking about the latest clothes and whether she should straighten her long blonde locks than what was happening in the world.

J.J. gave herself a mental kick. That wasn't really fair. At that age, she herself had also been interested in fashions and style, which is probably why she'd drifted into the world of advertising on graduating from Champlain College in Burlington. It had beckoned like the call of the ocean and a wide strip of white sand. In fact, her first campaign had been for a travel agency. And she had lucked out with a free trip to those sands, a trip of a lifetime. But she'd also been aware of the extreme poverty just outside the gates of the resort. She shouldn't dismiss Brittany so quickly. Maybe she had a charity or concern that she was into but just never talked about.

J.J. finally shut down her computer and grabbed her briefcase. "Gotta go. I've got a hot date myself tonight."

"Connor? Hot?" Skye joked.

"Yes and yes. Have a good weekend, both of you."

"Good luck with your dinner club on Sunday."

"Thank you. Not worried. See, no nerves." She held out both hands in front of her, then quickly grabbed her purse when she noticed the slight shaking. "Ciao."

She'd already checked the mirror three times before Connor knocked on her apartment door. She took a final glance at herself before opening it. She'd realized how it was odd that she be so conscious of how she looked when going out with Connor.

There were no sparks there. Nothing to suggest future passion. But she did have fun with him, and Connor always looked ready to step into the limelight. There was a certain buzz about that. As the morning man on local radio station WHMB, he'd been chosen as the face of the place for all their advertising. His dark good looks, enhanced by a perpetual five o'clock shadow, always turned heads wherever he went. And J.J. had decided, without even realizing it, that she should at least try not to embarrass him when they went out. The look of pleasure on his face when he eyed her reinforced her decision to wear a silky red swing blouse with skinny black pants.

"I'm ready," she said after a quick kiss on the cheek.

Connor had booked them a table at Ettore Trattoria, a fairly new Italian restaurant in downtown Burlington. J.J. was impressed. She also realized it might be quite some time before her recent penchant for Italian food was forgotten.

"I'd heard you had to book months in advance to get a spot here," she whispered after the maître d' had held her chair for her. She looked around. It seemed to be full even at this early hour.

Connor grinned what she'd come to label his real smile. "I don't play the media card very often, but I really wanted to eat here and I thought you'd find it cool." He ran his right hand across his chin and reached for the menu.

She nodded. "I do."

"So tell me," he said after they'd placed their orders, "are you all set for Sunday's feast, or do you think it would jinx it to talk about any questions you might have?"

J.J. smiled. "I have it all in hand, thanks to some friendly advice from a certain Italian who's in the food business."

Connor looked suddenly serious. "Do you mean Antonio Marcotti? I'd heard you were interviewed by the police."

"No, not Marcotti. But you're right, I'm on their suspect list. I meant Rocco Gates."

"Also on that list."

"How do you know that? Oh, of course, the media knows all." She knew she sounded sarcastic, so she smiled to take the edge off.

He shrugged. "We try. So tell me, is this bothering you a lot?"

"It is, of course. I was the last person to talk to him, or so it seems, except for the murderer that is. And I don't like being thought of as a suspect. But I'm also worried that two friends are on that list, too."

Connor nodded. "I know about Evan."

"Hm. See what I mean?"

He stared at her until she looked at him. "I'm not the bad guy here. I have a job and I do it and, I might add, being a radio host is a far cry from being a newsperson. And I do understand how it can turn your life upside down to be involved in something like this."

"That's a good description. I try not to dwell on it, especially since I do have deadlines at work, but sometimes . . ."

He covered her hand with his and gave it a comforting squeeze. "I know you're innocent, and I also know that Evan is, too."

"What about Rocco?"

"I don't know much about him. I've been to his bistro a couple of times and he seems like a nice guy, but we've never really talked. I would think, though, that if you like him and trust him, he's gotta be okay."

"Thanks." J.J. took a sip of the wine that had been served while they were talking. "He's been good to me. I feel I owe him."

"Have you talked to Alison about all this? She is a police officer, after all." Connor offered her a slice of still-warm bread and pushed the butter dish closer to her.

"I haven't seen Alison since we were all at the Cups 'n' Roses. I can't keep track of her work schedule."

"Well, why not give her a call? Get her take on how it's going. I bet she'll help put your mind at ease."

J.J. thought about it. "Sounds better than just sitting around worrying."

CHAPTER 14

Sunday morning, J.J. woke with a start, checked the clock on her bedside table, and flopped back on the pillow. Within seconds, Indie had jumped onto the bed and snuggled in beside her.

"Good morning, Indie. Did you do your early-morning rounds looking for bugs?" She ran her hand along his back, enjoying the softness and the resulting calm she always felt. After ten minutes, she eased away from him and pushed herself to get up. She had a busy day ahead.

She really needed a morning walk to clear her head and run over the list of to-dos for today's dinner. She put the cat food out, chugged a tall glass of water, and left.

The morning was cooler than she'd supposed but held the promise of sun and therefore warmer temperatures by the afternoon. She turned toward the bay and by the second block was into her power-walk stride. She would head straight to the water and walk along to one end, then circle back home.

She met several dog walkers, none of whom she knew, but she greeted them with a smile. She loved walking down Gabor Avenue and looking in the shop windows. This was where the tourist quality of the village really shone through. She'd have to come back later and have a closer look at the brightly striped cushions she spotted in the window of Accent. The store next door, Imagine That, showcased an equally tempting orange throw in its window. Oh, to have the time, and the money, to indulge.

She reached the boardwalk and was happy to see only one other person around, and she was jogging in the same direction but well ahead. J.J. took the stairs down to the sand and continued walking north, putting all thoughts out of her mind. The to-do list could wait for the walk back. At the end of the sandy part, she stopped where a wild thicket of brush and undergrowth provided a natural buffer to keep interlopers away from the estates that lay beyond, and veered right. That brought her within viewing distance of the gates to the Portovino estate. She stopped abruptly and sucked in her breath as the memory of her shouting match with Marcotti flooded back. Such a beautiful setting for such a tragic happening. She wondered if the Portovino family felt the same every time they stepped out of the house. *Maudlin.*

Time to head back and get the show on the road.

By two, the kitchen was a mess, and everything had been measured and prepared for the final stages in the cooking process. She glanced around. Why could she not clean up as she went along? Other cooks did. Those cooks were also less frazzled when it came time to dish up, she'd bet. She sighed and gathered all the dirty dishes and equipment, ran a sinkful of water, and washed down the countertop.

She'd loved the apartment when she'd first seen it two years ago. One of the major selling features for her was the open concept and resulting brightness in every room.

However, that was also the main problem, especially when it came to having dinner guests. The kitchen had to be totally cleaned first. Counters cleared and washed. Nothing extra to clutter the space.

She glanced at the clock and realized she wouldn't have time to Skype with her mom. She'd tried yesterday but it had been a rushed day for the Tanners, June and Adam, with her mom showing several houses to a client in town for the weekend, and her dad busy painting up a storm. Or maybe it wasn't a landscape he was working on this time. As a successful Realtor, June Tanner's days were filled with activity, quite different from when J.J. was growing up. Then she'd been a stay-at-home mom until the youngest child, J.J., entered high school, and then the floodgates opened and June was all about the job.

J.J.'s dad was usually found at his easel in his studio that had been added to the north end of the house. That had been a given all though her childhood. It had led to a prominent place in the artistic community and a house full of original paintings. J.J. had many of them adorning her walls, too. She'd chosen the ones having to do with water, complementing the seashore colors she'd chosen for her rooms. The water had always been a source of comfort and relaxation for her, and after her turbulent life in Montpelier, she'd decided to make her new apartment an oasis. And it had worked. Until the murder.

She looked at the sink and sighed again but was spared having to actually stick her hands in the water when the doorbell rang.

She checked through the peephole and saw Ness Harper staring back at her. He waggled his eyebrows and held up a bowl at eye level.

"Good afternoon. This is a surprise," she said, pulling the door wide open.

"I know this is your big cooking day, so I thought it would

be a good idea to share my special lunch with you. Help you get into the right frame of mind without actually having to do anything yet. That's if you haven't already eaten. I know it's a bit late for lunch."

"That's so thoughtful, Ness. I just worked straight through without taking a break to eat."

"I thought as much."

She reached for the bowl. "What is it?"

"Just some chili." He shrugged. "Haven't tried this particular recipe before, but it looked interesting."

"Will you share it with me?"

"Nope. I've eaten."

"Well, how about some coffee?"

"That I will do." He led the way into the kitchen as she shut the door.

She set the bowl on the counter and peeked at it. "Looks and smells yummy," she said.

"I tried it with some vegetables this time. Carrots and celery along with some different herbs. It should still have a kick, though." Ness sat at one of the stools at the counter. "So, what's new with the cops?"

J.J. shook her head. She finished making their coffee and carried it over to the counter. "I was hoping I was off the hook after what Ty Devine told them, but Detective Hastings called yesterday and asked a few more questions. He admitted I'm still on the list because I could have doubled back after Devine left."

Ness swore under his breath. J.J. smiled, feeling pleased to have his support. At least, she thought that's what it meant.

"I'm less worried now, though," she lied. "Their suspect list is getting longer by the day."

"Oh yeah? How so?"

"Well, my friend Evan Thornton—you remember him—has been questioned, as has Rocco Gates, the owner of Rocco

G's, although I'm certain neither of them had anything to do with it. That makes three of us who are actually innocent, so I'm hoping they have another list of people more likely to be the killer. I wonder if Candy Fleetwood has been added to that list." She debated over whether to tell him about her upcoming appointment with Candy and decided *Why not?*

"I'm sure I don't have to tell you that you can't come right out and ask her if she did it," Ness commented when she'd filled him in.

"I know that. But I hope I can get a feel for how their relationship was going. If it was on the rocks, she could be a suspect."

"The wife sounds like a better suspect, especially if she knew, and I do believe every wife knows, at some point."

J.J. took a sip of her coffee and pondered that. She wondered if Ness was speaking from personal experience. "Well, we know that she realized there was an affair, because she hired Devine to find out who it was with, even though he won't admit it to us. And as far as we know, he was still trying to find the person at the time Marcotti was killed. That's why Devine was tailing me."

"Or so he says. I wouldn't be too quick to believe everything that shyster tells you."

"Is this instinct or knowledge speaking?" J.J. smiled.

"Humph. Thirty-five years, partly on the street and then working as a detective. Look, I gotta go. You keep out of trouble, you hear?"

J.J. saluted him. "Yessir. And, thanks, Ness."

He made a gruff sound in his throat and let himself out.

So, he doesn't trust Devine. I don't, either, but he may be the best chance at finding the killer. If I can't. Where did that come from? I don't know how to do this, and I don't want to. Not really.

J.J. went back to tidying the kitchen. As much as she appreciated Ness's gesture, her stomach was too tied in knots to eat anything right now, even though she had skipped lunch. She stuck the chili in a covered glass dish and set it in the fridge. Her mind kept going on the sleuthing track. *She pictured finally cornering the killer, although his face was in the shadows and unidentifiable. She tried talking tough, but he came at her with a large knife, which she couldn't escape.* So much for a worst-case scenario. Her mind then landed her behind bars, in jail, charged with murder. Maybe this was the worst-case scenario. Either way, she shuddered and blinked, glad to have that over with.

Now, dishes first, then maybe a short lie-down with Indie. She shrugged her shoulders and held in that position for a count of twenty, then released. After doing this three more times, she tilted her head to each shoulder and then shook out her arms and hands.

Tension begone.

"The cookbook was a good choice, J.J., with lots of tempting recipes, but I sort of missed there not being an appetizer section," Evan said as he scooped a spoonful of the fettuccine with mushrooms, marsala, and mascarpone onto his plate.

"Are you complaining?" Alison asked. "And by the way, I believe the correct term is *antipasto*, not *appetizer*."

"Point to you, Alison. You know I never complain, but it is unusual. Am I the only one feeling this way?"

"You're right," Connor answered. "Usually, there's a variety of antipasti—at least that's what's on the menu in an Italian restaurant, so I'm sure other cookbooks include a section."

"Well, the cover does call them 'Italian-inspired recipes.' So I guess Nigella is using her favorites or recipes that complement each other. I mean, it's like any author crafting a book, be it a novel or nonfiction. They get to choose what they want to include or leave out," Beth added.

J.J. nodded. "I'm with you on that. And another thing the cover says is 'easy.' I'm sold."

Everyone laughed, and Evan passed the basket of *pane*, the crusty Rosetta rolls provided by J.J. The rules allowed the host to add such items to the menu, even if they weren't included in the cookbook being used.

Silence followed while they each savored the flavors on their plates. Too nervous to eat, J.J. scarcely touched her food. And what she did try was tasteless. Had she chosen the wrong cookbook? Had she made a mess of her dish? Had she known what she was getting into?

"Absolutely delicious," Beth pronounced at last. "I love the pizzaiola. Like it says in the cookbook, it reminds me of a pizza topping, and you know how I love pizza."

J.J. gave a quiet sigh of relief. She glanced around at the others. Looked like they all agreed.

"You've really done it, J.J. It looks inviting and tastes great. I'll bet it wasn't an easy choice for you to make, no matter what the cover says." Evan added a second helping of everything to his plate. "In fact, I think all of the dishes are delicious, and we have chosen a very compatible meal. By the way, I noticed the beef—or rather, turkey—pizzaiola called for anchovies." He looked directly at Alison as he said this and she made a gagging sound. "I'm assuming you got around that, or Alison would not be faking her ungracious gesture."

"I asked Rocco Gates for some suggestions, and he came up with using miso. I hope it's worked."

"It's seamless," Beth agreed. "And it smells wonderful, just begging you to stick a fork in."

"You can relax and eat now," Alison said, giving her an elbow nudge.

J.J. smiled. "That obvious?"

Alison nodded and took another mouthful of the piz-zaiola.

J.J. did the same. She took a couple seconds to savor the flavor before swallowing. The turkey was tender, and a tang came from the garlic, olives, and capers. *Yay!*

"Okay, so what did you like best about this book?" Con-nor asked J.J.—the standard question at all their dinners. "Besides the pictures, I mean."

J.J. waited until the chuckles had stopped. She'd prepared for this part, too.

"It really is a helpful book. Nigella Lawson has included all sorts of cooking tips and sections that give an explanation about the ingredients. It's like she was here, sitting at the counter, talking me through it. I actually picture her with a glass of red wine in hand, leaning of the counter, encourag-ing, sipping. Of course, I have to give a lot of credit to Rocco Gates, also. He's a great teacher."

"Speaking of Rocco, is he still a suspect?" Beth asked.

"Why are you all looking at me?" Alison asked. She popped a black olive in her mouth. "I told you, this has nothing to do with me. And you should stay out of it. I know nothing, I tell nothing."

"Well, then you should hear nothing," Evan suggested. "So, plug your ears."

"What?"

"You heard me, therefore you haven't plugged your ears. Just give us a minute to bring everyone up to date, and no lip reading, either."

"Huh. I do not plug my ears, but I do have to excuse myself and visit the powder room. So talk quickly." Alison pushed back her chair, nodding at Connor, who was about to pour her some more wine.

They all looked at J.J. and waited.

She gave herself a few moments to organize her thoughts.

"Here goes. I've hooked up with a personal trainer at High Time Fitness Center because she's the mistress of the deceased. Some of you may know some of this already." She glanced at each of them quickly before proceeding.

"Then there's this private eye who was following me because he thought I might be the mistress." She heard Connor choke on his wine.

"Of course, I'm not and he knows that now. But he keeps getting in the way, and even though he could have alibied me for the murder, he sort of left me dangling in the suspicions, so to speak." She avoided looking at Connor. "That's about where it's at right now. Except that I'm not guilty, Evan's not guilty, and I don't believe Rocco is, either."

"Do you think the mistress did it and if not, what's next?"

"I haven't decided about her yet, and even so, we need more suspects anyway. The police have got to know there are many more people out there who hated the man and could have done the deed. We just have to figure out who they all are."

"And that, my friends," Alison said as she walked back to her chair, "is a job for the detectives."

CHAPTER 15

By Monday afternoon, J.J. felt back in charge of her life. No surprise calls from the police. No Ty Devine crossing her path. She was still getting e-mails from her dinner cohorts with kudos for her Sunday meal. The only negativity in her life came from her three-times-a week visit to the health club that she'd committed to. Today had been only the first day, and not only had she learned nothing about Candy Fleetwood's relationship with Antonio Marcotti, but she'd also developed a slight tilt to the left, as Skye pointed out when she entered their office later that morning.

"Are you sure this is what you want to be doing to your body?" Skye grabbed the latte that J.J. held out to her and took an appreciative sip. "Hmm. This is what works for my body. So, tell me: is the torture worth the payback in info?"

J.J. sat down gingerly in her chair and took a sip of her own latte. She could feel its restorative effects as it burned its way down her throat. She blew on it, then took a sip. "It's really hard to get any casual conversation in when Candy is timing me and checking the the amount of weights I'm lifting all the time. I think I'll give it the week, and if no opportunity arises, I'll ask her to meet me for coffee—to talk about my workout plan, of course."

"If you last that long."

"There is that." She set her latte on the desk and turned on her computer. Skye took an incoming call and was in the middle of a conversation when J.J. let out a yelp. Skye eyed her and raised her eyebrows.

J.J. stared at her computer screen and kept shaking her head and groaning. Finally, Skye hung up and scurried across the room to read over J.J.'s shoulder.

"What the frig does that mean?" Skye demanded, pointing at the offending e-mail.

"I have no idea," J.J. managed to squeak out. "How could another event planner come up with exactly the same plans for Olivia Barker's retirement party? That's just not possible."

"No, it's not. You suggested an afternoon patio party at the very exclusive Walkton Club with their staff catering, right?"

"Uh-huh." J.J. felt her words leave her.

"That's not the go-to venue these days. Most groups want something more modern, down by the water if possible."

"They do, so that's why I thought, because we're talking about someone on the older side since he's retiring, that an aging-but-still-grand location would be better suited. Obviously, I was thinking too much in the box."

"Are the proposals exactly the same?"

"From what Ms. Barker says, they are. No wait. The other anonymous planner has suggested a private catering firm rather than the club's. But that's about all that differs. This can't be happening." J.J. stood and started to pace.

"Hold on. You've got another chance at it. Read on."

"I know. Barker wants one unique, dynamic suggestion

from each of us by end of day Friday and that will decide who she goes with. Friday! Something unique!" She started pacing faster. *She pictured herself racing up the stairs in the Carter building to Olivia Barker's office on the twelfth floor. Of course, the elevator wasn't working. As she struggled up to the receptionist's desk, the clock struck twelve, and a gorgeous blonde wearing a formfitting orange jersey sleeveless dress that stopped midthigh and fab multicolored heels at least six inches high, came out of Barker's office. She sneered at J.J. as she swept past her and out the door. Olivia Barker appeared at her door and told J.J. she was sorry, but J.J. was too late.*

J.J. realized Skye stood watching her. J.J. gave her a weak grin and slumped on the couch. "Oh boy."

"Understatement."

J.J. sat staring out the window for several minutes, then sat upright. "I will not lose this one. I'll come up with something so brilliant it will live on in the annals of event planning. But what?"

Back at her own desk, Skye asked, "Are you wanting to brainstorm or trying to psyche yourself up?"

"I think I'll get my brain in gear first, then try to storm the little gray cells. If all fails, I'll draw you into the loop. Okay?"

"Fine. In that case, I'm taking an early lunch with Nick. He wants me to take a look at a new condo he's thinking of buying."

"Whoo-ee. Does this involve a ring in the future?"

Skye thought about it a second. "We pussyfoot around it, so I doubt it's anytime soon. He just wants my input. Superior taste, you know." She winked as she slid her arms into her pale blue jacket, pulled her purse out of her desk drawer, and patted J.J. on the head as she walked past her. "I have complete and utter confidence in you, sweetie. You'll pull it off."

J.J. grunted and went back to staring out the window. What

to do? She usually loved coming up with ideas; in fact, that's the part of the job she enjoyed the most. The follow-through could be tedious and tiring at times. Of course, time management was not her strongest suit. Skye held the trophy in that area. And there were always those pesky obstacles that popped up every now and then, derailing the critical path she'd worked so hard to create. Relying on other people could be a downer sometimes, too. Uh-oh, this wasn't good. She was spiraling into a funk. *Time to think positive.*

The wrap-up of a job well done was the most positive feeling ever. But the ideas were her spark. How could someone else have come up with that same spark? She sat up a bit straighter. She wouldn't let this anonymous person get the better of her. She could do it. She just had to relax, let the ideas flow. Start jotting ideas on the whiteboard they'd attached to the wall, behind the door when it was open. That was it. Every time she walked out the door, she had to first jot down an idea. *Great start.*

The phone rang, and she pushed herself off the couch with a slight groan. Sitting in that position for a prolonged length of time hadn't been such a good idea. She was limping slightly when the office door opened. She looked over to find Ty Devine staring at her, a look of amusement on his face.

"I see you're taking to the fitness project with ease."

She shook her head at him and grabbed the phone, but it had already gone to voice mail. She hung up, took a deep breath, and turned to face him.

"What can I do for you, Mr. Devine?" That was good a good start. "Or are you here to share some information with me?" Time to start pumping him.

"About what?"

J.J. bit her tongue before exploding at him. He was goading her; she knew that. She could handle it. "Perhaps about the murder investigation of Antonio Marcotti. It appears I am still a suspect since you volunteered information about it being possible for me to slip back to the scene of the crime." She glared at him until he answered.

"First of all, I didn't volunteer any information. I answered the questions I was asked. And second, it is true. However, if you're innocent, you have nothing to worry about."

"*If* I'm innocent. Of course I am. But given that, do you really believe I have nothing to worry about?" she asked, unable to hide the quaver in her voice. She sank into her chair.

He looked at her and sighed. "No, I don't believe it. I was just trying to make you feel better. I've worked with the police before. Hell, I was a cop at one point, and I know how easy it is to have tunnel vision. You find a suspect that fits the bill, and suddenly you make it happen."

"You were a cop?"

He grinned. "Yes, in another life."

"Where? When?"

"Boston. And like I said, another life." He sat on the edge of her desk. The edge nearest her, she noticed.

"Why did you quit? Or were you fired?" *The devil made me say that.*

He glanced sharply at her. "Like I said, it was another life. Now, I know you're pretty uptight about all this, but I have a question for you."

Despite herself, she felt intrigued. "Shoot. Oops."

He grinned again. She almost flashed him one in return.

"Not today," he said. "I want you to tell me all you've learned so far, and before you try to stonewall again, I'm talking about the Marcotti investigation. If you think I'm not clueing in to the fact that you're questioning Candy Fleetwood and Rocco Gates, not to mention that you're friends with Evan Thornton, then you're delusional. Four equally viable suspects. And you're the constant here. So, what do you know?"

She shrugged. "I'm flattered you think I have the ability to figure this out when neither the cops nor you have, but really, I don't have a clue. Honestly. I know I didn't do it; equally certain it wasn't Evan; very sure Rocco is innocent; and, not sure what I think about Candy. How's that?"

Ty grimaced. "One of us is not trying hard enough."

"You mean you're clueless, too?" She tried to keep a straight face.

"That is correct; however, it's early days."

"I thought the cops always say if it's not solved in the first forty-eight hours, it probably won't be solved."

"You've been watching too much TV but that's generally how it goes. However, for a high profile case like this one, they'll keep digging, and deeply, for some time. They'll want a solid case before it goes to trial."

He stood and looked down at her. That made her uncomfortable, so she also stood, trying not to groan, and faced him with the desk between them.

"What makes it high profile? Marcotti wasn't a politician. He wasn't overly wealthy, was he? No celebrity status. Or am I missing something?"

"His wife is independently wealthy, and with that status comes some pull. I'm certain she'll make sure this is followed through to the end."

"Is she your client?"

He grinned. "Nice try." He glanced at his watch. "Gotta run. But I'll leave you with some advice: since you haven't dug too deeply yet, don't. There is a murderer on the loose, and he won't stop at getting rid of you if he thinks you're getting too close to finding him, no matter how cute."

"Excuse me? Cute? Are you using that word in the same thought as a killer?" Her cheeks felt on fire. "As you can see, I'm not getting in your investigative way, nor am I a threat to anyone, so I may or may not ask a few questions here and there. Have a nice afternoon." She limped to the door and held it open for him.

He flashed her a smile as he left but said nothing.

She caught the door before it slammed. No good letting him know he'd gotten under her skin. Cute was not her style. Nor was playing sleuth, but she wanted to find out who had murdered Marcotti and save not only herself but also her friends from further anguish. She did not include Candy Fleetwood in that group.

She was at home later that night, having finished the leftovers from Sunday's dinner and nursing a glass of red wine, when the thought came to her. Of the group of four, as she had started thinking of them, Candy was the only viable suspect, so what was her motive? And, if it wasn't Candy, then there were others to be added to the list. How long was the list the police had, and how could she find out who was on it?

Alison wouldn't give names, but maybe she would nod or something in answer to questions like *Are there more than four suspects?* Maybe Tansy's spy could then fill in the details. J.J. reached for the phone and punched in Alison's home number.

"Alison, I have a quick but important question to ask you," she said when voice mail kicked in. "If you're free for coffee tomorrow morning, I'll be at Cups 'n' Roses at seven forty-five. Let me know."

There, that would have to do for now. Except for the list of possible Candy motives. She grabbed a pad and wrote down a heading. How about jealousy? Anger? Or both? She had wanted to be Mrs. Marcotti and he, after months or years (how long had they been together?) had finally told her in no uncertain terms that he would never leave his wife. Candy then plotted, waiting for the right moment when he'd be alone, late at night, possibly leaving a client's event, which of course he would have told her about. And she lay in wait, stabbing him to death when the coast was clear. That would work.

However, would her anger have been that raw after a few days of waiting for the perfect killing time? Probably not. So she'd have been better off disposing of the Mrs. and then just stepping into that role.

Oh no. J.J. had just ruled out Candy as the murderer.

CHAPTER 16

J.J. had just paid for her latte when she got a text from Alison saying she was on the way. Within minutes, Alison, in uniform, walked through the door. J.J. had chosen the table nearest the cash and watched as she made her way over.

"I can't stay long. Just need to get me and my partner some java."

"Let me get them. My treat."

"You must want something real bad," Alison answered, pulling out a chair.

J.J. smiled. "Hear me out, then we'll get the coffee. I know you can't divulge anything about the Marcotti investigation." She reached out to touch Alison's arm when she saw the look on Alison's face. "But, if you could just maybe, like, *nod* if I'm right or do nothing if I'm wrong, that would help me so, so much. You know that neither I nor Evan are killers. I have to clear our names."

"That's what we have detectives for," Alison hissed, leaning toward her. "Just trust them and leave it to them."

"I'd love to, but I've been told by two ex-cops within the past three days that might not be such a good idea—the first part, that is. So all I want to know is if there are more than four suspects being looked at. The ones I know about are me, Evan, Rocco Gates, and Candy Fleetwood. Are there more?"

Alison sighed and lowered her head then looked up and over to the window. J.J. took that to be a nod. "Oh man. Thank you so much. I feel much better. I don't suppose you can get me those names?"

Alison remained still. J.J. sighed. "I didn't think so. Oh, well, it really is good to know the police are still looking into other possible suspects. Let's get those coffees. I know you're rushed."

As Alison grabbed the two cups, she said in a low voice, "I do not consider these to be a bribe. You are just being thoughtful to your friend."

"Absolutely."

J.J. added another two lattes to her tally and headed for the office. After depositing one of them in front of Skye, she stashed her own on her desk, and crossed over to Tansy's office. The assistant's desk was empty, so J.J. knocked on the inner office door and entered when Tansy called out.

"I'm sorry to bother you," she began, "but I need your help."

"I told you: keep a lawyer on speed dial." Tansy started rifling through her Rolodex. "I know just the person to help you."

"No, sorry, that's not what I want. Let me explain." She waited until Tansy sat back in her chair, giving her full attention. Today's outfit was a navy suit, the jacket of which was hanging on the back of her chair, and a white blouse with navy polka dots. *Power suit. Must be an important day. Maybe a court date.*

"I have it on the best authority that the police have added more suspects to the list in the Marcotti murder. I know of four names, but I'm hoping your spy—uh, *source*—can give you the names of the others. Do you think that's possible?" J.J. used her best smile and hoped that would be enough.

Tansy shook her head. "Not possible. I won't even ask her. I can't use her for insignificant things like that. I save her for the big stuff, like if I need some background info for a trial. You can understand that, can't you?" Tansy's smile seemed sincere.

J.J. sighed. "I suppose so, but I'm not sure how else to find out what's going on."

"Why do you need to know? You already said they have over four suspects now. That means you're off the front burner, at least. Have the police brought you back in for questioning in the past few days? No? You see? Now, I have a meeting in twenty minutes. Come back and see me anytime. My door is always open, and I'm always ready to help." Tansy waved her away, and J.J. left feeling totally dismissed.

"'My door is always open, and I'm always ready to help,'" J.J. mimicked as she flopped down at her own desk.

"Tansy, I take it. You know with her it's always quid pro quo. What does she need from you? Think about it. I'm having an early lunch with the corporate team-building trainer who'll be working with me on the weekend retreat project for the city. How about you?"

"I'm still trying to come up with a dynamite zinger for Olivia Barker."

"I see you've added, and subtracted, a few ideas to the whiteboard. How's that working for you?"

"Just great. At this rate, I'll hit the brilliant idea by, say, Christmas."

J.J. finished her latte, now cold, and turned her attention to her e-mail. By the time noon rolled around, she had come up with a couple of ideas, both of them non-starters, so decided to heed the call of her stomach and head to Rocco G's for something to eat. She also hadn't told him about how well her dinner had gone, and she knew he wanted to hear all about it. She quickly scribbled an idea on her way out. She knew she'd cross it out on her way back in.

Only one table stood vacant when she arrived at Rocco G's. She snagged it and then made her way to the counter to order an espresso. "You look a bit frantic, Zoe. Has Rocco deserted you?"

"OMG, that's just it. I don't know. He had to go to the police station a couple of hours ago, and he's still not back. I'd just walked in the door to start my shift, and he walked out. I'm getting a bit worried, but Hank Ransom—he's the cook—says it's nothing." She shrugged. "I hope you don't mind, but it might be a bit of a wait for your food." She smiled an apology.

"No problem. Could I just sneak back there and ask Hank something?"

"Sure. I guess it's okay."

While Zoe busied herself delivering two plates of food that had just appeared on the pass-through, J.J. scurried through the swinging door into the kitchen. Probably not the best time to bother a chef, she acknowledged, but she was worried about Rocco.

"Hank Ransom, isn't it?" she asked.

He grunted. He had his back to her, and all she could see were white runners, blue jeans, a long white apron that had been tied in the back over a navy T-shirt, and long dark hair caught back in a ponytail. His body looked very thin. *Obviously, he doesn't sample while cooking.*

"I'm J.J. Tanner, a friend of Rocco's."

He shot her a quick glance without turning to face her. "You've been in here before. You're the one with the questions about cooking Italian, right?"

"Yes," J.J. said, pleased that Rocco had mentioned her. "I know this is a bad time to disturb you, but I won't take a minute. Zoe just told me about Rocco going down to the police station. Did he say anything before going? He's been gone a long time, hasn't he?" Although her interview had taken just as long, she realized.

He turned to look at her and then glanced up at the clock. "He's been there since ten, but like I told Zoe, he'll be okay. It's about the Marcotti murder, but he's not a killer. They won't keep him long."

"I'm happy to hear you have confidence in him. How can you be so sure he didn't do it?" She had her own reasons, but she wanted to hear others'.

He almost put his hands on his waist, but then remembered the bread crumbs coating them and turned back to the counter and the fish he was coating. "He just didn't. He's a good guy. He has a short fuse, but it's out just as fast. Look, I really don't have time to talk."

"Sure. I know. I'm sorry. Thanks," J.J. mumbled as she backed out of the kitchen.

By the time her food was set in front of her, about half the crowd had finished eating and left. She thought about her short chat with Hank. She was pleased they agreed on the fact that Rocco wasn't the murderer. But she had wanted to ask him some more questions. She'd obviously have to come back another time.

She watched Zoe smooth back her long curly dark hair and secure it again with an elastic band. She really looked the part of a harried mom of twin seven-year-olds but maybe, as Rocco said, that's what made her so capable of handling the noisy lunch crowd. She'd be heading home shortly and would hopefully have a bit of a break before the kids arrived home from school. Try as hard as she could, J.J. couldn't imagine that lifestyle. Maybe she'd remain single forever.

Rocco hadn't returned by the time J.J. had finished her lunch. She checked with Zoe, but there hadn't been a phone call from him either, so she headed back to work.

She dialed Alison's cell phone as she waited for her computer screen to load. From the background there were sounds of traffic when Alison answered, and J.J. guessed she was working and away from the station. "I'm sorry to bother you but I really need to find out something."

She could hear Alison take a deep breath, or at least that's what she thought it sounded like. Maybe that was her conscience prodding her.

"I might not be able to help you, J.J. You know that."

"I do know, but I need to ask, anyway. Can you find out why Rocco Gates is spending so long at the police station? Apparently, he's been there since ten this morning."

"You're just curious, right? You're not going to do anything. Right?"

"Absolutely."

"Okay. Give me a few minutes. I'll call you back." She hung up without waiting for a response.

J.J. was getting caught up on her e-mail when Alison's call came through. "I have some bad news for you. Or maybe it's good news in a way. Rocco Gates is being detained for further questioning about the murder of Antonio Marcotti."

"Arrested? But that's all wrong. He's not the killer." J.J. felt a flutter of panic.

"Pardon me, but I think the detectives are better able to make that call. However, I did not say he was arrested. They can hold him for twenty-four hours for questioning without having to charge him. You should be pleased. That means you and Evan are off the hook."

"Well, I am pleased about that, but I'm worried about Rocco."

"I didn't know you two were such close friends."

"Maybe we're not, but he's been good to me. Besides, he's a nice guy, and I'm sure he's not a killer."

"Nice guys are bad guys sometimes. I gotta go. We'll talk later."

J.J. sat staring at the phone. She couldn't believe it. She was certain Rocco wasn't a killer. She didn't really know how she knew, but way down deep, she believed in him. Maybe she was a little naive for feeling this way after having known him for such a short period of time, but sometimes people just click and that's what had happened. She realized she thought of him as a good friend.

"Who's been arrested?" Skye demanded. She put a hand on J.J.'s shoulder and gently rubbed.

"Rocco Gates. Although Alison says he's not yet charged, just being held. And that's just jargon. Bottom line, he's in jail."

"You sound pretty certain he's innocent."

"I am. He's such a sweet guy and I feel really bad for him. He took a lot of extra time to explain the intricacies of Italian ingredients to me. And he wanted my supper to turn out just right. What's going to happen to his bistro?"

"Do you know if he has someone to take care of it?"

J.J. sat back in her chair, a surprised look on her face. "I don't know a thing about his personal life. We've only talked food and murder."

"And that's what you base your conviction on?" Skye shook her head. "You are so trusting. So who would know?"

"Rocco's cook, Hank, might, but he's already kicked me out of the kitchen once today. Besides, I'm pretty sure he works only part-time for Rocco, and once the lunch hour's over, he's out of there. I wonder where he goes."

"Would Evan know anything?"

"I don't even know how well he knows Rocco." She picked

up a pencil and tapped it lightly on the desk. "I think I'll see if Tansy can find out anything."

"Again? She's going to start the clock on you soon, you know."

"I have an idea." J.J. stood and straightened her blouse. "Wish me luck.

She heard Skye doing just that as she closed their office door behind her. She opened Tansy's door to find Izzy, Tansy's assistant, on the phone. J.J. motioned to Tansy's office, and Izzy gave her a thumbs-up.

"Tansy, do you have a minute?" J.J. asked as she stuck her head around the inner door.

"Depends. What do you have in mind?" Tansy had her suit jacket on, which probably meant J.J. had better make this quick.

"I've been thinking about the paint situation, and I think you're right. We do need and deserve fresh paint on this entire floor." J.J. kept her expression earnest.

Tansy clapped her hands. "Yes. I knew you'd agree. Come in and sit down."

"Have you thought about a color?"

"Have I." Tansy reached into a desk drawer and pulled out a stack of paint color chips. She had a thick elastic band marking a spot about halfway through the two-inch stack. "What do you think of this, in two or even three tones?"

"I like it." J.J. was truly impressed. She'd expected something more "in your face." "It looks classy and cheerful at the same time. What are you thinking, the pale cream—or I guess it's called maize—for the walls and then one of the darker tones for all the trim?" She looked around at what that might entail. Windows, doors, and crown moldings.

"Exactly. Now, you'll talk to Evan? Take this with you and it should help you convince him."

J.J. reached for the stack and held the chip away from her, closing one eye to help with her imagining the entire wall that color. "I will."

She stood but paused before leaving. "It might take me a while to get to Evan today, though. My friend Rocco Gates is being held for questioning in the Marcotti murder and I'm worried about him. I'm not sure if he has a lawyer or what. I don't even know if he has family who might help."

Tansy shoved her glasses above her forehead. "Hm. I wonder if I were to make some phone calls if that might ease your mind so you can concentrate on that talk with Evan?"

"Would you? How wonderful, Tansy." J.J. sat back down. She worried that Tansy might put off doing it once she left the room.

Tansy sighed and punched a number into her phone. She picked up the receiver as the number connected. After several minutes of asking questions, and even more of waiting, she finally had an answer. She hung up and focused on J.J.

"He has a lawyer and the police have twenty-four hours before they have to release him or charge him. If he's charged, he can appear in court before a judge to see if bail can be set. That might not be possible, though."

"Why?"

"It is a murder case. They don't often let go of their prime suspect."

"But he's a businessman with ties in the community."

"Have you ever thought of becoming a lawyer? No? Probably a good thing. We'll just have to wait and see, but the lawyer is all over it, so don't you worry. Now, I think Evan might be in his office this afternoon." She looked pointedly at the door.

"Thanks, Tansy. I'll let you know how it goes."

J.J. wanted to head back to Rocco G's to see if there was

anything she could do, but she had promised Tansy. She squared her shoulders and took the stairs down to Evan's domain. A smile spread across her face when she saw the Closed sign on his office door.

She ran back upstairs, dropped the color chips on her desk, and grabbed her purse. "I'm just heading over to Rocco G's to check on things. I'll be back real quick," she told Skye.

"Don't worry. I'll hold down the fort."

J.J. walked as fast as her heels would allow but found another Closed sign when she reached Rocco G's. The lights were all off and nobody seemed to be moving around. Of course not. Both Zoe and Hank had done their jobs and then locked up when their shifts were over. A flicker of light caught her attention, and she cupped her right hand against the window and tried to peer in. There was somebody in there, she was certain. A burglar? The bistro would be a prime target for anyone who knew Rocco was in jail and that the part-timers had left by now. What to do? Call the police?

She pulled her smartphone out of her pocket and was about to punch in 911 when the person pushed open the door to the kitchen. There was enough light with the door open that she could recognize Hank Ransom. J.J. started pounding on the door. Ransom looked over at her and, without a moment's hesitation, backed into the kitchen and flicked off the light. J.J. tried knocking twice more but that didn't get her anywhere.

Had it even been Ransom? If so, why wouldn't he open the door? Probably because he didn't want to answer any more questions. That hadn't been her initial reason for going to Rocco G's, though. But what had she been thinking, that she could offer a helping hand? She wasn't in the restaurant business. It was really none of her concern. Except, in a way, it was. Rocco had been really nice to her, giving her all that advice about cooking Italian. She felt she owed him for that.

And they both had issues with the same guy, who was now deceased. There had to be something she could do.

Okay, Hank Ransom. You're definitely on my to-visit list. But at the moment, the best she could do was go back to the office, come up with a dazzling idea for Olivia Barker, and check one more thing off her list.

CHAPTER 17

J.J. knew the black car parked in front of her office building. A 2014 Acura driven by Ty Devine, if she was correct. She approached with caution, wondering what he was doing there, but at the same time wanting to avoid him.

On second thought, she needed to talk to him and at least let him know about Rocco. That is, if he didn't already know. But knowing Devine, he was well aware of everything happening with the case.

She leaned over and tapped on the passenger window and felt a bit pleased when he looked startled. He got out of the car and leaned on the roof to talk to her.

"Guess you caught me unawares." He grinned.

"Looks like it. Am I right in assuming you were waiting for me?"

"No. Actually, I didn't know you weren't here. I was just listening to the end of the newscast on the radio, and then I planned to pay you a visit. Maybe you'd like to hop in the car and we could go get a coffee and talk."

"Or maybe we could walk the block over to Cups 'n' Roses and get a coffee and talk." She raised her eyebrows in challenge.

"Okay by me." He pocketed his key fob and joined her on the sidewalk. "Lead the way."

"You don't know Cups 'n' Roses?" she asked in mock shock.

"Can I plead to not knowing this entire area at all? I recently moved to Burlington and haven't really had the need nor the opportunity to visit the outskirts."

"Outskirts? We don't take kindly to that kind of talk. Half Moon Bay is a very important part of the greater Burlington area. Besides, how can you not know about a scene like this?" She gestured in front of them. Gabor Avenue appeared to end right in the bay.

"It looks great, but it also looks like many other parts of the city that border Lake Champlain. How long have you lived here?"

"Almost two years."

He stopped and looked at her in surprise. "You were sounding like a born and raised Burlingtonian there."

"And I'm surprised you didn't know. Haven't you been digging around in my private life while trying to find out if I had a fling with Marcotti?" She was surprised and pleased that maybe her privacy hadn't been invaded.

"I look at the details relevant to a case. Your childhood would have no bearing on this matter, unless of course there was an even more sinister, deeper motive at play."

She couldn't tell if he was kidding or not, which irritated her. "There isn't." She stopped and pulled open the door to Cups 'n' Roses. "This is Half Moon Bay's finest coffee shop, owned and run by my good friend Beth Brickner."

Devine followed her to the counter and paid for two lattes.

"Thanks," she said as she sat down at one of the tables for two.

"Don't mention it." He took a long sip of his latte. "This is good."

"I told you. So, what did you want to talk to me about?"

Beth appeared at their table with two biscotti on a small plate. "This is on the house."

"Wow, thanks so much, Beth. This is Ty Devine."

"The PI? Really!"

Devine looked pleased. "Absolutely. And besides being the bearer of really delicious-looking treats, I gather you're also the owner?"

"Beth Brickner." She stuck out her hand. "I throw all modesty to the wind and avow that I am the owner of this place, voted number one in the *Half Moon Bay Village News* for one straight month in a row. And, I'm also a member of Culinary Capers."

"I should know that name?"

"Well, duh. You're sitting here with one of our newest members. Superb Italian cook J.J. Tanner. She didn't tell you? Or rather, you didn't discover that in your investigating?"

J.J. smiled. Score another one.

"Actually, no to both. What is it?"

"The best darn dinner club around." Beth pulled over a chair from the next table and sat. She broke off half of one of the biscotti and chewed on it. "There are five of us who take turns hosting a dinner each month. The significant part is that each person chooses a cookbook, and from it, an entrée. The rest of us then pick something to go with it from the same book." She leaned over and patted J.J.'s hand. "J.J. did a mean turkey pizzaiola Sunday." She sat back and cocked an eyebrow. "Do you cook?"

Devine laughed. "I know my way around a kitchen. Well,

I am impressed." He looked at J.J. "And is that how you know Rocco Gates?"

J.J. nodded. "He's my Italian-cooking guru."

"Then I'm sorry. I have some bad news for you."

Beth glanced at J.J. and then over at the line forming at the counter and stood and excused herself, pushing her chair back in its place.

"What? It can't be much worse than what's already happened," J.J. said, bracing herself.

"He's being detained for further questioning."

"I knew that."

"Of course you did. Why am I not surprised? And I'll bet you're still certain he's not a murderer." Devine stirred his latte but didn't take a drink.

"Of course he's not. They had history, but that doesn't always lead to murder. Is that really why you wanted to talk to me?"

"Yeah. I suspected you had a connection there, beyond your pumping him for information last time we met. I thought you should know."

J.J. smiled. "That was thoughtful. Thanks. Now, if you can just come up with the name of the real murderer, you'll be my hero."

Devine laughed. "Such an easy task. On the upside, this places you closer to the bottom of the suspect list."

"So I've been told. Do you think the police will still keep investigating, or will it be a slam dunk now with a prime suspect in hand?"

"Hard to say. I haven't worked with Detective Hastings before, but he seems to be thorough. I'd like to think he'll keep looking."

"Which is why I'm still on the list." She looked down at the plate. Empty. *Oh, well. You snooze, you lose.*

"Yeah. Tell me what you know about this feud between Gates and Marcotti."

"Well, Rocco didn't talk much about it. In fact, all he admitted was that the feud was over a woman, when they still lived in Italy. He did say they left at about the same time to come to the US, but I'm not sure why they settled in the same area."

"Hm. Seems rather odd if they were enemies. I'll look into that. Maybe Mrs. Marcotti will know. Is Gates married?"

"I think he's a widower. We didn't talk about family, just mainly about olive oils and anchovy substitutes. So is the wife still looking for the other lover?"

Devine grimaced. "Nice try."

J.J. leaned forward on her elbows. "And you really don't think that Candy Fleetwood is the murderer?"

"She'd be better off to murder the wife, don't you think?"

"Well, what if there is someone else and she didn't like being cheated on? How weird would that be? He's still with his wife but cheating on his mistress, as well as on his wife. Huh. What a crud. What?"

Devine looked like he was trying to suppress laughter. "You just can't help it, can you?"

"Huh?"

"Digging around in it."

"You're the one who wanted to tell me about Rocco." She tried to look affronted but knew she hadn't pulled it off.

Devine looked at her a moment before answering. "But not to get you involved any deeper."

"Not true. You were hoping I'd know something and tell you." She stood. "Not today, sorry. But thanks for the latte."

Devine beat her to the door and held it open for her. She mumbled another thank-you and walked beside him in silence until they'd reached his car.

"He didn't do it, Devine. I truly believe that."

Devine nodded. "See you."

∘ ∘ ∘

J.J. sat at her desk staring at, but not seeing, the photo of a snow covered bridge on the wall opposite. She felt like pounding her head on the desk. Maybe that would unleash the brilliant idea that was just floating around inside her brain, waiting to be harnessed.

"That photo's not going to tell you a thing," Skye finally said. "You've got a good start on the whiteboard. Would you like me to brainstorm with you? It would be less painful than watching you."

"Why are you watching me? I thought you had your own proposal to finish." She looked at Skye. "Thanks for the offer but I'm almost there. I can feel it. The trick is, if this competitor is thinking along the same lines I am, I have to totally switch tracks to best him or her on this. I can't suggest anything predictable."

"Hmm. Good thinking. Good luck." Skye answered the phone, and J.J. went back to staring at the photo.

"The thing is," she continued when Skye had hung up, "right now, I'm much more interested in figuring out who killed Marcotti and getting Rocco off the hook."

"Not your job. How about a choir made up of his coworkers singing lyrics you write that are set to a popular song?"

"Too ordinary, in an unusual kind of way." She closed her eyes. When she opened them, the door was flung open and Connor walked in.

"Hi, gorgeous. I've just finished taping an interview for tomorrow's show and I'm ravenous. Join me for an early dinner? Hi, Skye."

Skye waved at him, then turned to her computer.

"I'd like to, Connor, but I have to finish off this proposal I'm working on. I'm running out of time."

"We'll make it a quick meal. I just heard about Rocco Gates being in jail, and I thought you might want to talk some more about it all. I've been thinking about the murder ever since you first got involved. Do you think they've finally got their man, or is there something they're missing?"

He looked so concerned and sincere and delectable in his beige chinos, black plaid shirt, and black leather jacket. Of course, Connor always looked his best. He ran his hand across his chin. He seemed to do it unconsciously, although she often wondered if he was checking the thickness of his facial growth.

J.J. sighed. She could always work on the project later that night. She did want to talk more about the murder and try to figure it out. Going over it in her head was leading nowhere. And Devine was her only real sounding board these days, not that he was encouraging. She turned off the blank screen on her computer and grabbed her purse.

"They're missing a lot, in my book. Okay, let's do a quick dinner, if you don't mind. See you later, Skye."

They walked a couple of blocks toward the lake and easily found a table at that hour at the popular O'Casey's. She realized that in just a couple of short months they'd be able to sit out on the wraparound porch with a wonderful view of the water, if they were lucky enough to get the right table. Summer. She was looking forward to it.

Connor ordered them each a glass of Shiraz and then asked, "So, what's the latest, and don't tell me you haven't been poking your nose into things. I saw how your eyes lit up when I suggested discussing the murder. Not the having dinner with me but the murder, I might add." He was smiling, but J.J. wondered if there might be a message there. The last thing she wanted to do was hurt his feelings.

"I can't help it, Connor. First, being a suspect, and now, having someone I like and admire being arrested. It's just too much."

"Okay, so who are the other suspects, according to Josephine June Tanner?"

J.J. cringed, regretting her moment of weakness in telling him her full name. She leaned forward and said in a low voice, "I asked you never to call me that."

Connor grinned. "Sorry, couldn't resist. J.J. it is. Now, what's the answer?"

A voice behind J.J. answered, "Answer? To what? Are you proposing?"

J.J. whipped around. "Evan!" She glared at him, hoping he got the "don't go there" message. "What are you doing here?"

"Waiting for Michael. We're eating early, then heading to the cinema. It's movie night and we've run out of DVDs, so we're splurging by going out."

"Why don't you join us?" Connor asked.

Evan looked at J.J., who gave a small nod. "Sure thing. This is really the time to be eating here, isn't it?" He looked around him. "Maybe we could ask for a bigger table?"

Michael arrived as they were settling at the new spot. After they'd placed their orders, Evan leaned forward with both arms on the table and asked Connor, "You know all the players in town. Surely you've heard talk about a motive for the murder. Or maybe even some names that are being thrown around as possible suspects?"

Connor cocked an eyebrow. "As flattering as that is, I'm not really that much in the know. I can dish all sorts of info about the celebs and media, but I don't necessarily have an in when it comes to the business world."

"I beg to differ," Michael stated and everyone looked at him. "You did that interview a couple of years ago that turned into a bit of an expose on the lack of regulations for the new food trucks. That got a lot of people talking and even brought into being a new bylaw. Don't sell yourself short."

Connor looked like he was blushing, which surprised J.J.

This really was another side of him that she hadn't encountered before.

"That's impressive, Connor. Are you sure you haven't dabbled in the restaurant world?"

He grinned. "Okay, maybe a little. I guess I should confess to having been part owner of Harry's Haven several years ago."

"I remember hearing something about that," Evan ventured.

"Seriously?" J.J. was surprised. "That's so cool. But you're talking past tense. What happened?"

Connor shrugged. "We had a falling out, and I removed myself from the business. It happens. I still get a discount when I eat there." He grinned somewhat sheepishly.

"So that's why we go there a lot?" J.J. asked and burst out laughing.

"Guilty."

"What if Mr. Marcotti had a business partner at one point," Michael suggested, "and it ended on a much worse note?"

J.J. looked from one to the other. "Wouldn't we have heard about that? Connor, do you know if that's possible?"

"I don't. You know, when I dove in it was at the beginning of the fusion phase, and we didn't have much to do with the others in the more mainstream restaurant business. I could ask around, though."

"That would be great." J.J. thought she could do the same, but the more questions being asked the better. Someone had to know something.

CHAPTER 18

Get with the program, Tanner. J.J. kept the mantra going in her head throughout the morning's workout with Candy. After what she'd eaten the night before, she had to make amends. Calories galore needed to be defeated.

She'd just finished her thirty minutes on the treadmill and stopped for a water break. It was now or never. She didn't think she'd make it through the week and get another shot at talking to Candy. "Candy, do you mind if I ask you something?"

"Is this a way to grab more of a break?"

J.J. laughed. "Not really. I'd heard some of the women in the locker room talking, and I wondered how you were holding up?"

Candy cocked her head and looked confused. "What do you mean?"

J.J. tried to look apologetic and uncomfortable. She didn't

want to throw Candy off by sounding too nosy. "You know, the murder and all. I heard you were very close to Antonio Marcotti."

Candy almost choked on the piece of gum she'd popped into her mouth. Her face ran through a series of emotional changes, from shock to embarrassment followed by something closer to horror. "Who told you that? No one is supposed to know. Is that really what they're talking about? OMG, I'm so mortified." She glanced all around her.

J.J. felt immediately abashed. "I'm sorry, I didn't mean to make you feel uncomfortable. Me and my big mouth. I may be way off base. You know how you sometimes hear bits and pieces and make an entirely different story appear? Forget I said anything."

Candy stared at her a few more seconds without saying anything, and J.J. feared she'd lost this round and seriously doubted she'd get another chance.

"You seem nice enough, not like some of the more catty shrews we get around here." Cathy sighed. "You know, I'm not really in the mood to continue the session right now. Do you mind if I make up the time to you next time? Can you stay a bit longer then?"

"I can. But I feel bad that I've obviously upset you. Do you want to go for a coffee? Can you get away for a short while?"

Candy nodded. "You're right. I probably should get out of here, until after the memorial service anyway. He owned part of this fitness club, you know? I try not to let my feelings show when I'm in here. But it's really hard, you know?"

J.J. nodded her head but was afraid if she spoke, it might stop Candy from continuing.

"Yeah, he hired me a couple of years ago, and then . . . Let's go next door to the Java Joint. I could use some caffeine."

Grateful for being rescued from the agony of doing

weights, J.J. quickly changed and found Candy waiting at the front desk. She'd thrown a light cotton sweater over her workout clothes. She led the way next door.

They grabbed coffees at the counter and found a spot at the bar set up to overlook the parking lot. J.J. waited for Candy to make the first move. She hoped it would be to continue with her story.

"It didn't take long for Big T and me to get it on. That's what he wanted me to call him, Big T." She pulled a tissue out of her pocket and blew her nose. "He was such a generous guy, always bringing me gifts. I love jewelry, you know, and he really knew how to make a girl feel special. He couldn't take me out anywhere, so he found me a condo with a gorgeous view and a romantic balcony, so we could eat out. Get it? He was a really sweet guy."

J.J. wasn't quite sure how to respond. She'd heard a lot more than she'd expected, and she tried not to be judgmental.

Candy continued after taking a long drink. "I know what people are thinking and probably saying. Here's this old guy and this young chick, young enough to be his granddaughter. And I'll admit, I was sort of turned off by the age difference at the start, but he was so kind and so gentle. You know, a lot of guys just take me for a dumb blonde. But not Big T. He listened to me like what I said really counted. And then the romancing started, and all the rest just didn't seem to matter. Can you understand that?"

J.J. nodded, although she couldn't relate. "This must all be very hard on you."

She nodded. "It is. You know, I was really blown away by him. We had so much in common, you know? I thought what would make it perfect was if he left his wife, but I knew right from the get-go that he'd never do that. He told me so, and after a while it didn't really matter so much. I knew I was special to him. And besides, they weren't *together* anymore, if you know what I mean." She sniffed and pulled another tissue out of her pocket.

"I'm sorry for your pain," J.J. said softly. She felt bad for Candy but knew she had to persist if she wanted answers. "Do you mind my asking, had you ever thought of ending it?"

For a moment she worried she may have pushed the boundaries, but Candy's eyes widened and she whispered, "Oh, I could never leave him."

Time for another approach. "I hope the police haven't been hassling you too much. I know they look really closely at the people closest to a victim."

Candy shrugged. "They did ask if I'd killed him, but I said I could never do such a horrible thing to him. I think I might have loved him even, you know?"

And they believed you? Funny, though: J.J. did believe her.

"Did he ever talk to you about either of his businesses?" What if they'd been focusing on the wrong one? Maybe it was the fitness center that needed probing.

"No. Not really. Well, maybe once or twice. Everything was going great guns with High Time. It was making money hand over fist, he said. But a few weeks ago, he looked really upset one night and I made him tell me. He was worried about his restaurant. He thought that his head chef might be leaving him and stealing some of his recipes, too."

Wow. Was that a great motive or what? "That would have been hard on him."

Candy tried to smile but it fell flat. "It was good to talk to you about all this, J.J. I don't know if you believe me or not, but I needed to get it all out. I think now I'll go and grab my stuff and take the rest of the week off. Friday is the memorial service and I plan to be there, wanted or not. After that, I guess I'd better start planning the rest of my life."

She gave J.J. a quick hug and walked out, head held high.

CHAPTER 19

J.J. hadn't been at her desk for more than five minutes the next morning when Tansy came rushing in. "I have some news for you. And for this, you'd better have good news for me soon."

J.J. nodded, although she hadn't even approached Evan about the paint job as yet. "What is it?"

"The police have charged Rocco Gates with murder. It seems they found the murder weapon. It's a knife, part of a set from the Rocco G's kitchen."

J.J. felt a sinking sensation but wouldn't give in to it. "You're sure?"

"That's what reliable contacts are all about. Of course, I'm sure."

"How bad does that make it?"

"Well, it may also depend on whose prints were found on the knife. I couldn't find anything out about that, but I'll bet his were on it for sure. It is his kitchen, after all. It doesn't look good for him, I'm sorry to say." Tansy did look sorry, and J.J. felt momentarily abashed that she hadn't yet done her part of the deal.

"Thanks, Tansy."

Tansy lifted her eyebrows and tapped her foot.

"I haven't had a chance to talk to Evan but I will, I promise." Tansy still didn't move. "Before the weekend."

"Okay. I'm trusting you on this." She left as quickly as she'd entered.

J.J. sighed.

"That doesn't sound good," Skye said. "Look, what if he is the murderer? You don't really know him all that well. You may be overly convinced he's innocent because he's like an Italian cooking mentor to you."

"I'm grateful and all that, but it goes beyond. I'm pretty sure he didn't do it. Call it instinct or a gut feeling. You know, he sounded entirely shocked about the news, and he readily admitted to the feud they'd been having over all these years. Would a murderer admit to a motive?"

"Maybe if he were super smart and trying to throw you off the trail."

J.J. gave that some thought. "I really don't think he'd do that. But if he is guilty, I'll be totally devastated and never rely on my own judgment again."

"I'm glad you're taking this in a calm, understated way."

J.J. made a face at her. "But how could someone get at one of his knives?" J.J. sat thinking for a few minutes and then flipped off her computer. "I'll be back shortly."

"I hope you're doing some brainstorming while doing whatever it is you're doing."

J.J. wiggled her fingers over her shoulder and added another idea to the whiteboard as she left.

It took just under ten minutes to walk to Rocco G's. She was pleased to see it was open and wondered who she'd find behind the counter as she opened the door.

To her delight, Rocco's cook stood there. It looked like he was wearing the same clothes as last time she'd been in.

"Hi, Hank, remember me? J.J. Tanner?" *The person you tried to avoid the other day?*

He gave her the same look of disinterest as the last time she'd talked to him. No guilt. No evasive glance. Maybe it hadn't been him later that day after all. Then who? Should she ask if there'd been a robbery?

Looking around the room, she walked closer and leaned against the counter. It looked just the same as the last time she'd been in, except this time it was empty. Where was Zoe? Where was the noon-hour rush? Did bad news travel that fast?

"I hope you don't mind if I ask you a few questions. I can see you're not busy right now."

"I have a takeout I have to prepare."

"Okay. How about if I go out back with you while you do it?"

Ransom shrugged. "Suit yourself."

"Where's Zoe?"

"Look around. Does it look like we need anyone else working here? I promised Rocco I'd keep the noon-hour business going. We're closed the rest of the day. For now."

J.J. followed him through the swinging door and immediately eyeballed the countertops, searching for the knives. A couple of knife blocks sat on the counter next to the fridge. She wandered over.

"I understand that the police have found the murder weapon and it's one of Rocco's knives." She noticed one empty slot in one of the blocks.

"He didn't do it."

"I agree, but how could one of his knives be used? Who has access back here?"

Ransom's face turned dark. "I do, of course. Are you accusing me?"

"No, no, of course not. There must be others who come back here."

"Zoe does. The delivery guys. Rocco, of course." He shrugged.

"Would it be possible for someone else to just wander in and, say, grab a knife?" She looked over at the door leading outside.

"Possible but not probable." He was still glaring at her.

"Hm. Do you have any theories?"

"No. But I do know Rocco wouldn't kill somebody. Him and Marcotti were always arguing, but it was like a good type of arguing. You know? When you've been doing it so long, it wouldn't be right not to? Do you know what I mean?"

"Maybe. That's interesting. How well did you know Marcotti?"

"Well enough to know he was a bastard." He stood up straight and folded his arms in front of him. "But not enough to have a reason to kill him."

J.J. tried to stand her ground. She didn't like feeling intimidated. "How long have you worked here?"

"That's none of your business."

"I don't mean any offense. I was just curious. Are you from the village?"

"Again, none of your business."

"Okay, one more question and then I'll leave. Why didn't you answer the door the other afternoon? I know you saw me."

The bell above the front door rang and Ransom suggested, with outstretched hand, that J.J. precede him through to the front. He stood behind the counter and watched as the new customer glanced at the board of daily specials and sat in a chair.

"I'm busy. Time for you to leave," Ransom hissed as he prepared to take the order.

J.J. took the hint and left, glancing back at him before

closing the door. Hank Ransom had been more talkative than she'd expected, so that was good. But she didn't really like the guy and tried coming up with reasons for Hank Ransom to kill Marcotti all the way back to the office, but she couldn't come up with any outstanding ones.

Skye had left for the day, according to her note. Another note, taped to J.J.'s computer, had one word on it: Ideas?

J.J. sighed and switched the computer on, poured herself a glass of water, and sat with a thud. Ideas, indeed. She'd have to abandon the ones she'd tried coming up with for the identity of the murderer and think of one, just one dynamite idea to blow Olivia Barker out of the water.

J.J. watched the second hand on the wall clock slowly inch along. This was not conducive to producing ideas.

She had to get an edge over her rival, J.J. knew, but what she didn't know was how to do it. She'd come up with this brilliant, if she did say so herself, idea for the retirement party. The patio party at the Walkton Club. Not many could get a booking there without being members, but it helped to know people. She wondered how her competitor would manage to book the place. She'd always been a bit hesitant in using contacts for anything other than ideas, but she'd had to give that up when she entered the world of event planning. She was trying to build a solid reputation for the unusual. Now, for the zinger. She started pacing, which was always guaranteed to get the juices flowing.

Something personal. That was it. So far, the party revolved around the guest of honor's place in the business community, but what about the real him? What were his outside interests? That was it, but how to find out? *The obvious way—just ask.*

She placed a call to Kirking Manufacturing and asked

the receptionist if she could suggest the name of a close friend of the retiree being feted. It took a few minutes, but she was finally put through to a coworker in the accounting department. After talking for about twenty minutes, J.J. knew she had her idea. Now she needed to do a bit of research on availability and pricing, write up the proposal, and make sure it sat in Olivia Barker's e-mail on Friday.

CHAPTER 20

J.J. glanced at the clock and shrieked. Where had Friday morning gone? She had fifteen minutes until meeting Evan to drive together to the Marcotti memorial service. She'd been so wrapped up in tracking the details for the proposal, she hadn't left time for much more than a quick bathroom break. She grabbed her makeup bag and dashed down the hall to the room they shared with Tansy.

She met Evan at his office right on time. They drove in his car, a 2008 yellow VW Beetle, arriving at the Southwood Mortuary in twenty minutes. The parking lot was full when they arrived, and Evan parked on the verge, as close to the circular driveway as he could get. They squeezed into seats beside each other at the back of the chapel just as the service was about to start.

J.J. disliked the formalized process of grieving in public, mainly because she'd been forced to go to the funerals of two of her grandparents as an adolescent. It had totally unnerved her, leading to several nights of bad dreams and unsettled sleep. At least, she thought that's why she had an aversion to them. She looked around and noticed Detectives Hastings standing in the back right corner. Hastings looked at her but didn't acknowledge her. She next spotted Devine sitting one row in front of her, at the far right. He glanced over and winked. Not very funereal, she thought. He did look good in black, though.

She listened half-attentively to the eulogy and many comments made by mainly business friends and some family. She sat a bit straighter when Candy Fleetwood walked up to the microphone. Oh boy. What would she say? As it turned out, very little, but just enough to make it appear okay that she'd attended. Things like how good a boss he had been and how he would be missed by everyone at the High Time Fitness Center. J.J. had to hand it to Candy, although part of her had been hoping for a bit of a cat fight.

J.J. tried to catch sight of the widow, but from the angle she was situated, she couldn't see her face. She did notice the woman sat ramrod straight and wore a large brimmed black hat with a short black veil. Was that to hide tears or the lack of them? she wondered.

Just when J.J. thought she couldn't sit another minute, the service ended. There were too many tall people standing in front of J.J. for her to get a good look at everyone as they left the chapel. She asked Evan to see if he could get a look at the widow's face.

By the time they made it outdoors, cars were already driving away, with the widow's black limo in the lead. J.J. and Evan looked at each other and shook their heads. They were just about back at his car when Devine caught up to them.

"I guess I shouldn't be surprised to see you here. Any thoughts?" he asked.

"Only that it was a very long service." She mentioned

her question about the purpose of the veil, but Devine just shook his head.

"Maybe it's an Italian custom?" he muttered.

"It's very Jackie Kennedy."

Devine's right eyebrow lifted ever so slightly.

"What? I've seen pictures."

Evan added that it had been interesting but he had to get back to work. Once they were in the car, J.J. turned to look for Devine and noticed his car waiting in line to leave through the main gates.

"So, what did you think, Evan?"

"It was a big one, but I guess that's not a surprise. I saw a lot of guys who'd bad-mouthed him at one point or other. I guess they wanted to confirm it was over. I'm not sure what I was expecting or why even I wanted to come. What about you?"

"Well, I was hoping to figure out who to add to the list of suspects."

Evan chortled. "What did you think? They'd stand up and announce it, or maybe wear a scarlet *S* on their foreheads?"

"That was another story, I think. No, I was wondering if there'd be any confrontations."

"I felt the widow would create one when the mistress got the mike."

"Me, too. That was well played by Candy. Maybe the widow held it all in check, or maybe she's not too devastated a widow."

"What do you mean?" Evan asked, looking over his shoulder to back up and get around the car that had inserted itself in front of his.

"Well, how do we know? She might be the killer, after all."

"What a jerk," Evan said, pointing at the car parked in front of him. "Did he pick up his car and drop it in that space? Look at it. There's no place to go. He's lucky he didn't touch my bumper. What makes you think she could be the killer?" he added without missing a beat.

"Always look to the spouse as the first possible suspect. I've heard that on many a TV show."

"Hmm. Since we weren't among the close two hundred friends to be invited back to the widow's digs for refreshments, what say we grab a coffee at Cups 'n' Roses on the way back to the office?"

"I'm there."

They found their favorite booth empty, and J.J. laid claim with her scarf, then lined up behind Evan.

"Go. Save," he said, giving her a slight push. "My treat. The usual?"

She nodded and went back and slid into the booth, checking her iPhone for any messages. By the time Evan got back with their lattes she'd answered a text from Skye and sent one of her own.

After a few minutes, Beth joined them, placing a plate with two orange-cranberry scones in front of them. "My treat. You two haven't had the most uplifting couple of hours, I'll bet. I hate funerals. If you weren't feeling bad about the newly departed before attending the send-off, you sure are afterward."

"You know, Beth, that giving away food is not considered good business practice?" Evan said, reaching for a scone. "Not that I'm complaining," he added.

Beth sniffed. "It's my business, and I'll go broke in the manner I choose."

She smiled and then sipped her coffee from a cat-shaped mug. "So, was it worth going to the funeral?"

J.J. looked at Evan before answering. "Not really. There were no revelations, just a regular service with a lot of platitudes. It was actually a memorial service. He'd been cremated last week, but the widow wanted to wait for relatives from Italy to make it here before having today's service. The place was packed. You'd think everyone loved the guy."

"But we know otherwise," Evan jumped in. "I'll bet half the folks there were feeling a tad gleeful on the inside while mourning on the outside."

"You could be right," Beth said. "Too bad you couldn't get into the reception after. If there's alcohol involved, there might be some dandy things going on."

"I wonder if Candy went," J.J. mused. She thought about it a bit longer, then asked Evan, "Why don't we go?"

"Uh, no invitation, that's why."

"But there may not be one—on paper, I mean. And we might be able to just waltz in."

Evan shook his head. "I know where you're going with this, J.J., but I really don't want any part of it. Besides, the police have their killer. As much as I respect Rocco Gates, the murder weapon belongs to him, so it looks like he did it, and that means both of us are off the hook. That should please you and also make you want to stay clear of anything to do with this case from now on."

"I don't believe Rocco is guilty. It just doesn't feel right. And if everyone is going to think like you, then he needs all the help he can get." She patted Evan's hand to take the sting out of her words.

"You probably don't have enough background in this sort of thing to go around believing in instinct, J.J.," Beth added. "Just saying."

"You may both be right, but I just feel I have to try at least. Ty Devine should be at the reception. He could get me in, if need be."

"That's probably the last thing he'd want to do," Evan said, finishing off the rest of his latte.

J.J. finished hers, thinking through the various scenarios

while Evan and Beth watched her in silence. She could see it all now.

She'd sail through the front door and a large, muscular hand would latch on to her shoulder and growl something she couldn't understand. Without being given a chance to simper or explain, she was being whisked back toward the front door when Ty Devine stepped forward to block it. "She's with me," he growled, ready to go up against the thug. Suddenly, the hand was gone, to be replaced by Devine's as he guided her toward the food table. His hand remained in place as she bent forward to snag a mini quiche, which she dropped into the punch bowl. Yikes.

She put her empty mug on the now-empty plate and took a deep breath. "I'm going. How about it, Evan?"

"Uh-uh. Sorry. I know my place and it's in my office. I will drive you to your car, though."

CHAPTER 21

J.J. tried one last time to convince Evan. He shook his head, pulled open her car door, and kissed her on the cheek before hurrying inside to his office. J.J. sighed but felt even more determined than ever.

That determination slid a bit when she approached the gate to the Marcotti estate. Not as large or lavish as Portovino's, but still impressive. Restaurant money or wife's? She was stopped at the front door by a man in a black suit, black shirt, and white tie. "Your name?"

"J.J. Tanner. I'm here with Ty Devine, although I'm a little late. He should be on your list." She tried to peer at the clipboard in his left hand, but he adjusted the angle and she had to be content looking around her. Yes, impressive was still a good word.

"He's here. All right." He stepped to the side and she walked in, trying to look more confident than she felt.

Now, should she let Devine know she was here and using

him as her cover, or should she try to avoid him? She spotted him at that moment in the far corner of the formal living room in deep conversation with a stunning redhead, possibly in her late forties. Devine seemed to be enjoying himself, not at all in work mode.

A loud laugh drew her attention to the dining room, where an older woman, decked out in a black silk pantsuit and loads of jewelry, held court. Although she'd changed her clothes after the service, J.J. recognized Gina Marcotti. She looked to be in her early sixties, trying for forty. Her hair was a dark mass of thick curls and waves, professionally styled. More Sophia Loren than Gina Lollobrigida, J.J. thought, remembering the photos she'd seen of the former Italian movie stars.

J.J. eased in her direction, grabbing a glass of champagne from a passing tray. She didn't want to join in the conversation, just eavesdrop. When she heard the woman referred to as Mrs. M, she knew this could be revealing, especially when the woman in question made a crude remark about Candy.

"I didn't see your name on the guest list," a voice whispered in her ear.

She jumped slightly, spilling some of her drink on her shoe and one black loafer belonging to her accuser. She started to apologize and looked at him.

"Devine. You scared me. Sorry about the spill but it's your fault."

"Nice to see you, too."

"Oh, I don't think so. It looked like you were very busy over there."

Devine grinned. "You saw me with the stunner? Yes."

J.J. sucked in her breath. She wanted to probe about the woman but felt that would give Devine the upper hand in whatever it was they were playing.

"Now, what are you doing here and how did you get in?" he asked.

"You know what I'm doing here. I'm trying to find an alternate suspect. As to how I got in"—she slipped her arm through his and smiled sweetly—"I'm here with you."

He shook his head. "All right, then. In order to avoid any possible scene at this solemn event, let's get something to eat." He unhooked her hand and held on to it, pulling her over to the buffet tables that stretched from one end of the dining room to the other.

"I wonder who catered."

"She does own a restaurant and catering service, you know. And that is staffed with chefs."

"I just hadn't thought it would be up and running. Not yet, anyway."

"She reopened last night. I think she was worried about the staff being without work too long."

"Is she keeping it?"

He shrugged. "I wouldn't know. Now, has this been enlightening? Have you added anyone to that list?"

"I have been wondering if the murder could be related to his co-owning the fitness center instead of his restaurant. What do you think?"

He stared at her, pondering. "Okay. I'll tell you this much just to avoid you sticking your nose in any further and causing any more havoc. I've checked into the business, and it was running smoothly. No money problems. No fights with a business partner. This was his own venture out in the world without his wife's backing. I don't think he'd do anything to mess it up."

"You know they charged Rocco yesterday morning?"

Devine nodded.

"He didn't do it."

"I know that's what you believe."

J.J. looked him in the eye for a few seconds before asking, "What do you think of the widow as suspect?"

"Why would she do it? You know she's the money behind

the restaurant business. It's all hers, comes from her family. And I don't think jealousy is a motive, either, because he's cheated on her before."

"So why would she hire you this time? What was so different about his affair with Candy Fleetwood?"

Devine grabbed a plate and filled it with a variety of food before answering. J.J. was doing the same.

"She did hire you, didn't she?" J.J. persisted

Devine just smiled. "This time he was spending money, lots of it, on his paramour."

"But you just said Gina Marcotti comes from money. It couldn't be enough to run her into the poorhouse."

"No, but what do you think it would mean for her to learn that?"

"That her husband might be more serious this time? Maybe he was thinking of leaving her, but the worst that could do is hurt her pride. Right?"

"Would you kill if you found your husband was having an affair?"

"That would be my first instinct, but no, I'd try to come up with something more physically painful."

Devine winced.

J.J. chose a small spinach quiche from a tray at the end of the table. She also took the time to look him over covertly. The black suit did look as fine on him as his usual casual wear of jeans and a pullover. Well, maybe he looked a bit better today. "Aren't you supposed to be defending her? She's your client, after all."

That smile again. "I'm keeping an open mind. But if you were to ask, I'd say she didn't do it."

"You're exasperating. You've just given her the ideal motive, and now you're saying she's innocent. I have to think about that, away from here." She looked around the room. "Anyone else on that list?"

"Not in this group, and I don't think anything's going to happen to change that."

J.J. looked around one more time. "You're probably right. Well, I'm leaving in that case. I have work to do." She shoved the final bite into her mouth and patted her lips with a napkin. "Thanks. It's been a swell date."

Back in her office, J.J. shelved any more thoughts about Gina Marcotti until later that night, when she could concentrate at home. She quickly read the note on her desk from Skye, explaining she'd taken off early and that Brittany wouldn't be in. A glee club rehearsal had been called, and she would do her hours tomorrow morning. Fine with J.J. She'd be sure to leave the list of website updates right next to the computer.

J.J. read over her proposal to Olivia Barker one final time before e-mailing it. She then printed out a copy for filing and was placing it in the basket on top of the filing cabinet when the phone rang. She dove for it, thinking it might be Devine calling after thinking it over and deciding to share information with her after all. The caller ID showed Portovino Technologies.

She answered a bit hesitantly, wondering if they were querying the final invoice that had been sent last week. She identified herself and held her breath.

"Lorenzo Portovino here, Ms. Tanner. I have your invoice in front of me, and I notice the funghi is not included in the breakdown of the food for the birthday party. Why is that?"

"Well, Mr. Portovino, it was a late addition by the caterer and not included in our original quote."

"So, who is paying for it?"

"Make It Happen is covering it, Mr. Portovino."

"Nonsense. That's not very good business on your part."

J.J. was getting a bit tired of being chastised for poor

business sense. "Oh, but I think it is. As I said, it wasn't in the original quote but it is our responsibility."

"How much are we talking about?"

She told him and waited for another blast about being a poor businessperson.

"I'll have a check in the mail to you today and it will include the cost of the funghi. It was a delicious addition, and although I also don't quite approve of how it was added, I am happy to pay for it. And, I must say that I admire your work ethic. Portovino Technologies will be using your company again in the future."

He hung up before she could thank him. If she'd been able to find her voice.

On that high note, she decided she'd done all she could for the day, and besides, the Culinary Capers gang was meeting for the big reveal of Evan's cookbook for the next dinner.

CHAPTER 22

J.J. was the last to arrive at Cups 'n' Roses for the Culinary Capers coffee klatch that evening. She sat in the empty chair next to Connor, who gave her a dazzling smile.

"Sorry I'm late. I got caught up in work."

"In that case, do you need some sustenance to go with your espresso?" Beth asked as she placed a cup in front of J.J.

"Mm, what's left at this time of day?"

Beth held up her index finger and disappeared into the back room. In less than a minute, she was back with a plate of biscotti and scones. "I was just about to package these up for home, but you've saved me from many extra calories."

"What about me?" J.J. asked in mock despair.

"You do belong to the fitness club, as I recall," Evan contributed.

J.J. made a face at him and grabbed a blueberry scone.

"Would you like that heated?" Beth asked.

J.J. took a bite and shook her head. After she swallowed, she managed to say, "Delicious."

Alison sat staring at the biscotti, so J.J. pushed the plate over to her. "Go for it."

"Thanks." Alison took one and dunked it in her coffee before biting into it.

"Okay, as fun as it is watching you two eat, let's get down to the basics." Evan pulled a hardcover book out of a bag. "This," he said with great drama and a sweeping gesture across the cover, "is my selection for next month's dinner: *The Scandinavian Cookbook* by Trina Hahnemann." He passed the book to Connor, who flipped through it.

By the time the book had made its way back to Evan, the others were enthusiastic.

"I thought I'd just continue on with the international theme that J.J. set this month. Of course, it doesn't mean we all have to carry through with it. And I have an ulterior motive. Michael and I have been planning a trip to Sweden in the fall. He has loads of relatives over there, so I thought I'd get a jump on the cuisine. Although it just this moment struck me that maybe I'm doing it backward and should wait until after we return." He held his hands up, looking a bit baffled.

"That's all right, Evan. We might let you get away with doing another one at some point," Alison said and giggled.

"That may come back to haunt you, Alison. Also, the book is divided by months, but we won't stick to that. I just bought it today and haven't yet figured out my main, but I promise to do so this weekend and I'll e-mail it. Everyone good with that?"

They all nodded.

"We haven't done a Scandinavian meal before," Beth commented. "That should be an adventure."

"And a challenge," J.J. murmured.

"Don't worry. You're up to it," Alison told her, finishing off the biscotti. "After your coup last weekend, I think you can handle anything."

"I meant that in a positive way, Alison. But thanks for the praise. You know I lap it up."

J.J. felt herself flush with pride. Never in her many, many years of reading cookbooks had she thought she'd reach this pinnacle. For her, the cookbooks themselves had been a secret pleasure. She had to admit, though, that there was that hidden part of her that really longed to be a good cook. To enjoy the cooking experience. Maybe she'd finally arrived.

If so, it had been a hard trek trying to put behind her the disdain she'd heard in her ex-fiancé's voice whenever she attempted something other than her usual fare. She knew it was his problem, not hers. But she'd been cowed by his superiority on many fronts over their three years together, and the fact that he truly was an excellent chef had made his judgment seem the truth. Thank goodness those days were gone and she'd gotten back to being her own self. Actually, *gone forward* was how she liked to think of it these days. She realized her mind had been wandering and that Evan was talking.

"I'm glad you're all so agreeable. I must also admit it's something I've been wanting to try for a while now, and wasn't that one of the reasons we started up Culinary Capers? To spread our culinary wings and try new menus? What I particularly like about our group is this putting together of an entire themed meal. Whoever first proposed Culinary Capers is a genius."

Alison threw her serviette at Evan as everyone started laughing. "You're so modest, Evan. That's why we stick it out, you know."

Evan grinned and turned to Beth. "I'd like to order coffee all around, madam barista, on me."

"Wow." Beth looked around the table. "The same for everyone?"

When she returned from giving the order to her two staff persons, she asked, "What's the occasion?"

"Well, our group is an occasion in itself. And also, I'm feeling relieved that neither myself nor J.J. are considered murder suspects any longer." He reached out to touch J.J.'s hand. "I know, you feel bad about Rocco Gates, as do I, but that doesn't mean we can't also be pleased for ourselves. Right?"

J.J. nodded. "Although Detective Hastings hasn't said in so many words that we're off the hook. I don't know if I'll totally believe it until the real culprit goes to trial."

"It sounds like you don't mean Rocco," Beth said. "He's a nice guy and all, but from what I hear, and it's village gossip mainly, they had a fierce rivalry going on and both were hot tempered."

"Plus, the knife," Evan added.

"What about it?" Beth asked.

"Apparently, a knife from Rocco's kitchen was found, and it's believed to be the murder weapon," J.J. offered.

"Wow. That sounds like a done deal, then."

"Is it?" J.J. asked. "What about your place here, Beth? Could someone get in the back there and steal something without your knowing it?"

Beth thought about it before answering. "It's highly unlikely. Unless during deliveries. Maybe one of the guys could do it then, and I wouldn't know it was missing until I went to use it. Or someone could sneak in while the back door was propped open."

"I hadn't thought about that," J.J. said, feeling pleased.

"Now wait a minute," Alison jumped in. "Don't go trying to track down deliveries or any such thing, J.J. I'm sure the detectives have already checked out that avenue."

"But what if they haven't? Alison, you have to find out."

Alison's face flushed. Her voice had an edge to it. "I do not. I told you—what I need to do is stay out of this."

"But you're a cop. You should want to help find the murderer."

"Leave it, J.J."

Connor put his arm around J.J.'s shoulder. "It's okay, Alison. If you don't want to do it, I'm sure J.J. wasn't being accusatory, just overly enthusiastic. Right?" He squeezed J.J.'s shoulder.

J.J. realized she was staring at Alison with her mouth open in total surprise, partly because of Alison's reaction but also because of her own. She scrambled to make amends.

"Yes, Connor's right. I'm sorry, Alison. I didn't mean it to sound like that. I guess I'm getting too involved in this. I just hate to see an injustice taking place. I truly am sorry, Alison."

Alison's face relaxed and she moved her head from side to side, stretching her neck. "I'm sorry, too. I shouldn't have jumped on you like that. I'm a bit stressed out these days, that's all."

Their coffees were delivered, and Alison took a long drink before continuing. "I think I owe you an explanation. You see, I got into trouble at work a few weeks ago. Nothing really major but enough to keep me under the sergeant's watchful eye for the next while. If I'm seen to take a wrong step, or overstep, I'll probably get a written reprimand in my file."

"Wow, I'm so sorry. I didn't know."

"Of course you didn't. I was embarrassed and wanted to keep it a secret, but I can see it's been affecting our relationships, so I want it out in the open. Maybe I can handle it better with the support of all of you."

Beth hugged her. "Do you want to tell us what happened? You don't have to, you know."

"I know, but it might do me some good. You see, sometimes I get to thinking I just know everything there is to know about a subject, especially if it has to do with police protocol."

"Well, you did ace your exams, after all."

"More or less. But the part I sometimes forget is the number one rule about not calling out your higher-ups on a topic, especially in front of others. I, in my know-it-all way, told the lieutenant that something wasn't considered probable cause for a forceful entry into a suspect's home. I was right, but he was steamed. Lambasted me in front of my platoon and told the Sarge to keep an eye on me. Consider me dutifully chastised and watchful." She smiled a little ruefully and looked from one to another.

"We're here for you, Alison. And just for the record, I don't think you've done a darn thing wrong," Evan stated with a nod of his head.

"Thanks."

"Well, now. Perhaps I should be the one to tell the detectives your theory, J.J.," Beth said. "After all, as the owner of an establishment, I do have a different take on things."

"That would be great, Beth. I'll go with you, if you want."

"We'll see."

"Have you come up with any other theories since we talked about it over dinner?" Connor asked.

J.J. shook her head. "Not really. Evan and I went to the memorial service today, but it turned out to be just that, with nothing happening that would point to anyone." She finished her espresso and looked around at them, hesitating when her gaze fell on Alison. "I also went to the reception afterward."

Alison groaned. "Did you get tossed out?"

"No, I didn't. In fact, I suggested I was there with Ty Devine and got in no problem."

"That guy. What's the story there?" Beth asked.

J.J. chose to misunderstand her. She could feel Connor staring at her. "Well, I did get in and just about managed to talk to the widow, and I could hear some of the things she was saying about Candy Fleetwood. She did in fact know about her and there was a lot of animosity there."

"Not surprising." Beth continued probing. "Then what happened?"

"Devine spotted me and whisked me away from her. He says he doesn't think she did it but he's keeping an open mind."

"Who is Ty Devine?" Connor asked.

"Oh, just a private eye."

CHAPTER 23

J.J. waved good-bye to the gang and realized she was still starving and also that she seemed to have gained her second wind. She glanced at her watch. Only eight thirty; there was still time to grab a light meal and some useful information at Bella Luna.

The same woman who had greeted J.J. last time stood at the tall podium-style desk just inside the front door. Lucy, if J.J. remembered correctly. She greeted J.J. with a warm smile and showed her to a table for two, tucked away from the crowd.

"I heard what had happened at the birthday party. I do hope you've forgiven us," she said, setting the menu down on the table.

"Of course. It was something done by your boss. I know there's nothing any of you could have done about it. And you have my condolences."

"*Grazie*, Ms. Tanner. Something from the bar?"

"A glass of California Shiraz, please. Lucy, do you mind if I ask you a couple of questions before you go?"

She looked a bit wary but nodded.

"Do you know of anyone who had it in for your boss? A member of the staff or even a customer?"

"A customer?" She gave a short laugh. "We get the odd one who's unhappy but not angry enough to kill over an overdone pizza crust. Not that it happens often. Mr. Marcotti was very proud of the quality of the food served here, and he made sure everything that left the kitchen was cooked to perfection."

"Did that bother the chef or anyone else in the kitchen? Was he particularly hard on any of them?"

"He was the boss. He was demanding but fair."

Right. "So you don't think the head chef, for instance, might be driven to do something desperate?"

Lucy shifted her weight from one foot to the other, obviously tiring of standing there. "No. Not Kevin. He's a very nice guy to work with." She shook her head. "I can't think of anyone."

"Where are you from?"

Lucy hesitated a moment before answering. "I'm from Italy."

"You have a very lovely accent."

Lucy blushed. "I've been trying hard to lose it but cannot do."

"Oh no. Stop trying," J.J. said with a smile. "How long have you been here?"

"Three years now, so there's really no excuse, but that's nice of you to say. I'm sorry but now I must get back to work. I'll have your wine sent over to you."

J.J. watched Lucy take the few steps over to the bar to place the order and then look back over with a small smile before resuming her place at the door. A server brought her a small carafe of wine and a glass a couple of minutes later. J.J. took a few minutes before checking out the menu and then spotted what she wanted right away. A roasted fennel and arugula salad with a citrus vinaigrette.

She'd decided to give a pass to the calorie-loaded desserts on the menu when she'd finished the salad, although the chocolate tartufo was probably to die for, and opted instead for an espresso. That led to a second one, and she was chasing it down with a glass of water, when Chef Kevin Lonsdale entered the dining area and started mingling with the diners. He seemed to have slipped into Marcotti's role quite readily. By the time he reached J.J.'s table, she had her questions ready. Brief and to the point.

"And was the meal up to your expectations?" he asked, stopping at her side with a small bow.

"It was delicious. Of course, I've enjoyed everything I've eaten here. And also, the food I've had catered. You don't remember me, do you?"

He looked puzzled. "I'm sorry, no."

J.J. offered her hand. "J.J. Tanner from Make It Happen. It was the birthday party at the Portovino estate."

"Of course. We met only briefly as I recall. Nice to see you again." He started to walk away.

"Yes, the food was delicious." She plowed on ahead, and he turned back to her. "It was certainly horrid how the evening ended, though. With Mr. Marcotti's death. I guess the entire staff here was devastated."

"Yes, we were very shocked by what happened." He started to turn again.

"Does anyone here have any ideas about the murder?"

"The killer is in jail. What else is there to know?" His eyes narrowed as he looked at her.

"That's just it. I think they got it wrong. Tell me, was Mr. Marcotti well liked here?"

"He was a respected chef and restaurateur."

"That's not what I asked."

Lonsdale leaned forward and put his right hand on the table. "Look, if you're trying to pin the murder on someone from Bella Luna, you're barking up the wrong tree. He was a hard taskmaster but that's because he was a perfectionist. How else would the restaurant have reached its stature? And it was an honor for all of us to work for him. Now, if you're really hung up on finding a different suspect, you might try Don Kelland, the councilor for this area."

"Why?"

"Marcotti had made an application every year for the past two years for a permit for an outdoor dining space, and every year Kelland opposed it. They got into a shouting match just a few weeks ago when Kelland came by for lunch."

"Why did Marcotti think it was Kelland's fault?"

"Because he's the go-to for that department. Nothing gets passed without his say-so, and not much gets his say-so without someone greasing his palm."

"You have evidence of that?"

"Not me. Marcotti. I don't know if he had evidence, but that's what he believed. Kelland threatened to sue him for defamation and left. That's all I know. Now, I need to get back to my kitchen."

She watched him go, sorry that she hadn't asked about the rumor that he'd been planning on leaving and taking some recipes with him. Of course, this hadn't been the best venue for asking those questions. She would come back another time, maybe before the place was open to diners but when the staff would be in getting set up. Or maybe she'd find out where he lived and surprise him at home. But in the meantime, she was happy to add Don Kelland's name to the suspect list. She wondered if the police knew this story. And if not, how best to tell them without actually having to go there and tell them.

She finished her water and then paid her bill. As she was leaving, she spotted Ty Devine's Acura parked a few spaces up the street. Funny, she hadn't seen him in the restaurant. She glanced around, wondering where he was. Oh well, probably just as good she didn't see him. At least not until she had figured out how to pump him for some more information.

She checked the street and stepped from between two cars to cross it when a van, headlights off, screeched from around the corner and headed straight for her. She froze for a second, then screamed when strong arms wrapped around her from behind and pulled her back. She fell across the trunk of a car, hitting her elbow on it.

She straightened herself and clutched her sore spot. "What just happened?"

Devine had run after the van but returned to her side, checking back over his shoulder. "Someone just tried to run you down in a white van. Don't you watch where you're going?"

She stood straighter and tried to catch her breath. "I did look. Both ways."

"Did you hurt your elbow?" He pointed to it as she continued to massage away.

"Yes, but I'll live. I guess I have you to thank that nothing worse happened." She hugged herself.

"No problem. Are you sure you're all right? You're shaking."

He looked like he was about to wrap his arms around her again, so she backed away. "I'm fine, really."

She could see his smile even in the dim lighting. He looked over at Bella Luna. "I take it you just came from there. Good way to stir up trouble."

"I didn't stir up anything. I had a light, delicious meal and then a few words with the chef as he greeted the guests, Marcotti-style."

"And no mention of the murder was made?" He sounded like he didn't believe her.

"I may have asked a few questions."

"And did he tell you anything useful? Or do you think

he's the murderer based on the fact that he might have been trying to leave and take some recipes with him?"

J.J. gasped. "How do you know that?"

"The police have him in their sights. Or at least, they did."

"Well, that answers that."

"What?"

"About whether the police know or not." She rubbed her elbow again. She was sure she'd have a bruise by morning. "We meet twice in one day. What are you doing here?"

"Mrs. Marcotti asked me drop by and take a look around."

"Still looking for girlfriends?"

He shrugged. "Just looking. Now, I think I'd better get you home."

"I'm fine. It's not too long a walk."

"Good, that means only a few blocks for the crazed motorist to try again." He grabbed her good arm gently. "Please. Let me give you a lift."

"Okay."

They remained silent until he pulled up in front of her apartment. "I think you're asking too many questions and this is starting to get dangerous."

"Well then, doesn't that prove my point about Rocco?"

"It could. We won't talk about it now because you're probably still shaken up. Go inside, have a strong drink, and go to bed."

She opened her mouth to protest and then closed it. It sounded like good advice.

"Good night," she said as she got out of the car. She leaned back in. "And thanks."

"Don't mention it."

CHAPTER 24

J.J. had forgotten that Brittany would be at the office the next morning, and considering the night she'd had, the unlocked door set her nerves tingling. She gingerly pushed the door open and breathed a deep sigh of relief at the sight of Brittany's back standing at the buffet-cum–file cabinet. Britanny spun around when J.J. closed the door.

"Oh, you scared me," Brittany said. She leaned back, closing the drawer at the same time, and held up her smart-phone. "Did you know you can use the camera function on your phone as a mirror? Just pretend you're taking a selfie."

She flashed a smile and went over to the spare computer set up on a credenza at the end of the room next to the closet. "I'm just about finished everything, so won't be in your hair if you're concentrating on anything special."

"No, that's okay. I'm sorry if I startled you. I hadn't planned to come in today, but I forgot my briefcase and I thought I'd just check my e-mail while I'm at it. I won't be long." *Why am I making excuses to her?*

"Sure," Brittany said with a giggle.

They sat working away at their own computers for about half an hour. J.J. kept feeling she should be chatty, but she couldn't think of a thing to say. *I must really be in a funk about last night. Come on, now.*

"How was the rehearsal yesterday?" J.J. finally thought of asking.

"Rehearsal? Oh, yeah, the glee club. Good." She nodded her head. "Yup, definitely good. We're getting ready for our spring concert in mid-May, you know." Brittany looked back at the screen and began typing again.

J.J. took it as a hint to get on with her own task. She was sort of hoping Olivia Barker might have already read the e-mail and replied. No such luck. She'd just logged out of her computer when the door opened and Ty Devine walked in.

J.J. looked at him in surprise. Brittany stood abruptly and practically danced over to him, J.J. noticed.

"Can I help you with anything?" Brittany sang out.

Devine smiled then looked over at J.J. "I'm here to kidnap your boss."

Brittany eyed J.J., then turned back to Devine. "You don't really mean that."

"Not in the criminal sense," Devine answered with a chuckle.

He walked over to J.J. and leaned toward her, both hands on the desk.

"We have some talking to do."

J.J. wondered what was up, then decided it might be better not to know. Or at least, not have it discussed in front of Brittany. She shrugged, then grabbed her purse and jacket before standing.

"Just lock up when you're finished, please, Brittany," she said as she followed Devine out the door. She realized as they hit the street that she'd forgotten her briefcase again. *Oh, well.*

When they were out on the street, she asked Devine, "What are you really doing?"

He held his car door open for her. "We're going for a little ride, and then we'll have a long talk and try to figure out just what you know about the murder that almost got you killed last night."

"Do you really believe that's what happened? It could have been a drunk driver or someone talking on their cell or . . ."

Devine turned toward her and put his hands on her shoulders. "Seriously? That van had no headlights and made a bee-line straight for you. You're living in a fantasy world if you think it wasn't an attempt, or at the very least, a warning."

J.J. tried to suppress the shiver that ran through her body. Devine must have felt it, because he started to pull her toward him but instead squeezed her shoulders before ushering her into his car.

"How did you know I'd be at the office?"

"I started with your apartment. The office was next. I know I'm not the only one who works on weekends. After that? I may have given up." He grinned.

They rode in silence until he turned into the parking lot for Laurel Beach off Lakeshore Drive. She looked at him in surprise.

He shrugged. "I'd heard you liked to come here and walk along the beach. I thought it might relax you enough to jog loose some information."

"You'd heard. When was this? Are you still checking up on me?"

He sighed. "No, I'm not. Now, do you want to walk?"

She looked at the water. Lake Champlain was so massive at this point, she could easily imagine she was at the seashore with nothing between her and Europe. Well, maybe it would technically be Asia. Or Hawaii, maybe. That's why it was her favorite spot, but she wasn't sure she wanted to share it or that information. *Oh, well.*

"Let's walk," she agreed.

Pleased it was warm enough to walk along the white sand and feel the grains caressing her feet, she pulled off her sneakers and socks. She was glad she'd worn jeans to the office. She could have done with a fleece top, though. Her lightweight Zenergy jacket from Chico's was no match for the wind.

She was surprised to see Devine do the same. They tucked their shoes beside a large log with an overhang making it look very similar to an alligator. After walking the length of the beach area in silence, Devine started talking.

"It's not the largest beach I've been on."

"I think it's just the right size. From here it's a twenty-minute walk to the start of the estates, and from there it's all private beach. Have you tried it since moving here?"

"Nope. I seem to be working a lot. It takes a concerted effort to start up a business, you know. I have to take on as many clients as I can possibly handle until I hit the mother lode."

"And what would that be?"

"Maybe a big corporate contract that allows me to drop the jealous-wife jobs." He smiled suddenly. "Don't get me wrong, I'd rather be doing this than being back on the force, but I'd also like to pay my bills with ease."

J.J. laughed. "Who wouldn't?" *So, how did you pay for your nice new car?*

"How's your elbow?"

"Not as bad as I thought it would be. Just don't punch it or anything, please."

He chuckled. "Good. Now, tell me who you've been talking to about the murder."

"You don't mean like the Culinary Capers gang, I'm assuming."

"I mean anyone you've considered a suspect or someone who you cornered hoping to get information out of them."

J.J. stopped walking. "Hm. I'd have to think about that a few minutes." She sat on a log and stared at the water. The wind was picking up and the waves lapping the shore were getting larger. She crossed her arms and bent forward to keep warm.

Devine stood throwing rocks, trying to make them skip across the water without much luck. Too much wind. His navy anorak blew in the wind, though, giving J.J. a fine view of his derriere, nicely clinging jeans and all. Not that she cared. He finally gave up and sat beside her.

J.J. glanced at him and started reciting her list. "I've talked to Rocco and Evan, of course, both being considered suspects. And, I guess Hank Ransom, Rocco's cook. Of course, Candy put me on to Kevin Lonsdale, Marcotti's cook, who put me on to Don Kelland, city councilor, but I haven't had a chance to get to him yet."

Devine interrupted, "And probably shouldn't, either."

J.J. frowned. "It does sound like the outdoor patio space is a weak motive for murder, but he and Marcotti did get into several arguments over the past month. And I've also talked to Candy Fleetwood, of course. Although I'm not so sure I'm thinking of her as a suspect these days. And Mrs. Marcotti, or rather, I tried but didn't luck out." She flashed Devine a withering look.

"That's the list? You've managed to ruffle more than a few feathers in the village, I'd say. And you still haven't uncovered the killer? I guess you'd better not switch jobs anytime soon." He chuckled.

J.J. punched him on the arm. "I don't want your job or to be a cop. I just want to get Rocco off the hook. I really believe he didn't do it. Neither did Evan. Nor did I, just for the record."

"I agree with your assessment of the three of you."

"You do?"

"Yes. Which is why we're sitting here having this conversation right now." Suddenly serious, he turned to face her. "But we've got to figure out who on that list either got worried enough to try to get at you, or said something to someone, who then tried to."

"If it's the latter, we'll never figure it out." She moved her head from side to side, stretching the neck muscles. She thought she should get moving before she stiffened up and if she wanted to be able to stand up gracefully. But she stayed put.

"Never say never. That's why I have a job. So did anyone raise any alarm bells in your head when you were talking?"

"No."

"Anyone react in an unusual manner?"

"No."

"How about anyone trying to cut your questioning short?"

"Well, Hank Ransom was in no mood to talk, but I figured it was because he was overwhelmed with trying to run the bistro without Rocco there. Although I'm certain I saw him there later the day Rocco was taken in for questioning. Most of the lights were out, and he wouldn't answer the door when I knocked, even though he saw me. The only other person working there is the part-time server over lunch, who doubles as the cashier. She really was no help at all and, I'm sure, not involved. What do you know about Ransom?"

Devine moved back toward the water, picked up a handful of rocks, and started throwing them again. "Not much."

"I don't believe that. I think you've thoroughly looked into the backgrounds of each and everyone involved with this case. Now, I shared my info; you share yours."

"I can't do that."

"Why not?"

He turned back to face her. "Because you'd just go ahead and poke your nose in even further. You're not trained to do this. I am."

"That's so not fair." J.J. stood abruptly. "Well, if you don't share, I'd say this conversation is over."

She started stalking back in the direction of the car. She heard Devine swear as he caught up with her.

"All right. I'll tell you anything I think you need to know that will help eliminate people off that list. But that's as far as I'm prepared to go. And you know, if you keep this up, the police are bound to catch on, if they haven't already. Then you could be in trouble for interfering in an investigation."

J.J. huffed and crossed her arms but she couldn't think of a comment that wouldn't sound whiney. She chose to keep walking in silence. She retrieved her sneakers and sat to put them on, then walked to the car to wait for Devine to catch up.

He drove her back to her office and pulled up to the curb. "I don't want you to get in trouble or to get hurt."

She squirmed a bit. "I know. If I promise to stop asking questions, you have to promise to find the murderer real fast."

"Deal." He smiled and she felt herself smiling back. She uncrossed her fingers, pulled her hand out of her jacket pocket, and let herself out of the car.

CHAPTER 25

"You could have been killed," Skye shrieked when J.J. told her about the incident with the van. They were sitting in Skye's living room on Sunday, sipping white wine while Nick grilled some salmon filets outdoors.

"That's what Devine said."

"Ah, he's a clever guy. And handsome." She wiggled her eyebrows.

J.J. shrugged. "I'll admit that he's clever but apparently not enough so to have found the killer."

"Well, what else did he say and when did he say it? Did you go out with him?"

"What? Of course not. He's not dating material, and we're talking murder here, not romance. We went for a walk and he asked me who all I'd been questioning."

"Where and when did you walk?"

"Really, Skye?" When Skye continued to look at her

expectantly, she finally relented. "Laurel Beach. Saturday morning."

Skye didn't reply. She just smiled smugly. J.J. knew that smile from the seven years they'd been friends. Whenever Skye knew she was about to get her way, out came the smile. Well, two could play the game.

"I really love that fitted top you're wearing. Dynamite color. Is it new?"

"Do not try to change the subject, and yes it is. Now, dish."

"All right." J.J. took another sip before doing so. She went through the details of Devine coming to the office and convincing her to walk and talk. "I told him who I'd been talking to about the murder, but that didn't result in any alarm bells going off and Devine leaping up to announce the killer's name."

"Hmm. Now you're getting dramatic. That's a good sign."

"Of what? No, don't answer that."

"Remember, in college, you always got overly dramatic when you talked about some new guy that you wanted to date."

"I did not."

"Did so. You still do that, not with the dating of course, since you haven't been serious about anyone since that jerk fiancé of yours back in Montpelier. Which is why I believe you when you say that you and Connor Mac are just really good friends. But look at you, when you start getting emotional about anything, you go off the deep end for a few seconds, work through to the worst-case scenario in your head, and then come out the other side able to deal with the problem."

"Wow, thank you. I'd have to pay big bucks to get that kind of analysis anywhere else. I'll admit, I do on occasion think the worst, but I don't see what that has to do with Ty Devine. My other news is, you'll never guess who called late Friday afternoon."

When J.J. had finished the play-by-play of the conversation

with Portovino, she threw her arms wide. "Voilà. What do you think?"

"Nice. He's a very honorable gentleman and an invaluable client. That's a relief, really. You know, sometimes the wealthier they are, the—dare I say—stingier they are. He sounds like a nice guy. Now, how about your other client? And this will be the absolute last talk of work this weekend."

"Olivia Barker? I had a brilliant idea and worked it up and e-mailed her Friday afternoon." She took a long sip of wine before carrying on. "I actually called up the receptionist at Kirking Manufacturing on Thursday and asked to speak to someone who knew the guest of honor really well. The guy I talked to was a wealth of information. Anyway, he said the honoree's favorite pastime was his model train work. He's built a miniature town in his basement at home—it takes up the entire space—and keeps adding to the town and the train. He's absolutely obsessed by it, I'm told."

She stood and started pacing, trying to contain her excitement. "So, I was thinking of decorating the side wall of the patio at the Walkton Club in décor that will transform it into a posh railway dining car. We'll use velvet draped around windows that are painted on the wall to show passing scenery. Everyone attending will be issued a train ticket, which will be punched by 'conductors.'" She used her hands to provide the quotation marks and was getting more excited as she went on. "We can rent dining-car china, crystal, and white linens from the railway heritage society in Campbellville. The servers will be properly attired, again all rented. Printed menus. The whole bit. I even suggested a subscription to a railroading magazine as part of his gift. What do you think?"

J.J. looked expectantly at Skye. She realized that, even after a couple of years working for her, it was the one opinion that really mattered.

"Dy-na-mite. The contract is yours, guaranteed. I wonder what the competition will come up with."

"You had to mention that. I know—reality check."

Nick knocked on the patio door at that moment, and Skye ran over to open the door for him.

"Ladies, your superbly grilled dinner awaits you," Nick said, depositing a plate with the salmon on the table and continuing into the kitchen with the grilling utensils. He came back carrying a bottle of cabernet sauvignon.

Skye scrambled into the kitchen to grab the veggies from the oven. They passed around the food, and J.J. noticed the smile that passed between them. She smiled also. She was happy for Skye. They'd shared a lot over the years, and J.J. was relieved Skye had ended up with one of the good guys. When she thought back to the long string of losers Skye had attracted throughout their college years, she remembered how often she'd wanted to give Skye a good shake. This was more like it.

Toward the end of the meal, Skye told Nick about J.J.'s van experience.

"This is turning out to be very dangerous," Nick said. He pushed a lock of hair out of his eyes. That must be really annoying for a dentist, she thought. But it did look good on him. He was much taller than Skye and leaner, but their fair complexions and blond hair were a match. "Skye's been telling me about all the questions you've been asking. Maybe it's time to stop."

"So I'm told. But I continue to believe the police have the wrong man in custody. The more I ask around, the more astounded I am by the number of possible suspects. Antonio Marcotti was not a very well-liked guy."

"I attended a banquet he catered once," Nick admitted. "It was put on by Grimswald Medical and Dental Equipment. They're one of the largest suppliers in the state. I remember toward the end of the evening there was some big to-do in the kitchen. Lots of yelling, and it sounded like some pots and pans being thrown. The Grimswald fellow came barreling out of there and told the orchestra leader to play louder. I heard him. I was sitting at the table right next to the stage, which in fact was his table, too."

"And?" Skye asked when it appeared that Nick had finished his story.

"There is no *and*." He poured some more wine all around. "J.J. said that people didn't like Marcotti and I remembered the evening. End of story."

"How do you know Marcotti was involved?" J.J. asked.

"Because Mark Erwin, my sales rep from the company, asked what had happened. The other guy said that Marcotti flew off the handle when questioned about a substitution that had found its way onto the menu."

Skye gasped. "The same thing that happened to you, J.J."

"How long ago was this?" J.J. asked.

"Oh, a few years ago. Before I met you, Skye."

"Probably too long for your Grimswald guy to carry a grudge, unless he lost his job over it or something."

"I don't think that would have happened. He was too high up in the company, as I recall. But I could tell it didn't sit well with him. He fumed about it most of the night. I'll bet he never used Bella Luna Catering again."

"Oh man, I wish we'd known before contracting with him," Skye said.

"It might not have made much of a difference at that point," J.J. pointed out. "I was desperate for a replacement."

"Well, let's forget about the late Mr. Marcotti and focus on this delicious dinner presented by our own chef, Nick Owens." Skye raised her glass in a toast.

"To Chef Owens," J.J. offered, clinking her glass with Skye.

Nick stood and bowed from the waist and then passed around the remaining piece of salmon, which he'd sliced into thirds.

CHAPTER 26

J.J. had to talk long and hard to convince herself to go back to the High Time Fitness Center on Monday morning. What eventually did the trick was telling herself that her conversation with Candy may have triggered some memory about something Marcotti had said or some other repressed clue. Not likely, but an acceptable reason for returning.

She'd just about caved when Indie jumped on the bed and snuggled in between the sheet and the duvet. Since his cuddle times were on his own schedule, J.J. really hated to miss any. She stayed put for another five minutes and then eased out of bed. By the time she made it to the fitness club, she was fully awake and raring to go, thanks to two cups of dark roast coffee.

Candy was waiting in the weight room by the time J.J. had changed and wandered in. She didn't look her usual peppy self and when she greeted J.J. she sounded even less cheerful than the last time J.J. had seen her.

J.J. wondered if it was memorial-service lag or maybe

too many memories over the weekend. She gave Candy a quick hug. "How are you holding up?"

"Oh, gee. Okay, I guess. I just feel so lost, you know? Big T used to spend part of the weekend with me and we'd have a lot of fun. This past weekend was no fun at all. I guess I'm just down in the dumps."

"It takes a while to get back to any resemblance of normal, Candy. But it does eventually happen."

"That's what everyone's telling me. So it must be true, huh?"

J.J. smiled, although she felt herself being dragged down by Candy's sadness. "Well, I'm ready for some more torture. Lead away."

She was rewarded with a small smile as Candy pointed to the seven-point-five-pound weights. "I hope you warmed up before coming in here," she warned.

"Oh yeah." J.J. tried to inject a little enthusiasm into her voice.

"To tell you the truth, I was wondering if you'd keep on with the program after our talk the other day. And then they said you didn't show on Friday."

"I knew you wouldn't be here on Friday so I played hooky. But I've signed up for this and I'll see it through."

"I'm happy to hear that." And she sounded so sincere that J.J. visualized them meeting for coffee, going out shopping together, even catching a movie. She shook her head to prevent herself from actually suggesting something like that.

The hour passed quickly, much to J.J.'s relief. They were heading out to the hall when Candy suddenly stopped. "I guess I should tell you something."

What, I'm hopeless? Might as well give it up? "What is it?"

"I don't know if it means anything— probably not—but Big T was thinking of going into politics."

"Really? At what level?"

"Well, in the city of course. He wanted to represent Half Moon Bay Village."

"That's Don Kelland's job, isn't it?" *Interesting. Some confirmation about the problem between the two?*

"For now. Big T said the ninny—well, that's not really the word he used—didn't deserve the job and he was just the guy to kick his ass. His words."

"I'd heard a rumor there was some animosity between the two of them."

"Yeah. Well, it wasn't Big T who started it. Every time he tried to get a variant or whatever they're called, Mr. Kelland would block it. Or he'd come back and say, once you've done so and so, we'll give it to you. So Big T would do it and go back to the guy and be told he had to do something else. They almost came to blows about it a couple of times."

J.J. thought for a moment. "I guess Kelland wouldn't have been too happy about the competition in the next election." *A better motive?*

"No, but I'm guessing he was even unhappier when Big T told him what he'd learned."

"What's that?" J.J. was all ears.

Candy quickly looked around her and lowered her voice. "Well, it had something to do with his nephew, and that he—the nephew—had it in for Big T and made sure his uncle saw it the same way."

"Big— I mean, Marcotti told you this? Did he tell you why the nephew was so angry?"

"Something about him having worked at Bella Luna when it first opened, but then he was fired."

"Do you know why?"

"Uh-uh. Big T didn't usually talk about his business, but I guess in this case, it was really bothering him. When I asked some more questions, he said he'd didn't want to talk about it right then but soon everyone would know."

o o o

J.J. had already been planning on paying Don Kelland a visit on her way to the office, but she was even more determined after her talk with Candy. She wanted to start off with some casual questions, not confront him right off, but she was happy to have knowledge of the nephew in her arsenal. She debated briefly about checking the information out first, at least finding out the name of the nephew and if he'd actually worked for Marcotti, but when she walked into Kelland's office in the municipal building on West Boulder Avenue, she left caution at the door.

The receptionist, a wide-eyed blonde trying to look many years younger than her age, was her first obstacle. J.J. needed to get past her. Being needy might do the trick.

"I'm afraid I don't have an appointment, but I've got a real problem and it won't take long to talk to Mr. Kelland about it," she said, trying to sound whiny and sincere at the same time.

"He's getting ready for a committee meeting at ten. You'll have to make an appointment for later in the week. He's really a very busy man, you know."

"I'm sure he is, but that just won't work. That's too late."

The door to Kelland's private office opened and he popped his head around it. "Cancel Drummond. He's late as usual and I won't be played the fool." He stopped in surprise when he noticed J.J. standing there. She recognized him from various news clips on local TV. She'd always had the impression he was a grandstander. And taller.

"Mr. Kelland, I need just a few minutes of your time. Please. It's really, really important," J.J. called out.

He looked at his receptionist, who shook her head. After another few seconds of looking at J.J., he invited her in.

"I'm really in a rush here—a day full of committee meetings, you know. Now what's bothering your pretty little head?" He indicated she sit in the upholstered chair across from his desk.

Pretty little head! She tried to look demure as she did so, even though she was steaming inside. Again, she tried for a sweet tone when she spoke.

"It really is very nice of you to see me without an appointment. I promise I won't take long. I just have a couple of questions."

"Oh?" He brightened and sat up straighter in his chair, sucking in his gut. "You're from the media?"

"No. I'm an event planner who used Marcotti catering. It was his final job as a matter of fact."

Kelland looked surprised, but J.J. pressed on before he could say anything. "I'd heard that you and Marcotti almost came to blows a couple of times. It seems he thinks you were unfairly blocking his requests to open a sidewalk terrace."

She didn't ask a question, just waited to see the effect and was pleased to see his face go from ashen to beet red in a few seconds.

"How do you know that? I can't talk about council business with an outsider, but I wouldn't go around spreading rumors if I were you." He stood and looked as threatening as his words sounded.

She stood her ground. "I'm sure it's a matter of record, the number of times Marcotti made the changes the council requested but was again turned down. Why were you so against it? Or were you against *him*?"

Kelland sputtered, "I'd like you to leave now."

He looked down at his desk and started shuffling papers around. When she still didn't move, he gazed at her again, and this time she actually felt a shiver run through her body. What was it about this guy that made her want to challenge him rather than retreat?

"I'd also heard he was thinking of running against you in the next election." Her heart was thumping so hard in her chest, she hoped she wouldn't do something embarrassing. Like expire.

"Leave and don't come back." He pointed at the door.

It was such a dramatic gesture, J.J. actually felt herself relax enough to ask, "Did you kill him?"

Kelland picked up the phone and told his receptionist to call security. This time J.J. took the hint. As she opened the door to leave, she turned and said, "I hope you were more forthcoming with the police."

The receptionist was on the phone, obviously talking to security, as J.J. breezed past her trying to look unconcerned. When she made it outdoors without being accosted, she let out the breath she'd been holding. When she was seated behind the wheel of her car, she started shaking. She'd never been so confrontational. Well, maybe once, with her ex-fiancé, when she'd found out he'd been sleeping with a mutual client. What had possessed her this time? She'd never get to ask him another question, the important one about his nephew, that was for sure.

She wondered if Devine had been to see him yet.

"You did what?" Skye's eyeballs almost popped out when J.J. finished running through her visit to Kelland's office. "Oh man. I don't know if you're spunky or stupid. Really."

"What could he have done? Had me thrown out, sure. And he was about to do so. But that's not being jailed or anything, and he certainly wouldn't raise a hand against me in his own office." J.J. felt a lot more nonchalant about the whole incident after a double latte and one of the remaining truffles she had stashed in her desk drawer.

"Oh, I don't know. Maybe he'll check the business—our business—and try to see if he can cite us on a few bylaw violations or something. He sounds that vindictive from what you've told me."

J.J. gulped. "I'm sorry. I didn't think about that."

"It's all right. It's very unlikely he'll do that, especially since I can't think of anything we've done that will cause us any trouble. And besides, if he does, we can always counter with your information. I guess I was just spouting off. After that van attack, I'm really worried about you, you know."

"Thanks, Skye. I do know that and I'm worried, too, but I can't let it stop me."

"What will it take to stop you?" Alison asked, standing in the doorway.

"I didn't hear you come in," J.J. said. "And what will stop me is the police taking a serious look into other possibilities as the killer."

Alison sank into the chair next to J.J.'s desk. "I know. And that's good to hear, because I'm just heading home after night shift and I wanted to tell you the scuttlebutt. You didn't hear it from me, though." Alison glared at J.J. and then Skye.

Both crossed their hearts and gestured zipping their lips.

"Okay, then. Detective Hashtag—that's what we call Hastings because he's always tweeting everything from football scores to drug busts—had us doing surveillance last night on someone he considers a suspect in that very same murder case."

J.J. sat up. "Yay. Who?"

"Candy Fleetwood."

"Candy? He's on the wrong track. Again. I'm certain it's not Candy."

"How would you know?"

"She's my trainer at the High Time Fitness Center, and believe me, she's totally broken up about Marcotti's death."

"You know about their affair?"

"Yes. In fact, I mentioned it at the last Culinary Capers gathering when we were talking about the murder. You were indisposed at that point."

Alison sighed. "And you've kept on talking about it, too. Why do you guys do that? I told you it was best to stay out of police business."

"Yes, and you also said you couldn't be involved in anything, so we waited until you'd left the room, as you'll recall. We didn't want to put you in a compromising situation."

"Very thoughtful, I'm sure. But it looks like I've gotten myself into it anyway. What else were you all talking about?"

"I can't really remember. So much has happened since then. I know I talked about Ty Devine."

"The PI? What's up with him anyway?"

J.J. shrugged. "All I know is that he's still working for Mrs. Marcotti, only searching for the murderer rather than the mistress. I did also say that I really don't think that Candy Fleetwood is the murderer and that there are tons more people out there with a motive to kill him."

"All right, I'm going to pretend I didn't hear anything about you investigating or the others collaborating, and I'm going home to sleep. I'm on nights again, and they roll round awfully quickly and pass by very slowly." She stood and adjusted her skinny jeans.

"Are you doing Candy surveillance again?"

"I don't know. We'll find out our assignment when we go in tonight. It could just be regular patrol, so don't get your hopes up."

They waited until Alison had left, and then Skye said, "I wouldn't have that job for any amount of money."

"Agreed. I hope she doesn't get into any more trouble sharing this."

"Agreed."

"Maybe her biggest problem will be with herself," J.J. said thoughtfully. "She's usually very tight-lipped when it comes to her job. I guess that's drilled into them."

"Fortunate thing for you, the drill is wearing off. Now you can stop snooping, because you know the police haven't locked into Rocco as the murderer."

"That's good, but when they discover that Candy didn't do it, what happens to Rocco?"

CHAPTER 27

J.J. knew she couldn't give any more time to thinking about Marcotti or any of the other suspects. Her time was better spent looking for a location for her new client, the Vermont Preschool Teachers Association or VPTA, to hold their conference. This was J.J.'s first time working with an association, as Skye usually handled the larger events. However, business was expanding, and they might not be able to afford the luxury of specializing as much as they had been. J.J. was sure she could handle it. She would just have to practice her time management and stay on top of the plans.

She'd compiled a short list of hotels in Burlington when the phone rang. The caller ID showed Olivia Barker. The confidence she'd felt when answering had turned to shock by the time she hung up. Skye noticed the look on her face and asked if she wanted some coffee or something stronger.

"Hemlock juice would be best. Just put me out of my misery. Now."

"Bad news, I take it." Skye stood, ready to offer whatever might be needed. She shoved the sleeves of her multicolored blazer up to the elbows.

"That was Olivia Barker. And you'll never guess what."

"I won't believe it if she says she doesn't like your new idea. I think it's terrific."

"Oh, she does also. The trouble is, my competitor had the same idea. Can you believe it?"

Skye stood up and walked over to J.J.'s desk. "No, I don't believe it."

"It differs in a few suggestions, but basically it's the same."

"There's no conceivable way you two could come up with the same proposal. Twice. Especially an idea like that. Something fishy is going on. What did Ms. Barker say?"

"She wants to meet with me and the other woman tomorrow afternoon in her office. She loves the idea or ideas and thought maybe we could work together."

"Uh-oh." Skye perched on the edge of her desk. "What are your thoughts on that?"

"I don't like it. Not one bit. This contract belongs to Make It Happen."

"I'm relieved to hear you say that. And normally I would think that."

"Do I hear a *but* in there?" J.J. began chewing on her bottom lip.

Skye went to sit in her chair again. "Just give me a few minutes to think this over. By the way, did she tell you the name of our competitor?"

"Ashley Rose. Does that ring any bells?"

"Off the top of my head, I haven't heard of her. Why don't you try Googling her?"

"Good idea." J.J. tried to find a listing by name, then searched for a Facebook site, tried the Yellow Pages, and finally the local bulletin board where contract workers often posted their credentials, looking for event planners in the area. Nothing.

"I can't find her anywhere. What do you think that means?" J.J. fanned herself with a ruler that was handy. She wasn't sure if the rising heat was external or internal, but she took off her black cashmere cardigan and carefully folded it.

"Maybe she's part of a corporate entity and not into any notoriety. Or maybe she's just starting out."

"If she were starting out, you'd think she'd want to have a profile somewhere. It's important to be on the Internet these days. Or even on LinkedIn. But she's nowhere. How can she expect to build up a business?"

"You're right. I don't have any answers."

J.J. tried Googling her own name and was surprised, maybe a little shocked, to find a listing of several pages pop up. There was even a mention of her engagement, an article from the community newspaper, a folksy paper with a social page, when she'd lived in the Coville suburb of Montpelier. She remembered getting the call from the reporter after someone in her office had phoned with the tip. J.J. had suspected it was the vice president in charge of public relations, who had always been on the lookout for a chance to get the company's name in the paper. She didn't want to read the article any further.

J.J. glanced at Skye, who sat deep in thought, so she checked her e-mails and spent a lot of time deleting old ones. Her favorite procrastination tool.

Finally, Skye said, "I've been thinking. Maybe you should sound agreeable to joining forces. We might then be able to figure out this person's game plan. Or at the very least, if you should have to go through with it, I'd bet it soon becomes apparent who's the creative thinker in the group."

"But what if it backfires? Also, we'd have to split the fee."

Skye shrugged. "I don't like it, but I don't really see what else we can do about it. If you refuse, the word could get out that you're uncooperative."

"Not good in this industry."

"No. Anyway, it's your client, your decision."

"Thanks for nothing," J.J. said, knowing she'd accept the suggestion, cooperate, and see where it led. At any rate, she wanted to meet this person of like mind and try to figure out what was happening. Surely, the other person was just as shocked and curious.

"By the way," Skye said, looking up from her computer, "I'm heading out of town tonight for a couple of days. You'll hold down the fort, I presume?" She had a playful look on her face that matched the tone of her voice.

"Natch. What's up, if I may be so bold as to ask?"

"I thought I'd drive to Stowe and talk to a few of the hotel owners there. It might be fun to set up some meetings or a conference with a little skiing on the side come winter."

"That does sound like a tempting location. Been thinking about this for some time now?"

"Uh, just since Nick mentioned going someplace snowy for New Year's Eve. Killing two birds with one stone."

J.J. gave her a thumbs-up. "So, back on Thursday?"

Skye nodded.

J.J. looked at the clock. She knew that any more thought would drive her crazy. Her original notes were ready for the meeting; her ideas were solid. There was nothing more to do about it.

She sighed and let her mind wander back to the murder. She'd love to get the widow Marcotti in a one-on-one situation where maybe some confidences might be shared. She also realized how unrealistic that was. But maybe, with Ty Devine at her side, the widow might get more expansive. He did have a way about him, and besides, she was his client. J.J. was positive about that. But would Devine agree? He'd tried awfully hard at first not to admit to the connection. On the other hand, J.J. was certain that if he thought she would be messing with his client, he'd want to be right there keeping an eye on things.

She picked up the phone to call him.

Devine's car was already parked in front of the Marcotti house when J.J. drove up. She hoped he hadn't gone in without her. She was prepared to give him the evil eye when she got inside but instead was pleasantly surprised to find him seated in the driver's seat when she walked past his car.

He opened the door and she scooted to the side. "Thanks for agreeing to this."

"I really didn't have much choice. If I want to keep my client happy, I need to be here or who knows what she'll assume after talking to you." He locked his car and followed J.J. to the front door. "Besides, I might have a few questions for her myself."

"Good."

Shortly after he rang the bell, the door was opened by a scowling dark-haired older woman wearing a dark-striped apron over a black dress. Sturdy black clogs encased her feet. J.J. wondered if this was the mother-in-law, and if so, whose?

Devine spoke while J.J. pondered. "Mrs. Marcotti is expecting us."

"Okay. You know the way." She turned and left them to close the door and find the widow.

"Who is she?" J.J. whispered as she walked with him toward the back of the house. She tried to take in the large winding staircase and open foyer, the walls lined with miniature art statues. It looked different minus the two hundred guests who had milled around the last time J.J. had been there. It reminded her of the Portovino estate in size but not in taste.

"That's their housekeeper. Not one for chitchat."

J.J. dropped behind Devine as he opened the glass doors to a room that looked like a cross between a greenhouse and a bordello. Gina Marcotti sat on a chaise lounge of red velvet immediately across from them. Her curly dark hair was styled a bit differently this time, with a dramatic sweep across her forehead. She was wearing black lounging pants and a periwinkle blue top with long sleeves and a cowl neckline. When she held out her hand, J.J. could see that her arm was draped in bracelets. She didn't stand up.

"Signor Devine. I'm so happy you're taking the time to update me. But who is that with you?"

"It's J.J. Tanner, the woman I mentioned." He gave J.J. a small shove toward the chaise, but Gina had lowered her hand by that time.

"Sit. Would you like something to drink? I can offer you a cosmopolitan." She held up her own glass and then took a long sip.

"No, I'm fine," J.J. replied.

Devine just shook his head. "If you don't mind, we'd like to ask you a few questions. It won't take long and it should be a great help."

"In tracking down the killer of my Tonio?"

"Yes."

J.J. sat on a gold brocade slipper chair facing at a right angle to their hostess while Devine took the matching chair across from her. Since Gina seemed to be fixated on Devine and totally ignoring J.J., she took the opportunity to give the room a thorough sizing up. It was too over-the-top for her. She knew that Gina came from family wealth, but their designer must have been nouveau riche. Not that J.J. was a snob. She came from a modest home life, but in her previous job with a large advertising agency and in this business, she'd seen enough homes where taste and wealth went hand in hand. She wouldn't dub this one as such.

She realized that Devine had said something to her. She looked at him and raised her eyebrows. He sighed and repeated what he'd said.

"J.J. happens to be the last person to see Antonio alive. Why don't you tell Gina about it?"

"Yes, all right. It was after the Portovino party had ended and the kitchen was packed up. I left at the same time your husband did, and we had a few words out by my car. Then I left. I didn't see anyone else in the vicinity."

Gina looked directly at J.J. and narrowed her eyes. "What were you discussing? Did he try to get you to go to bed with him?"

"No!" J.J. gasped. She knew, though, that she shouldn't have been surprised by the question. "Really. Nothing like that. In fact, we had an argument over his having slipped an extra high-priced dish onto the menu without my approval. I wasn't going to pay the extra charge for it."

Gina laughed, and J.J. was surprised by the lightness of the sound. Definitely the most pleasant thing about this woman. "That sounds like Tonio, all right. He has—had—a mind of his own, and you played it his way or not at all."

J.J. nodded. "Exactly. May I ask why you hired Mr. Devine to follow him?"

Gina glanced at Devine, then shrugged. "I guess it doesn't matter anymore. I knew he was having an affair. I've known about all of them. But he was spending more money on this one, so I wanted to find out who it was."

"And do what?"

"Stop his bleeding my bank account, that's what."

"By killing him?"

Devine shook his head. Gina looked shocked and then started laughing again.

"Oh no. I would never do that. Despite all his failings, and I know he had many, we were well suited."

"Really?"

Gina narrowed her eyes. "Yes, really. When he was with me, he was a devoted husband and he was great in the bedroom."

"But it must have hurt to know he had other women on the side." J.J. thought it best to take the straightforward approach.

"It did at first. That was many, many years ago. But I'll tell you the solution to that. I started having my own lovers."

J.J. gasped again. This woman was candid, if nothing else. "Did your husband know?"

"Probably, but we never discussed it. If we had, he would have had to 'fess up' himself or else make a big fuss about it. He knew that as long as he kept me happy and didn't cause me any public embarrassment, everything was simpatico."

"And yet you hired Devine. Was this the first time you'd hired a private eye?"

Gina finished her drink and went to fix another one at the bar tray beside the door. "No. The first time I had a suspicion that he was playing around, I did the same thing. That's because I was so shocked and wanted to know for certain if it was true. Once I found out that it was, I made the decision to carry on with the marriage."

"Would you have done anything to Candy Fleetwood?"

Gina smiled a Cheshire cat smile. "I was thinking about it but I hadn't come to any grand ideas. And before you ask, I wouldn't have killed her, either. I would have simply bought her off. She obviously was in it for the money."

You don't know Candy. "Can you think of anyone else who might have wanted to kill him?"

"Well, I think you had a good reason."

J.J. gasped.

Gina smiled and carried on. "And so did anyone else in the same boat. He was not an honorable man in business, I know that. But I can't think of anyone specific."

"What about Rocco Gates?"

"Rocco?" Her voice rose a little. "It's not likely. I know the police are very interested in him, but their feud was in the past. I think they just kept it going out of habit or maybe because they really didn't know how to properly end it. You know, without either of them losing face. No, Rocco had no reason to kill Tonio. Have you come up with any leads, Mr. Devine?"

Devine looked surprised to be pulled back into the conversation. "A couple of names have come up. We'd heard that his head chef might be leaving and that there had been some arguments over that. Do you know anything about it?"

"Yes, it's true. Tonio told me about an offer from some competitor downtown, and he was worried Kevin might take it—and worse yet, might take some kitchen secrets with him. Now that really got him angry. I know they had a very serious shouting match a couple of weeks ago, but I'm not sure what's been happening lately."

"Do you know Kevin Lonsdale very well? Do you think he could commit murder?" J.J. interjected.

Gina thought about it for a few seconds. "I really don't know. It doesn't seem like a powerful enough motive, though, does it? Killing over recipes?" She gave a sharp laugh.

"I guess, when you put it that way . . ."

"We also have reason to believe that the local councilor, Don Kelland, had been at loggerheads with your husband," Devine said, watching his client's face.

"Yes. Tonio had been angry with him for a long time over zoning issues, but he was about to fix all that by running against him in the next election. And you know, with the Italian community and my money behind him, he would have won. Now, does that make Mr. Kelland a murderer? I don't know. Do you?"

"I'll find out."

Devine waited a beat and then looked over at J.J., who gave a small nod. "We'll be leaving, then."

J.J. stood and suddenly asked, "Are you having an affair right now?"

Gina drew herself up. "I don't think I'll answer that."

"But don't you see? This guy could be the killer, wanting to get your husband out of the way so that he could marry you."

Gina blanched. "He wouldn't do such a thing." Her voice was steely as she bid them good-bye.

They were walking toward the car when J.J. asked Devine, "Why didn't you pursue the question about her lover? It sounds like she is still in an affair. We need to know who the guy is."

"I didn't ask because I know and I'm not going to tell you."

"Why not? I thought we were in this together?"

"Really? At the most, we're helping each other by sharing leads. Now, let it drop, J.J. The man is not the murderer. Now, do you have anything else to tell me?"

"No." *Two can play this game.*

She stewed about their conversation all the way back, and by the time she walked up the stairs to her office, she was more determined than ever to find out the name of the mystery lover. She had her hand on the doorknob when a thought struck her: what if it was Ty Devine?

CHAPTER 28

Later that night, she knocked on Ness Harper's door. In one hand, her excuse: a plate of profiteroles. What she really wanted was a sounding board and another take on where the case was going. He answered on the first knock.

"Ah, she comes bearing a bribe. Must want something pretty bad."

J.J. still wasn't totally used to Ness's wry sense of humor. She looked hard to see if there was any sign he was joking—twitchy mouth, dancing eyes, anything? Nothing. She chose to take it as such, anyway.

"Precisely, and I'm glad we can get right down to the point," J.J. said, equally seriously.

"Only after we have coffee and one of those delicious looking whatchamacallits. Homemade, of course?" He smiled and J.J. started laughing.

"Not likely. You know, I have to admit, sometimes I'm still not quite sure how to take what you say."

"So you've said." Ness shrugged. "That's me. Come in. I'll start the coffee brewing."

She followed him down the short hall, the mirror of her own apartment, at least as far as the layout. She perched on a stool at the counter while Ness went through the process of grinding coffee, measuring it out into the basket, and adding water to the glass Pyrex coffee percolator. She knew he loved his coffee and was always very precise about how he made it. She couldn't remember the last time she'd seen one of those percolators on the store shelves.

"So, what's troubling you, missy?" he asked, his back to her.

"It's this whole Marcotti business."

"I could have guessed that. What's new?" He pulled out a stool beside her and sat to wait for the coffee to finish perking.

"The latest is that Mrs. Marcotti was and is still having an affair. She's had several, apparently, just like her husband."

"Hm. A possible candidate for the murderer. Do you know who the guy is?"

"I don't, but Devine does."

Ness raised his eyebrows. "Devine does. How do you know that?"

"Because we talked to Mrs. Marcotti together. He told me to leave it alone when I tried pressing her for details about the latest lover."

Ness thought about it a few seconds. "Any ideas?"

"No. Well, not really. Well, maybe. Just a question, really. What if it's Devine?"

"Devine!" Ness gave it some more thought. "Don't see why it couldn't be. What are you thinking?"

"Well, he was at the Portovino estate, he admitted it. And we only have his word that he left when he said he did. Maybe that's why he told the police about me—he wanted to divert attention."

"It's possible. And he's continuing with the investigation

in order to deflect any suspicion from himself, should it arise."

"Exactly. That's probably why he's popping up all the time and harassing me."

"Harassing. That's a strong word. It sounds like you two joined forces for the Marcotti meeting." Ness looked over at the coffeepot, which was just starting to perk.

"Well, yes, we did. But he could have manipulated me to do that."

"Hm. Who called who?"

"Okay, I called him, but that part might not be important. He did tell me not to pursue it, after all. Oh, I know, there's quite an age difference between the two of them, but it's happened before, hasn't it? And she is a wealthy woman, and he's a . . ."

Ness tilted his head. "He's what?"

J.J. felt her face turning red. "Some would say he's a very attractive, sexy guy."

Ness stood and went to turn the stove burner down to low. "Let's move into the living room. Much more comfortable there. I'm not really sure why I have these stools. Hate sitting on them."

J.J. perched on the edge of the worn tweed-covered sofa while Ness sat in his leather recliner across from her. She hoped he wouldn't get back to the topic of Devine. She looked at the coffee table that separated them. The top was cluttered with magazines, newspapers, and what looked like a paper plate with some dried food on it. She tried not to judge.

"So, what's your next step?" Ness asked.

She sighed. "That's just it, I don't know. Should I tell the police?"

"I'm sure they've already checked him out every which way, but they should be told about the affairs, in case it hasn't been mentioned before. Let them draw their own conclusions."

J.J. visibly relaxed and leaned back. "That sounds like a plan."

"I sort of get the feeling that you like this Devine guy."

She looked startled. "Like? Why would you say that? Well, I guess he's okay. But I'm still a bit ticked off at him for spying on me, and he sure tried pushing me around when I made contact with Candy Fleetwood. That I don't like. And if he's having an affair—and worse yet, if he's the killer . . ." She didn't know how to finish the statement.

"Hm. I'll check on the coffee."

J.J. tried not to think about what Ness had said. Like the guy? Sure, in a casual, "we keep bumping into each other, so might as well be friendly" way. But not anything more. That was for certain. Her cheeks felt a bit flushed again, and she touched them.

"Here you go, fresh coffee the way it should be made, not with these pods and cups and what have you. Here, take one of your decadent whatevers. I tried one already. Feel free to bribe me anytime with this stuff."

He put the tray on the coffee table and sat across from her again. After looking at her a few moments, he smiled and shook his head.

She had a hard time getting to sleep. Of course, it was the coffee. She knew she shouldn't have had one at that time of night, much less the second cup she'd accepted. And then thoughts about Ty Devine kept flooding her brain. How could he be so deceitful? How could he be having an affair with a married woman? Okay, she wasn't so naïve as to believe it didn't happen all the time. But Devine?

He was handsome in a rugged sort of way. It was the eyes.

That intense blue got her every time. It should have been a warning. Her ex-fiancé also had blue eyes but not so piercing. She thought about him for a while, remembering their good times and then the brutal betrayal, him sleeping with a prospective client their company was wooing. He swore he'd done it strictly to get the account, but he knew that J.J. had also wanted it. That whomever brought it in would get a promotion. She gave herself a mental head slap. *Stop thinking about the scumbag.* Great word for him. She smiled and tried to calm her mind, but Devine crept in again.

She should have been glad if he was the lover, and hence the murderer. Her search would be over. But how to prove it? She doubted he'd slip up in any way if she tried sweet-talking him. He was an experienced investigator, and she was sure he'd faced any number of tough guys—and manipulating ones—in the past. Could she go back to Gina Marcotti on her own and play on her feelings, hope she'd name Devine as her lover, which might give him a motive to be the killer? Surely she wouldn't want to continue with him if that were the case. Unless she was in on it.

J.J.'s eyelids shot open. That had to be it. No, it didn't. She'd already decided that Gina had no need to be rid of her husband. Not for money, that was for certain. But what if for love? Oh man, this was driving her crazy.

Eventually, she dropped off, but she felt every bit of the lack of sleep the next day, and she had the big meeting with Olivia Barker coming up. She scrambled to get ready the next morning, and ordered an extra-large double-shot latte on her way to work.

As she was walking past Evan's open door, she heard him call out. She detoured into his office. "Good morning, Evan. You wanted to talk to me?"

"Yup, it is a good morning. And I do want to talk if you have a minute. It's about Tansy."

Uh-oh. "I hate to ask, but what now?"

"She said you were going to speak to me about the paint? Did we have that conversation?" He leaned back in his chair, and she noticed for the first time a small paunch straining at the buttons of his yellow dress shirt. She'd heard that Michael was a great cook, although it was usually Evan who did the honors whenever she'd been invited over.

"No, I forgot. There's been so much going on lately. But I did promise her, so here goes. She's right, you know. We do need to freshen the place up. Think of the clients."

"You're right."

"I am?"

"Yes, I've been thinking about it, and she's right, too."

"Did you tell her that?"

"No, I thought you'd like to, since it was your task to talk me into it." He smiled and sat forward abruptly. "She knows how to change tactics all right."

"It was in exchange for her doing something that had to do with the case."

His smile faded. "You know, the police came by to see me again yesterday."

"Oh no. What did they want?"

"They'd really like for someone other than Michael to give me an alibi, but what they asked was, had I ever been to Rocco G's and when?" *Access to the knife.*

"That at least means they haven't closed the case." J.J. jumped up. "I'm sorry you're under fire again, Evan. Tell me if there's anything I can do."

She meant it, but she was now anxious to get out of there and find out if Rocco was still in jail. This, along with what Alison had mentioned about the surveillance on Candy, must mean the major heat was off Rocco.

He waved his hand. "Nothing. There's nothing at the moment. Thanks, anyway."

J.J. went over and gave him a kiss on the cheek. "Don't worry. I'm sure this will be resolved soon. But let me know if anything crops up, okay?"

Evan nodded.

J.J. ran up the stairs and stopped at Tansy's office door, hoping she would agree to call the police and check on whether Rocco had been released, especially once she heard the good news about the paint.

"Tansy is out at the county records office," Izzy told her.

Okay. It could wait. Maybe she should call Rocco G's and ask. She went back to her desk and was about to do so when the phone rang. A new prospective client. Mrs. Jewels Stanton, wife of Clayton, well-known Burlington defense attorney and always in the local top-five wealthiest list. J.J. tried to contain her excitement as she spent the next half hour supplying some background about Make It Happen and gathering details about the upcoming Stanton fiftieth wedding anniversary celebration in return. They agreed to meet the following week.

J.J. silently thanked Lorenzo Portovino for recommending them to the Stantons, as she gathered her jacket and purse to head for Kirking Manufacturing. Her call to Rocco G's would have to wait.

J.J. was asked to wait in the reception area until Olivia Barker joined her. She wondered where the other event planner was. She hoped Ms. Barker wasn't in a meeting with her. That wouldn't bode well.

She could picture them sharing a coffee and a laugh as they delved into plans for the retirement party. At some point the interloper, as J.J. had come to think of her, would ask what J.J. had proposed, already knowing, of course, and would then introduce her own latest idea in such a way that

*anything else sounded amateurish and second rate. Barker
would absolutely love the ideas. They'd end up with a quick
hug, and Barker's secretary would appear to tell J.J. she
wasn't needed anymore.*

Talk about a worst-case scenario.

J.J. tried not to fidget. *Just stay calm.* She picked up the
latest issue of *Vermont Life* from the end table and flipped
through it, all the while going over in her mind all that she
wanted to make sure to say at the meeting.

Finally, the receptionist looked over at J.J. and told her
Ms. Barker's assistant was on the way. J.J. swallowed to dis-
pel the panic and looked up to see a young and pert woman
wearing a navy pantsuit, white shirt, and flat shoes, obviously
trying for an older and in-charge look, heading her way.

"I'm sorry you had to wait, but Ms. Barker is just finishing
up with a supplier." Her smile was sincere, as was the tone
of her voice. J.J. relaxed as she continued, "Sometimes these
things run over, you know. Let me show you to her office
and I'll get you some coffee or water if you'd like."

J.J. followed her to a small but tastefully decorated corner
office with a fourteenth-floor view of the lake on one side
and the Burlington skyline in the distance from the other.

"Those views are amazing," J.J. said, taking it all in.

"Aren't they just? Now, would you like something? It
may take her a few more minutes." She leaned closer as if
sharing some news. "We just got this marvelous espresso
machine and it makes really, really good brew."

"That sounds perfect," J.J. answered.

And it did. She could do an extended wait with an espresso
in hand. She was just finishing it off when the door opened
and a very tall, imposing-looking woman entered. J.J. scrambled to stand and still couldn't quite get on an equal eye level.

The woman covered the space between them in two
strides, hand outstretched. "I'm Olivia Barker. I'm so sorry

to have kept you waiting, but I see you've been treated to our new find." She gestured to the empty cup.

"It was as tasty as advertised."

"Good. Now, Ms. Rose is running late, so why don't you and I get started. You said you'd never met Ashley Rose?"

"No, I haven't." She hoped they weren't jumping right into the "working together" phase.

Olivia nodded as she sat behind her desk. Her light brown hair framed her angular face in a bob and the purple reading glasses she'd pulled out of her desk drawer complemented the lavender silk blouse she wore. J.J. wondered if she always coordinated with her glasses. Olivia had slipped out of her tailored black suit jacket before sitting down, and it now draped over the back of her chair.

"I'm truly amazed that two proposals that are so similar have been tended. In fact, the ideas are exactly the same, only some of the words have been changed. To protect the innocent," she added with a chuckle but watching J.J. She picked up a stack of paper in each hand. J.J. wondered which hand her proposal was in. She also wondered whose had arrived first but thought it better not to say so aloud. Might sound childish.

"Even the additional was almost word for word," Olivia continued. "You don't have a twin, do you?" She laughed as she said it, but J.J. detected a note of concern.

"Guaranteed not. I don't know what to say. I've never had this happen before."

Barker sat back, her eyes on J.J., who kept her cool and tried to look calm and innocent. But innocent of what? That internal light bulb in her head flashed on. Copying. Someone had obviously copied J.J.'s proposals. There was no other way this could have happened. But how? Were her e-mails intercepted? By someone in Barker's office?

The phone on her desk rang, and Barker answered, all

the while watching J.J., who suddenly had an answer to her questions. Brittany? Who else? But why?

Barker hung up and asked, "What's on your mind, J.J.? It looks like something's occurred to you."

"Uh, I've just had a thought, but I'd like to check something out before I say anything." She hoped that would be enough to keep Barker from prying any further.

"Well, that will be all right, but let's get on with discussing this proposal. That was Ms. Rose on the line. She's not able to make it after all, so we'll just continue and then you two can arrange between yourselves to talk. Will that work for you?"

"Yes."

"Fine. I'll have my assistant give you Ms. Rose's particulars as you leave. Now, I wanted to say how pleased I was that you'd suggested mixing up the personal life of Will Gowling with his corporate persona. I think that's the perfect touch. In fact, I totally approve of everything in both proposals. Of course, if you can bring the event in under cost, that's even better. But I won't quibble about money. The guest of honor has been a valuable asset to this company and will be sorely missed. I want this to be a party that will show him exactly that."

"That's the message I got from our last talk. I'm so pleased you think this fulfills that."

"Now, what's the next stage?"

"I'll get to work on all the elements—the catering, the décor, the invitations, the media release, the entertainment—and send all the details to you for final approval before continuing."

"That's after you've met with Ashley Rose?"

J.J. swallowed. "Of course."

Barker smiled. "I have complete confidence that you'll handle this well." She stood and held out her hand. "Let me know if you need any more information."

"I will, and please be in touch if you have anything to add."
J.J. shook her hand and left. The assistant handed her a piece
of letterhead notepaper with the e-mail and phone number
for Ashley Rose on it as she reached the reception area.

Okay, Ashley Rose, the game is afoot.

CHAPTER 29

J.J. had her computer off, her jacket on, and her hand on the light switch when the phone rang. She was pleased to hear Rocco Gates's voice on the line.

"You're out of jail?" She clamped her hand over her mouth. Not very tactful. She quickly recovered. "How wonderful, Rocco. I'm delighted to hear from you."

"My brother-in-law bailed me out this morning. I've been spending most of the day just walking around, but now I'm at the bistro and ready to rock and roll. If you have no plans tonight, I'd like to invite you to stop by for an espresso on your way home."

"I'd love to. I'm just leaving now, actually. I'll see you shortly."

J.J. decided to leave her car at the office and enjoy the mild early evening. She practically skipped downhill to Rocco G's. She did remind herself, though, that being out on bail wasn't the same thing as no longer being a suspect.

As far as she knew, Rocco was still number one on that list. But maybe now that he was free, she could ask him some more questions.

She pushed open the door to the bistro and spotted Rocco shaking hands with some customers at the cash register. He saw J.J. and flashed her a wide smile. After the customers left, he went to her and kissed her on each cheek.

"It's a so good to see you, my friend. I understand I should thank you for all you've been doing on my behalf. Please, come and sit and I will make you that espresso."

She sat at a table for two next to the window, facing away from the counter, so she was surprised when her espresso arrived. Rocco also placed a small dish with an assortment of biscotti, baicoli, and pevarini in front of her.

"Please enjoy." He looked around the room. "I think I have a breather right now. May I join you?"

"Oh, please do. It must feel good to be back in here."

"You cannot imagine. That place chills the soul. And if you are innocent of all charges, it's a double crippling." He shivered in emphasis.

"Did the police say anything to you, like who else they're suspecting?"

"Are you still worried you might be on their list?" He covered her hand in reassurance.

"No, actually I'm not, which surprises me when I say it out loud. I hadn't thought about it in a while, I guess. I was so worried about you. But they must be looking elsewhere."

"I certainly hope so. I've heard from a few sources that you have been doing the same thing. And I understand you've been checking around. Have you found anything out?"

J.J. nodded. "I've found out that Kevin Lonsdale, Marcotti's chef, might be leaving and there may have been some concern about his taking recipes with him. There's also the local city councilor, Don Kelland, who Marcotti had some issues with and was even thinking of running against in the next election. So a few possibilities."

"Yes, that sounds hopeful. You have been busy." He smiled, although she could still see the concern etched in his face.

She took a drink of espresso, enjoying the flavor. "I also know that Gina Marcotti is having an affair, but she won't say with whom. I'm wondering if it's Ty Devine—you know, the private investigator—and if that makes him the killer."

There, she'd said it aloud to someone other than Ness. Did it sound any more right?

Rocco turned to look out the window. When he didn't say anything, J.J. asked, "Do I sound way off base?"

"I don't know what to say." He looked back at her. "I don't really know this Ty Devine, just the time he came in to question me when you were here—remember? And then another time when he visited me in the jail. He seemed really interested in finding the killer."

"What if that was to throw everyone off his scent?"

"Let me ask you, what makes you think he is this mysterious lover?"

"Because he told me not to ask Gina about it anymore. He knew who it was, and he didn't believe that person was the killer. But if it was Devine, he'd say that, wouldn't he? So that we wouldn't realize he's the lover and he's the killer."

"It don't think it sounds very likely to me. Besides, he's too young for her."

"It wouldn't be the first time." J.J.'s thoughts flashed briefly to her ex-fiancé and the client, at least fifteen years his senior, whom he'd bedded.

"I think you are wrong about this man. As much as I want the real killer to be found, I don't think it's a him. You must look at the other choices rather than a lover."

J.J. searched his face. Why was he so adamant? Did he really trust Devine that much? What had Devine said to him during that jail visit? What was Devine not telling her?

She shrugged. "I'll remember that. However, I still think he's a good bet. Don't worry, I won't stop trying to figure this out." She was trying to make him feel better.

"As much as I appreciate what you're doing, I am worried about you and think it's a probably better left to the police and Mr. Devine. Promise me you won't do anything dangerous."

"All right, I promise." She stifled a yawn and realized it must be late. She glanced at her wristwatch. Eight. She'd better get some dinner before she waited too long and could fall asleep while eating.

"I didn't realize it's so late. I should be going. It's really good to see you. And thank you for the espresso and goodies."

Rocco laughed. "My pleasure, *cara*. Now, come and see me again soon."

He helped her shrug into her jacket and was collecting the dirty dishes when she glanced back in the window.

Who would know about Gina's lover? Someone in the Italian community? Did they all know about Candy? Well, Rocco was a someone but he certainly wasn't blurting a name, even though he thought it wasn't Devine. Would Candy know? Only if Marcotti had known, and surely he would have done something about it in that case. Who could she ask? Who was in a better position to find out?

She was so intent on her thoughts, she screamed when a hand shot out and grabbed her arm.

"Don't scream. It's me," Devine said, hanging on tightly and quickening his pace. "Just keep walking and don't slow down. You're being tailed by that white van again. Where's your car?"

"At my office."

"Mine's just around this corner. We'll walk to it, get in without looking back, and drive off."

"But don't you want to see who it is?"

"I'm hoping he'll continue to follow us right into a parking lot just down the street, where I can quickly turn the tables and box him in." They approached his car and she heard him unlock the doors remotely. He opened the passenger door and she slid into the seat. When he was behind the wheel, he glanced in his rearview mirror.

"Is he still there?" she asked, afraid to turn around and take a look.

"Oh yeah. This could get interesting. Buckle up."

They drove around for several minutes before J.J. asked, "Why were you following me this time?"

"I wasn't. I was headed to Rocco G's and saw you come out, then noticed the van start up. Rocco made bail, I take it?"

"Yes, his brother-in-law bailed him out this morning, and obviously he's delighted to be free. What do you think it means? They have another suspect in mind?"

"It means what it is. He was granted bail and someone came up with the money. It doesn't diminish the charges or anything like that. He's still their top man for the rap."

"But Evan Thornton said the police had been around to see him again."

"Yes, and they'll probably be paying you another visit, too. They have to check and triple-check to make sure they haven't overlooked anything. I'm thinking, even though they have the link to the murder weapon and a possible motive, there are no prints and no witnesses. And no confession. They still have a lot of homework to do in order to make their case stand up in court."

"All right, but— Ooh." She let out a big breath as Devine

took the corner without slowing down. "That sure won't let him know we're onto him," she said with sarcasm.

"Don't turn around. I just wanted to see how desperate he is to keep up with us. Okay, the parking lot is coming up on the left. I'm going to lure him in then double back to block off the entrance. I want you to stay in the car, no matter what happens. Got that?"

"Yes. Shouldn't I be calling 911?"

"Right. Now would be a good time to do that. Here we go. Hang on."

J.J. had been digging around in her purse for her smartphone when Devine made a sharp left turn and she dropped it. She glared at him but he didn't look over. She glanced in the side mirror and saw the van pull in, then stop. She was leaning down to the floor trying to recover her phone when Devine gunned the engine and did a 180-degree spin, speeding over to the entrance.

He sat staring at the van but no one got out. "Can you make out the plate?" He passed her some small but powerful binoculars when she straightened.

"I can." She made the phone call and gave the 911 operator the details.

"What's he waiting for?" she wanted to know. "Do you think he has a gun and will shoot us?"

"Possibly. He's trying to sort through his options. He could decide to ram us. Shoot us. Or give up. I think the last one is highly unlikely."

"You make us sound like sitting ducks. What did you think would happen when you did this?"

"I'd hoped he'd jump out of the van, mad as hell, and try to punch me out."

"Also a good option."

Devine chuckled. "Glad you're on my side. Or he could

just as easily have tried to run away and I'd be right after him. My other plan was to just sit here and wait for the police to arrive." As he said it, they could hear sirens in the distance getting closer.

"What if he hears them, too, and tries to shoot his way out? Or even worse, tries to ram us? Why aren't you more upset about this? You don't really believe any of those bad things are going to happen, do you? You already know who's in that van, don't you?"

Devine looked at her. "I've got a pretty good idea."

Three police cars pulled up and officers jumped out of their cars with guns drawn. Devine opened his door. "Stay inside until it's over."

He walked over to talk to one of the officers as the others surrounded the van. Two other officers then joined them. Devine had pulled his own gun out from his holster, worn under his bomber jacket. The officer he'd been talking to sidled alongside the van, up to the driver's door, and hit the butt of his gun on the frame.

J.J. opened her door so she could hear what was going on.

The officer yelled, "Open the door and throw out your weapon, then follow it, very slowly. You are surrounded, so don't try anything fancy."

They waited several moments until the door swung open and a male voice yelled out, "I don't have a gun." Hands followed the voice. "See?"

"Come out. Slowly."

J.J. strained to see the driver's face, but Devine was blocking her view. She got out of the car and walked around to where she'd have a better look.

Hank Ransom.

She wasn't prepared for that. Of course, she hadn't been too focused on possible drivers. She hadn't even been totally convinced her life was in danger. But now . . . Could he have killed Marcotti? He certainly had access to the weapon. But what about a motive? He had seemed secretive when she'd spoken to him, although at the time she'd also wondered if he just wasn't much of a talker.

She watched as the police escorted him to a cruiser. Devine finally returned to the car, and she asked, "What has just gone on here?"

"He's not saying anything, but he certainly was trailing us. It makes him look very suspicious in the murder investigation, although I don't take him to be the killer."

They both got back in the car.

"Why not?" she asked.

"Motive. I can't figure out what his motive would be."

"My thoughts exactly."

Devine glanced at her and smiled. "Of course, you've given this a lot of thought."

"Well, yes. I've talked to him a couple of times and didn't get a sense of anything sinister. But I may not have been asking the right questions when it came to Marcotti. I was mainly searching for reasons it wasn't Rocco. So, what now? How do we find out what he tells the police?"

"There is no *we* in this. I'll give Hastings a call tomorrow and see what information he'll share." He sighed. "Okay. I'll let you know if there's something."

She settled back in the seat. "Thank you. So he wasn't who you thought would be in that van?"

"No. I have to admit, I didn't see that one coming."

"But he's not Gina Marcotti's lover, because you know who that is. You know, for a while there, I wondered if you might be her lover, and therefore the murderer." She needed to say it, if only to check his reaction. She knew of no other way to find out the truth of it.

He turned to face her, but she kept looking straight ahead.

"Me? Whatever gave you such an asinine idea?"

"Well, you say you know who this lover is but you won't share the information. And we know that Gina has the money, so she didn't kill her husband for it. But she might have colluded with her lover to smooth the way for them to be together."

"Wouldn't it be easier for her to just divorce the guy?"

"Maybe. Maybe not. I don't really know what's important to her. Saving face in her cultural community? Religion?" She studied the dashboard as she thought about what she'd just said. "Okay, maybe it wasn't a conspiracy. Those could be pretty lame reasons. But the first part of my statement stands. You're not telling me who the lover is because it's you." She glanced at him.

"If I was the killer, don't you think I'd have disposed of you by now?" His face looked serious, but his body language certainly wasn't threatening.

"Actually, I was just thinking that." She looked at the door handle but she didn't feel afraid.

"And, if I was her lover, do you think I'd do this?" He leaned toward her, grabbing her arms, and kissed her. Thoroughly.

She felt a bit dazed when he released her. It took her a few seconds to make the words work. "Maybe. I mean, men often have more than one fling going on at a time."

She wished she could rip her tongue out when she saw his face. Followed by wishing she would grab him and kiss him right back. She did neither one.

His anger was palpable as he started the engine. He said nothing to her on the drive home, and her mind seemed to have gone blank. She mumbled her thanks when he'd pulled up outside her building. He nodded but didn't look at her.

Bummer. Her car was still at the office.

CHAPTER 30

"He did what?" Skye's voice rose a couple of decibels. "Should I be horrified or pleased?"

"A bit of both, I think," J.J. admitted, glad that Skye was back from her out-of-town trip but now wondering if she should be sharing the details of her adventure with Devine.

"Oh, come on, now. You've known the guy, what, two weeks? He's been stalking you, accused you of being a murderer—well, almost—and is extremely handsome in a rugged sort of way, with sexy blue eyes. Okay, I guess I can understand your ambivalence."

"I'd just accused him of being Gina Marcotti's lover and/or a murderer."

"And he kissed you? Oh man. That's gutsy."

"He did say that if he was the murderer he could have killed me a long time before now, or something like that."

Skye shuddered. "Now, that's plain creepy. Well, I guess

you've got your answer. Maybe plural, if you so choose. And at least he saved you a second time."

J.J. sat down at her desk and started her computer. "Enough about Ty Devine. I have work to do."

"It is rather an appropriate name, though." Skye grinned. "By the way, did you have any luck reaching Ashley Rose after your meeting with Olivia Barker?"

J.J. had called Skye while she was in Stowe, bringing her up to speed on her client visit.

"I'm just checking my e-mail again. Nothing."

"So, what now?"

J.J. was ready for the question. "I think Brittany is a spy. A mole. Whatever."

"Brittany! Explain yourself, girl."

"Well, it came to me when Olivia pointed out that the ideas were exactly the same but some of the wording had been changed in both proposals. The only way that the ideas could be exact is if one us had known what the other was proposing. And since it wasn't me doing the tinkering, that means someone stole my idea. Don't you think?"

Skye looked like she was giving it some serious thought. "Possibly. Okay, probably."

"I first wondered if it might be someone in Olivia Barker's office, which it still could be, but why? Then I thought of our office, and the only likely person is Brittany."

"Again, why? We pay her adequately for the work she's doing, and it's only a part-time job. We're good employers. We don't force her on coffee runs—okay, maybe I did that one time, but we don't beat her or keep her there till midnight."

"You're right, we don't, but she did want to stay late not too long ago, remember?"

Skye nodded.

"And she was there all by herself when I went in on

Saturday morning. That was the morning after I'd sent the e-mail about the train idea and she was supposed to file it in the binder."

"All right, suspicious. But again, why would she do it?" Skye asked.

J.J. shrugged.

"I guess we have to ask her to find out."

J.J. pursed her lips. "As much as I want to, we can't just out and ask her. What if it's not her?"

"You said it probably was. But you're right. Think of something."

J.J. stared out the window. "Something clever and devious. Planting false bait and seeing if she takes it."

"Well, we'd better do something if you want to hang on to that contract. Olivia Barker won't wait for long. If she thinks you haven't picked up on her suggestion, she may go directly to Ashley Rose herself."

"I am well aware of that. So I've written an e-mail, which I'm not sending, to Olivia stating that the cost of the train motif is too high, so instead we should consider a choir singing "Fifty Ways to Leave Your Workplace." She glanced at Skye and was pleased to see her grinning.

"You could do both," she said.

J.J. snorted. "I'll leave a copy of the e-mail for Brittany to file in the binder. Let's see where it ends up by Monday. I have worked on the original proposal, so that's all set to go if Olivia gives me the okay to do it alone."

"And how will you know if Ashley submits this suggestion?"

"I've asked Olivia's assistant to tell me. She told me all of Olivia's work e-mails go to her first, and she prioritizes and forwards them. I decided to let her in on what's happening. It's the only way we can control where the project is heading, don't you agree?"

"I suppose. Can you trust her? What if Ashley has already made a similar deal?"

"I can't be paranoid about everything that happens. I have to take this on trust or I'll drive myself crazy."

"Er."

"What?"

"Craz*ier*. Just saying." Skye ducked as the stuffed beaver was launched at her head. "What will we do about Brittany? Fire her? If she's guilty, I think we need to. How can we ever trust her again? I'm sure curious as to why she's doing it—if she is."

"And what, find someone to replace her? This isn't the type of job, with so few hours, that kids want for the summer, which is just around the corner."

"Do we really need someone in the office? After all, we were taking care of our binders before we had Brittany. Maybe all we need is a person to take care of the website updates. What do you think?"

"Well, if one of us learned how, we wouldn't even need another person." J.J. was quick to add, "Not that I'm volunteering."

"Nor I. So hiring one web mistress it is."

"Or webmaster."

"Exactly."

By noon, J.J. felt she needed to get out of the office for a break. Skye was eating at her desk, so she knocked on Evan's office door, and he gladly joined her for lunch at Cups 'n' Roses. Beth waved at them as they entered, but it was several minutes before she could make it over to their table.

"Looks like business is really booming, Beth," Evan said, craning his neck to see around the person at the next table. He spotted the daily-specials chalkboard and was ready to order when Beth pulled out her pad.

They both ordered the sweet potato soup with a half

panini of ham slices with brie and watched as Beth swiped at her forehead with the back of her hand before heading to the kitchen.

"I wonder if she's taken on too much, moving to a larger lunch menu."

"Well, it's not like it's an active kitchen with a chef or anything," Evan pointed out. "All the wraps and pasta salads are made earlier in the day, and the panini just gets pressed in the grill."

"Such a sympathetic view."

"No, really. I think Beth knows her limits, and this is where it ends. Coffee, baked goods, and ready-made light lunches. I admire her."

"Okay, you're right. Now, catch me up on what's been happening in your life," J.J. demanded.

"Hah. Not much." Evan picked up the pepper grinder from the center of the table and started playing with it. J.J. had to stop herself from grabbing it out of his hands and setting it back in place.

"I've been thinking about the murder," Evan continued. "I can't be the only one who got into a public display of tempers with the guy. Have you heard anything else?"

J.J. filled him in on what she'd learned about Don Kelland and Evan seemed to brighten.

"Kelland. I know a thing or two about him."

"Of course you do."

"Darn right. I redecorated his house just last year, and when you're wandering around taking measurements, you get to hear the darnedest things."

J.J. wasn't sure she was up to hearing any gossip. She tried to focus his thoughts. "Anything that could tie in to the murder?"

"No admission of a simmering motive but Kelland does have a nephew. Do you know what he does?"

"I know he has a nephew but I don't know his name. Should I?"

"Well, as a member of Culinary Capers, you really should be up to date on all things food in this village. So pay attention. His name is Warren Young and he owns the Tender Grill on Lakeshore Drive, the one with the great view of the lake— and on the same street as Bella Luna."

"And?"

"I'm getting there. Let me tell the story. I'm measuring the window in the great room and Kelland and nephew are talking in the hall, within listening distance. You know, that's the great thing about being a decorator: once you start working, you sort of fade into the surroundings and people don't really notice you."

"Evan. This is a lot of buildup. It'd better be worth it. And, I can't imagine you fading into anything." She grinned.

Evan wiggled his eyebrows. "Thank you, sweetie. Now, back to my story."

"Please."

"Kelland tells nephew not to worry, he'll get his outdoor seating but Marcotti won't get his. In other words, hog-tie the competition. Nephew gets all the hungry folks who want to eat outdoors and enjoy the weather." Evan finished with a flick of his left wrist and sat back, a *ta-da* look on his face.

J.J. gasped. "That's underhanded. And possibly illegal, don't you think? If Kelland did everything in his power to get the city council to turn down Marcotti's proposal but give it to his nephew without stating they're related, then he's—he's scum."

"You're probably right. There must be council rules about full disclosure. Do you think Marcotti knew there was something underhanded going on?"

"And confronted him, as Marcotti was apt to do? And Kelland, worried that he might be thrown off the council or even charged with fraud or whatever, decided to eliminate Marcotti before he talked."

"Yes." Evan realized his enthusiasm was turning heads their way. He lowered his voice and continued, "Or even nephew could have done it. A conspiracy. I like the sound of that."

J.J. sat thinking it over. It made sense, or so she thought.

"You know that Marcotti was planning on running against Kelland in the next election," J.J. stated.

"No, I didn't. But this gets even better."

When Beth returned with their orders, J.J. asked her to sit with them for a few minutes.

Beth looked around and nodded. "I think everyone's happy for now. What's up? You two are really getting into something."

"Can I run something by you?"

Beth nodded, and J.J. recapped what they'd just discussed.

"Why, that creep. I never did like Don Kelland. He never seemed to think big, like about what would be good for the entire village. And then when he voted against letting the high school band hold outdoor rehearsals in the band shelter at Grosvenor Park, I voted against him from then on."

"Do you think that the threat of exposure would be enough to turn him into a killer?"

"Definitely. He has shifty eyes."

CHAPTER 31

J.J. finished adding some details to her new proposal for the VPTA. She hadn't worked with a professional association before nor had she done a conference completely on her own, but she was looking forward to the challenge. She'd been culling the Internet and her stash of brochures searching for the ideal venue in Burlington, a hotel with enough meeting rooms to accommodate a small conference of two hundred as well as a large enough hallway outside those rooms for a series of displays and coffee break central.

She'd also wanted to find a place with room enough for the banquet to be held and catered on site. And she'd need a good room rate for the delegates. What else? Walking distance to such places as the historic district and its wonderful shops. Attractions such as the ECHO Lake Aquarium and Science Center or the Robert Hull Fleming Museum. Easy access to the airport, train, and parking.

She would next whip up a list of possible extra side trips

for the conference committee to take a look at. Burlington was a gold mine when it came to possibilities. Maybe a cruise on the *Spirit of Ethan Allen*, the wonderful replica of a twentieth-century steamboat. She'd love to sign on for that one.

Even with a little over a year to work on preparing the perfect conference, J.J. wanted to get on top of it as soon as possible, leaving time to develop the anniversary party and also keep her schedule open for any other new opportunities. She'd then have the new ones take a backseat just when the last-minute stuff for the conference would take the lead again. It was always a juggling act. At least she'd harnessed her original method of running right up to a deadline, which had been okay for the advertising world, and could now describe herself as someone who planned first before taking the next steps. She felt comfortable putting this project aside and getting on to the main task at hand.

It was unfortunate they had to wait until tomorrow for Brittany to take the bait. She did need to touch base with Olivia Barker before then and reassure her that all was well. It turned out to be a quick call, fortunately, as Barker was on her way out of the office. At least all was well. So far.

On the way home, she stopped in at the bookstore to pick up a copy of Evan's choice of cookbook. She found one copy on the shelf and wondered if she was the last of the Culinary Capers group to pick hers up, or if the others would be in trouble. She'd debated buying it as an e-book, but when she saw the colorful photos in it she was hooked. That's all it took. When she'd joined the club, she had readily admitted that she bought books for the pictures and didn't always follow up by making anything she found in the cookbook. Now, being a member, she was forced to follow through, but the imagery still played a major role in her choice of books to buy. It was turning out to be an expensive although totally enjoyable hobby.

She would thumb through it tonight and choose her side dish, then make a list of ingredients to pick up on the way home from work tomorrow, and do a trial run of the recipe on the weekend. She'd have to choose a suitable guinea pig, though. It couldn't be anyone from the Capers, which narrowed it down to Skye and Ness. Hm.

She'd just gotten in her front door, hung up her jacket, and sat down with her new book when the doorbell rang. Thinking it was Ness, she pulled open the door without checking the peephole.

"Rocco. What are you doing here?"

"I'm sorry to intrude at your home, but I wanted to talk to you in private, with no one around to intrude."

"Come in. How do you know where I live?"

"I asked Evan Thornton. I hope you don't mind." He looked so earnest that J.J. smiled at him.

"Of course not. Please come in and sit down. Can I get you anything?"

"No, no. I will be fine. As I said, I just want to talk. Well, to tell you something, I guess." He sat down on the nearest chair, next to the love seat.

Intrigued, J.J. sat on the white wicker chair across from him. She waited while he looked around the room, obviously not wanting to jump into what he was about to say. That made her even more uncomfortable than his just turning up at her door. She hoped he wasn't going to confess to the murder. She didn't know how she'd handle that. Call the police? She'd have to, but it would pain her to do so. What if that set him off and he attacked her? Not Rocco. He would never hurt her, just like he would never hurt anyone. Of course not. He wasn't a killer. She knew that. He had not come to confess. She breathed a sigh of relief and waited.

Finally, he cleared his throat and sat forward, elbows on

knees, hands clasped. "You asked about Gina Marcotti's lover. I know you think it is Mr. Devine, but you are wrong. It's a me."

J.J. gasped. "You?"

Rocco shook his head. "Yes, for many years now. And I'm not at all apologetic or ashamed. Antonio was playing her for the fool, only she knew what was going on, so who was the fool? I have been alone now for over ten years since my Anna died. I have been lonely. Gina was lonely, too. We are good companions to each other. Now I have said it. You needed to know, but I do ask that you will not tell others about our secret *affare di cuore*."

"Of course not. And thank you for telling me."

"If I had not, you may have found out eventually, and that might have done more damage."

J.J. felt her face turning red. She hadn't even thought about the fallout from her dogged pursuit of the facts in this case. She would have hated to have caused Rocco any more pain.

"I realize that now. I'm sorry to have put you in this position. But you have my word: I won't tell anyone."

He nodded and she relaxed.

"Can I get you some coffee, some wine?"

Rocco suddenly smiled, and she felt even happier. "Yes, wine would be fitting. Red, if you have it."

"I do. I picked up a nice Valpolicella ripasso for the dinner I did and liked it so much I bought some more."

"That's always a good choice."

As she handed him a glass, she asked, "Have you had any further thoughts on who the killer might be?"

"No. A lot of people wished him harm, but I do not know anyone who would actually do it." He chuckled. "I think I would have to put myself on that suspect list, if I were a detective. But like the others on it, I didn't do it."

"Someone sure did. Have you heard anything about his dealings with the city councilor Don Kelland?"

"Sure. Everyone knows Antonio detested the man because of being stonewalled in getting the outdoor patio license for his restaurant. In fact, he had planned to run against Kelland in the next election."

"What do you think Antonio's chances of winning would have been? Any motive there?"

"That depends on how badly Mr. Kelland wants to remain in politics. Antonio was well known and even respected in the Italian community. His reputation in the restaurant world was less so, but those qualities that had his competitors on edge may have made them vote for him. Being underhanded can be useful for a politician. Personally, you couldn't pay me enough to do that job."

J.J. nodded. "I totally agree. But it can be tempting for someone who likes power."

Rocco finished the wine and looked at his watch. "Agreed. Now, I must be going. I have a hot date tonight with a beautiful lady. I am glad we have had this talk, but I don't think my Gina will be very pleased. I will have to try to make it up to her."

He winked, and J.J. felt her cheeks getting warmer.

CHAPTER 32

J.J. had just finished checking her e-mail after returning to the office from a visit to her newest client when the phone rang. Skye was already on the other line, so J.J. answered, identifying herself.

"Good, I'm glad it's you. This is Gina Marcotti. I would like you to come out to my place right now. Does that work?"

J.J. recovered quickly from her surprise. "Yes, that will be fine. I'll see you shortly."

Gina had already hung up after hearing the word *fine*. J.J. wondered if she should be worried. Was Gina really upset about what Rocco had said last night? If so, what did she plan to say, or do? It could be a trap. Gina might be seething about the fact that she'd been found out, but she could also still be the murderer. More likely, though, that she was stricken at the thought that her secret was now out. Feeling embarrassed, even mortified, she might be planning some-thing dramatic, like an overdose of pills and J.J. would be the one to find her. A fitting punishment. She suddenly felt the full weight of her snooping. What was she doing anyway, messing about in other people's lives?

J.J. signaled Skye that she was going out, and on second thought wrote down where she was going on a Post-it note and stuck it to the corner of Skye's computer screen, just in case. She grabbed her purse and jacket, and left. She was grateful she'd brought her car today. It took about twenty minutes to reach her destination. Gina Marcotti seemed to be hovering near the door, because she opened it immediately after the knock.

"Come with me, please," she commanded. The politeness did nothing to mask that hardness in her voice. She pointed to a chair in the family room. "Sit."

J.J. did as told, keeping her eyes on Gina. She had felt an initial relief that Gina looked hale and hearty, but now her anxiety had returned. She could tell this wouldn't be a pleasant visit.

"I understand that Rocco told you all about us." Gina stood in front of her, feet slightly apart, hands on hips. The dramatic pose was in total contrast to the supple red silk lounging suit she was wearing. Her hair had been held back from her face by a red-and-black-striped scarf, the ends of which draped over her shoulder.

J.J. gulped. "Yes, he did. He felt I could be trusted."

"And can you?" Her eyes seemed to find their way to J.J.'s soul.

Get a grip. "Yes, I can."

Gina stared at her a few moments before nodding. "Good, because if the word does get out and I can track it to you, you will no longer be in business. That is not a threat; it is the reality."

"I understand."

"Good, because I still don't understand why he told you."

She walked over to the lounge she'd been sitting on the first time J.J. had been over, and sat back on it.

"I had told him that Ty Devine knew the name of your, uh, friend but wouldn't say anything, so I wondered if it was Devine himself."

Gina barked out a laugh. "You have got to be kidding. All right, he's very macho and handsome, I'll give you that. But I think only a woman who is interested in that man would jump to that conclusion. Are you?"

"What? Me? Devine? No way." *Neat way to turn the tables, lady.* She could feel her cheeks heat up, though.

"Hm. Well, I think it is time we have a good conversation. Tell me, who are the other suspects for the murder of my husband? Maybe it is you I should have hired to investigate."

J.J. shook her head. "That wouldn't have been a good idea. I've been looking around mainly because, as you know, I'm a suspect, as is my friend Evan Thornton."

"Evan. I love that man. He is the most talented decorator in town." She waved her right hand around the room as she spoke. "I must get him in here to work his magic once this has all died down. He would no sooner kill Tonio than kill a fly. I know he was upset with Tonio, but who wasn't?"

So I keep hearing. "I'm still wondering if Don Kelland is involved in any way."

Gina stood and started pacing. "You think it's because of the problem with the outdoor patio?"

"More likely because of the possibility of your husband running against him in the election. That is, if Kelland knew about the plans."

Gina sat back down next to J.J. this time. "Tonio did say just a couple of weeks ago that he finally had Kelland where he wanted him. Those were his exact words."

J.J.'s heart started racing a bit faster. "Do you know what he meant by that?"

"No. I know nothing more, except that he did say he had evidence of something illegal. And knowing Tonio, he wouldn't hesitate to use it in one way or another."

"Oh?"

Gina nodded. "It could come in handy during a campaign, don't you think? If it was bad enough, a little blackmail could go a long way."

"Wow. That could be quite an accusation. Do you know where that evidence is or what it was?"

Gina shook her head.

"Well, we'd better start searching," J.J. said, sounding more determined than she felt.

J.J. thought about that all the way back to the office. She'd asked Gina to go through her husband's desk at home to see if she could find anything that might be pertinent. And Gina had offered to also check his office at the restaurant. J.J. was hoping to hear back from her by later in the afternoon.

As she pulled into a parking spot behind the office, she decided to put aside any more thoughts about the murder until she heard back from Gina and, for now, to concentrate on her real job. Brittany was due at three, at which time J.J. and Skye would leave for a "business meeting." They really just planned to go to Cups 'n' Roses for a latte then head back to the office in time for Brittany to leave work at six. Of course, they wouldn't know until Monday at the earliest if their plan had taken hold.

She also realized that, even if any information surfaced about Kelland, she couldn't follow up on that until Monday, either. An entire weekend to wait.

There sure was a lot of waiting these days, something J.J. didn't do easily.

CHAPTER 33

Someone pounding on her apartment door wasn't the way J.J. liked to greet Saturday mornings, especially when she'd decided to sleep in. She almost tripped getting disentangled from the sheets after a restless night of tossing and turning, and ended up running to the door without slippers or robe. She did think to check the peephole before opening. Ty Devine.

Devine turned sideways, facing toward Ness's doorway. J.J. couldn't see what was happening, but she could see Devine's mouth moving, so she opened her door just as Ness asked Devine what he thought he was doing.

"I'm trying to awaken Sleeping Beauty."

"Sounds like you're trying to wake the dead. Uh, good morning, Sleeping Beauty," he added, seeing J.J. peering around Devine's shoulder.

J.J. nodded and then repeated what she'd heard Ness saying. "Just what do you think you're doing?"

Devine turned back. "We have to talk." He reached for her arm. "Now."

"Hold on a minute," Ness said. "J.J., do you want to talk to him?"

J.J. looked at Devine's face. It looked neutral, maybe leaning toward grim. "I guess it's okay."

"All right, but I'm right down the hall if you need me." And with that, he closed his door.

"You might as well come in."

"Thanks," Devine said, looking at her from head to toe.

She grimaced. Sleep pants with a cat-chasing-mouse motif and misshapen gray T-shirt was not the glam look she longed for when facing a handsome male early in the morning. She turned and stalked off to her room with as much dignity as she could muster, returning quickly after adding a short white terry towel robe to her ensemble. Indie, who had stayed in bed the entire time, trailed behind her.

"Espresso?"

"Thanks," Devine said and slid onto a stool at the counter while she ground the beans and made two cups.

When the noise of the espresso machine had subsided, she asked, "What do you want? What's so important?"

Devine waited until he had taken his first sip. "I understand you visited my client yesterday."

"I was asked by your client to visit her and I did." She leaned back against the counter, facing him. She was not about to be browbeaten.

"So you have the answer to your question."

J.J. sighed and closed her eyes a moment. "Yes. It seems I owe you an apology." At least he no longer seemed angry at her.

"Accepted. Now, tell me what's going on with Don Kelland."

"What did Gina tell you?"

"I asked first."

J.J. picked up her cup and walked over to the wicker chair. She sat and waited until Devine had settled on the love seat before answering.

"Gina thinks that her husband had something on Kelland and would have either used it to get his outdoor patio or against him in the next election. Sounds like just the sort of thing he would do," she added almost under her breath.

"Marcotti or Kelland?" Devine asked, with one eyebrow raised.

" Marcotti."

"All right. But Gina didn't find any information like that in his desk at home. She'd been meaning to go to the restaurant but got tied up. She'll go in early this morning and look around."

"I'm glad to hear that. When she hadn't called back last night, I wondered if she'd just been saying that to get rid of me."

Devine chuckled. "It would have served you right. Anyway, why don't you get dressed and we'll have breakfast at the Tender Grill, then meet up with Gina at her restaurant."

J.J. brightened. "I'm starving. And, we might get to quiz Kelland's nephew if he's there. That's his restaurant, in case you didn't know. But I'll bet you did. Be ready in a jiff."

She showered in record time and fed Indie before they left in Devine's car. Once there, they snagged a table at the window and were able to watch the few but hardy beach walkers enjoying their morning strolls.

J.J. had almost finished her vegetarian omelet when Devine got back to work. "Even if we find that Kelland was into something illegal, I have a hard time believing it would be so bad that he'd murder Marcotti to avoid being outed."

"We don't know that, and won't know how incriminating it is until we find the proof."

"I understood what you said. That's scary."

J.J. kicked him under the table. "Be nice. Well, if it has to do with the nephew, maybe he's the killer, not Kelland."

"Lots of possibilities." He turned in his chair, searching for their server. "Let's just see if the nephew, Warren Young, is in. He may not realize anyone's onto Kelland and let something slip." Unable to get the young man's attention, he walked over and returned very quickly.

"He's not in until later this morning. Guess that will have to be another visit. Finished?"

J.J. nodded. Devine insisted on paying the check, and they drove the two blocks to Bella Luna. Gina's Cadillac Escalade—a mate to the one her deceased husband had driven, only cream in color—was the lone car in the parking lot. Devine pulled in beside it.

"Maybe she's already found something," J.J. said as they tried the front door. It was locked, so Devine pounded on the door.

"You're very good at that," J.J. said with a smirk.

"Fifteen years of police work will do that for you."

The door opened and Gina let them inside. "I haven't found anything yet, but I only got started. Come with me."

They followed her into a small office down a short hallway beside the kitchen. It was big enough to hold a large wooden desk with two drawers on each side. A stack of six banker's boxes was tucked into the far corner next to a bookcase that filled the remainder of the wall space. The six shelves of the bookcase held more cookbooks than J.J. had ever seen in one place, along with several recipe-card drawers. Stacked on the floor in front of it was a pile of binders that looked like wallpaper samplers. There were only two chairs in the room—a wooden swivel one behind the desk and a leather club chair that had seen better days.

Gina sat down at the desk and pulled out a drawer. "I've already searched the top drawer. J.J., why don't you look through those cookbooks on the shelves? He might have tucked something in one of them. Ty, those boxes on the floor in the corner are the filing system." She picked up a box cutter and set it on the desk. "I never could convince him to do something with this office. Get it redecorated, bring in good furnishings." She glanced around. "Good luck."

J.J. was impressed. Gina sounded like she'd really thought this through. Of course, she'd already pegged Gina as an in-charge type of woman.

After about an hour, they heard noises down the hall in the kitchen. Gina explained that her employees were arriving and that it took several hours of prep time before each meal service. The kitchen would be a busy place until the restaurant closed later that night. She went out to talk to the early birds.

Devine stood and stretched. "It's going to take more than a couple of hours to search all those boxes. How are you doing?"

"No luck, but I don't think he'd put something in his cookbooks, do you? After all, any one of his staff might need to make use of them, don't you think?"

Devine shrugged. "Only if he would allow them to use them. He didn't seem to be a real sharing-type guy."

"I wonder if there's a safe."

Devine had been staring at the shelves behind the desk and walked over to them.

"What's up?" J.J. wanted to know.

"Does this wooden divider between these two shelves look different than the others?" He walked over to it and started tapping it.

"It's wider, I'd say."

He tried to jiggle it, then grabbed it with both hands and yanked. It came off to reveal a narrow space.

"What is it?" J.J. wanted to know, trying to look over his shoulder. "Is anything in there?"

Devine pulled something out and turned it over. "It's not what we were looking for, nothing that implicates Kelland, but it is interesting. It's an old photo." He held it so that J.J. could also see it.

"Wow, that is old. Hard to tell with the fading black-and-white tones, but it sort of looks like maybe a young Marcotti, don't you think?"

"I'd say so. Maybe a forty-years-younger version."

"Let me see," J.J. said, holding the photo closer. "If he's in his late teens that means the woman may be the one he and Rocco fought over back in Italy. Wow, she was a beauty. I can see why they'd both be courting her."

"Interesting place to keep the photo."

"So that Gina wouldn't see it? Maybe this girl was the true love of his life and he never forgot her. But he didn't want to upset Gina, so he hid his only photo of her at the office so he could take it out and daydream every now and then. How does that sound?"

"Like a romantic talking." He looked at her and smiled. "But you could be right."

"She looks sort of familiar. Are you going to show it to Gina?"

"It is her property."

"And I guess she's beyond being hurt by it."

"Show me what?" Gina asked, pushing the door to the office open farther. "What have you got there? A photo?"

She held her hand out and Devine placed the picture in it. She looked at it closely and shook her head. "It's Tonio and his first love."

"Is that the girl in Italy that your husband and Rocco came to blows over?"

"So you know about that? Of course, Rocco told you." She nodded. "Yes, that is the one. It took many years, but eventually Tonio told me about her and showed me this picture. Only once and after much alcohol. I didn't see it again." She looked at the open space in the wall. "I guess I know why."

She sat in the chair behind the desk. "I knew by the way he talked about her that she was still in his heart." She handed the photo back to Devine. "So, it is over. And that's all you've found in here? Have you checked on his desk?"

"No, I thought you had," J.J. said.

"I'm still not certain what it is we're looking for. Maybe one of you should go through it again, and probably the one at home also." She walked to the door, more slowly than before. *Sadder, maybe.* "I'll be out front finalizing details with my manager when you're ready to leave."

J.J. looked at Devine and then sat in the chair that Gina had vacated. "I'll quickly check this while you finish with the shelf."

She sorted through a pile of papers that turned out to be mainly old menu inserts with specials listed. The next pile, in a wire basket marked Bookkeeper, held several bills. But under it, she found a typed sheet of paper in a file folder marked Private. She read it over quickly.

"This is it. I've found it. This is what Marcotti had found out Liston to this. He's noted that he has proof, and he's attached it, that Don Kelland and his nephew bribed a city official in order to get a variance."

She handed Devine the attached paper and he read it over. "It's a signed affidavit from an inspector in the Planning and Zoning Department stating that that Don Kelland, councilor for Half Moon Bay, and his nephew approached him and offered ten thousand dollars for him to grant a variance. He agreed and took the payment. That's pretty damning. What was the variance for?"

J.J. quickly read the next page. "Marcotti's jotted down some notes. It says that Kelland and his nephew bribed a city official to secure a zoning change in order for the nephew to build an upper level to his restaurant. Up until this point, all buildings along Lakeshore Drive were restricted to being one story, but the nephew wanted an even better view along with an outdoor deck." She looked at Devine. "So that would mean not only did the nephew get the outdoor patio but also a second story, if that went forward. And Marcotti would get nothing."

"What are you thinking?" he asked.

"I think that's a good enough motive to kill Marcotti, wouldn't you say?"

"Why? Because he had this piece of paper? Because he threatened to expose him?"

"Yes, to both. And that's why Kelland, not his nephew, is the more likely killer. He had more to lose. Public disgrace and maybe a criminal charge." J.J. felt they'd finally hit the jackpot.

"Ten thousand dollars seems like a small amount as a motive for murder." Devine handed the document back to J.J.

J.J. took it, glanced at it again, and slumped back in the chair. Was he just playing devil's advocate? *Infuriating.* "It's not the amount, it's the disgrace. We're talking about a career politician here. And an ambitious one at that, from all I've read."

"But wouldn't it make more sense to kill the official, if someone needed to be murdered? He was the one who took the bribe and would testify to that. And is still able to, I might add."

"Oh, I see what you mean. But what if, in the heat of anger, he tossed logic out the window and attacked Marcotti, who had just threatened to expose him?"

"The murder appears to have been premeditated, remember? The knife from Rocco's kitchen? And how could he have gotten his hands on it?"

"Hm. His nephew would know about delivery schedules and all. He's in the same business."

"But why frame Rocco Gates?"

"Because everybody knew about their feud."

"Everybody? Are you certain about that?"

"Well, that's what I've heard." She shrugged. "I still think I'll confront Kelland about this."

"You will? Since when did you become the investigator? We turn this over to the police." He snatched it off the desk, tucked it away in his pocket, and held out his hand to her. "You've done good, though. He would have made a prime suspect except for a few facts that get in the way."

She accepted his helping hand, which pulled her out of the chair. "You may smile now, but you will see that I am contributing a lot to solving this case. At some point, you'll realize that."

"I'm happy to live with that. Time to leave."

Gina met them as they left the office. "We've found what we were looking for," Devine told her, "but it doesn't definitively point to Kelland as the murderer, unfortunately."

Gina frowned. "That's too bad. I would like for this entire thing to be over. Can I offer you some coffee?"

"I'd love an espresso," J.J. answered, and Devine nodded.

They walked back into the restaurant and sat at a table for four while Gina made their drinks and brought them over on a tray.

J.J. looked surprised. "That's impressive."

"You think I do nothing but sit around and be waited on all day?" Gina barked out a short laugh. "When we were starting this business, I actually worked with Tonio for the first year. Even though money wasn't the problem, he liked the illusion that he was making a go of it without my bank account, and I thought it was very romantic to be working with him. Later, the romance wore off. Everything. I find myself missing the business every now and then. That's why I decided to keep the restaurant going, and I'm taking an active role in running it."

"Of course, you have a seasoned staff to help out," Devine observed.

"I do, and I'm clever enough to keep them on. Lucy Vennos has been the hostess-cum–maître d' for a couple of years, and most recently Tonio made her the manager for when he wasn't around. And of course, Kevin has been head chef here for at least five years. I intend on keeping him also by giving him a raise."

J.J. raised her eyebrows. "Even though he was planning to leave and with recipes?"

"I know how to handle him. Money will help, as will freedom in the kitchen now that he is master chef. Kim Schaffer has been working more in the catering side of the business, and I will also continue to rely on her. She really is indispensable. The others seem to fit in well. So, you see, it is easy for me to replace Tonio." She smiled what J.J. thought was her most genuine smile yet.

Lucy approached them, saying that there was a phone call for Gina.

"Please, take your time and enjoy the espresso. We'll talk later."

She left them, but before Lucy could depart, J.J. said, "Mrs. Marcotti was just saying what an integral part of the business you are. Would you happen to know anything about Mr. Marcotti's dealings with other restaurateurs or even with the local councilor?" It was a wild stab, but who knew.

"No, I know nothing. I don't involve myself in anything except for Bella Luna." She tucked a stray curl back into a plain black barrette. "Maybe Kim Schaffer, our catering person, would know."

Devine's cell phone rang, and he excused himself to take the call over at the bar.

Lucy started to walk away, but J.J. said quickly, "I just find the Italian community in Half Moon Bay is much larger than I'd imagined. And everybody seems to know each other so well. Is there anyone in it that you think might have had a grudge against Mr. Marcotti?"

Lucy looked to be giving it some thought. "I'm not really a part of that set. I don't have the time. Besides, I came here to become an American, not to settle into reminiscing about the past. I do think Mr. Marcotti got along with everyone, though, except for Mr. Gates."

"Back to him. I'd heard their feud was more of a habit than anything violent these days."

Lucy gave another shrug. "Italians are known for their hot tempers. And their long memories."

Sunday turned out to be rainy and foggy, a condition predicted to remain the entire day. For J.J., it was as if her apartment had arranged the weather so that she would have to stay inside and actually give it a thorough going-over.

By the time she'd finished the vacuuming and dusting, she ran out of ambition. She made herself a hot chocolate, grabbed the phone, and sent her mom a text message asking if she had time for a Skype call. It felt like they hadn't talked very often these last few weeks, and J.J. wondered if she'd be in for a bit of a reprimand. The answer came back immediately; now was a good time to connect, so J.J. set up her computer on the kitchen table. She, as usual, had to remove Indie from the keypad several times before the connection finally went through.

"Hi, Mom."

"Hi, J.J. And Indie, I see," she added as the cat took a final stroll across.

"You're looking good. All set for a date or is it work?"

June Tanner showed none of her fifty-three years and, when the two were together, often heard the comment that she didn't look old enough to have a twenty-nine-year-old daughter. Much to her delight, J.J. suspected. J.J. was used to seeing the change in intensity of her mom's auburn hair on a frequent basis and knew that, as a Realtor, she tried to look her best at all times.

June laughed. "Why, thank you. I have a open house in an hour so this will have to be brief. Is everything okay?"

"Of course it is."

"Well, we haven't talked much in the last little while, so I just wondered but didn't want to interfere."

Uh-oh, here it comes. "No, really, I'm fine. It's just been a bit hectic here lately. I'm sorry."

"Well, you look a bit, what . . . uh, down?"

"I'm just tired. It's been a housecleaning day. Also, it's raining. I must have that seasonal disorder syndrome or something. Maybe I should move to the southwest."

"Maybe you should plan on coming home for a weekend. I hope you're able to make it for Easter weekend. That's just two weeks away, you know. Time to start planning. Both your brothers will be here, and of course, Quinn and the two babies."

J.J. could almost picture the happy holiday scene with Grannie June and her older brother, Rory's, two children, aged three and one. Of course, daughter-in-law Quinn was a perfect fit with the Tanner family. J.J. really should go home. She loved playing the doting aunt.

"I'll be there." *There, one decision made.*

"Good to hear. I've written it down in ink and chiseled it in stone." June laughed.

J.J. could hear her father, Adam's, voice in the background. "How is Dad?"

"He's just allowed himself a late lunch break but won't stop to talk. This landscape he's painting is a commission and it's due before Easter. How he hates commissions, but they do help pay the bills. He sends his love. Now, I've got to get moving also. Talk about hectic. I have an open house this afternoon and a special client showing tonight. Talk soon. Be good and keep safe." She blew a kiss to her daughter, and the computer screen went blank.

Really. "Be good"? Just like she'd never left home.

CHAPTER 34

J.J. was primed with two espressos and a handful of chocolate-coated espresso beans by the time she left her apartment on Monday morning. She'd decided to visit Don Kelland one more time at his office before he could escape to any meetings. She needed to confront him with the bribery accusation. Could the fact that Marcotti might have released the information to the council, and the press, be motive for murder? She didn't even know if Marcotti had even challenged him with the evidence.

And what if the bribery accusation wasn't the reason for Kelland to commit murder? He may have had another one, maybe even something as basic as hatred. There had been a lot of antagonism between them over the years.

She asked the pert young blonde at the reception desk if Kelland was in, and when she nodded, J.J. ran down the hall to his office, leaving the receptionist calling out to stop. She didn't even knock on his door, just barged in to take him by surprise. That was her planned attack. She hoped he would be so taken off guard, he'd blurt out the answers to her questions.

She hadn't counted on his assistant being in the room. They seemed to be going over notes and both looked equally shocked at J.J.'s unannounced arrival. It did register with her momentarily that she might be making a fool of herself, and with a witness present, but she went right on with it anyway.

"Mr. Kelland, I found something very interesting in Antonio Marcotti's papers this weekend. I think you have a lot of explaining to do, along with a lot of convincing that you're not his murderer."

"This is outrageous, Ms. Tanner. I thought I'd seen the last of you. However, I guess you'll continue to just barge in and disrupt my life whenever you feel the urge, so I'd better deal with you now, once and forever." He stood abruptly, dismissing his assistant.

J.J. took a step back and wondered who would shoot her, Kelland or the assistant. *She saw him pulling a gun from the drawer, adding a silencer to it, and shooting her right where she stood, unable to flee, paralyzed by shock. Afterward, the assistant would help to roll her up in the area carpet and stuff her in a closet until later at night, when everyone was gone. That would be the right time to cart her body away and dispose of it. She shuddered to think how that might happen. Or where that might be.*

"Ms. Tanner," Kelland said in a loud voice. "Take a seat. Please. Now, tell me what you've got that makes you so certain about all this."

"We found an affidavit signed by a high-ranking city official that you and your nephew, Warren Young, offered him ten thousand dollars to grant a variance so that Young could add a second story to his restaurant."

She could see in her peripheral vision that the assistant

hadn't left the room, but only moved to her right, and was shaking his head.

Kelland sat down at his desk and sighed. "That's not going to do you any good, nor would it have done Marcotti any good. That official has already been questioned by the police and criminal charges have been filed against me and my nephew. It's being done in quiet right now because of delicate negotiations the city is immersed in. So you see, that is non-news, and therefore, not worth murdering somebody over. Now, will you please leave while I explain this whole mess to my assistant?"

J.J. felt her mouth hanging open. Not at all the answer she'd expected. She'd make one more stab at it.

"So you didn't attack Mr. Marcotti in a fit of rage?" she stood as she asked.

"No, I did not!" He was almost yelling now.

"What about your nephew?" She was now edging toward the door.

"He did not. Do I have to call security again?" He looked pointedly at his assistant, who hurried back to the desk and reached for the phone.

She shook her head and had her hand on the doorknob when Kelland spoke again. "And believe me, Ms. Tanner, if I read a word about this in the media, I will know who it came from, and I do know where to find you."

J.J. swallowed hard as she left.

She had just exited the building when she spotted Devine walking toward her.

"I had a feeling you'd follow up anyway. So, what did he tell you?" Devine fell in beside her, and they walked toward the parking lot at the side.

"He told me he's under investigation and criminal charges have been laid. So, he didn't have a motive. He wasn't trying to silence Marcotti."

"Don't sound so disappointed."

"I even asked if his nephew was the murderer, and that nearly got me thrown out by security." She sighed. "I was really hoping it was someone I didn't like, and he certainly fit the bill."

"Seems like I did at one time, too."

J.J. felt her cheeks growing hot. *Don't go there.* "Yes, well. I do admit I can sometimes be wrong. At this stage, I just want this to end. I hate thinking my friends, and possibly still me, are under suspicion."

He squeezed her arm and turned back toward the building. "It will end and soon. Just try to keep out of danger."

What does that mean?

J.J. had a phone message waiting when she got to the office. Olivia Barker's assistant wanted her to call. She dialed immediately and held her breath after identifying herself.

"How freaking crazy is this? You were right," the receptionist said in a hushed voice. "That new proposal you mentioned was sent in by Ms. Rose on Friday night. I found it this morning when I went through Ms. Barker's e-mail."

"You're certain it's the same one?"

"It's almost word for word what you sent me earlier. What should I do now?" Her voice was hushed, and J.J. couldn't tell if she sounded excited or scared.

"Can you just sit on them both for a few hours? I know it's asking a lot of you, but I'd never meant for mine to get past your desk anyway. It's a bogus proposal. I'll have to figure out how to handle this, and I will get back to you later today. I promise."

"I guess I can do that as long as you're sure Ms. Barker won't get angry at me, or worse yet, fire me." There it was. She was scared.

"I will take full responsibility should she find out. You can count on that."

J.J. heard a sigh at the other end of the line. "Well, all right, then. I'll hide them in another folder and wait for your call. It is sort of exciting." Her voice had changed. "Agent Carter over and out."

J.J. chuckled as she hung up.

"I take it that was Olivia Barker's office and Brittany took the bait?" Skye asked.

"She did, and now we have to figure out what to do next. The receptionist is a bit worried about how this will play out."

"Hm. It would be good to keep her out of it. Since we have only a cell phone number for Ashley Rose and no address, it'll be hard to track her down and confront her. I think Brittany is our only solution."

"What if she is adamant and denies it?" J.J. could just picture Brittany digging in her heels and putting up a good front.

"What if we trick them into meeting and confront them both?" Skye had a sly look on her face.

"What are you suggesting?"

"Well, we could ask Brittany to come in later tomorrow to do something urgently needed on the web page. And then we leave a voice message on Ashley's cell pretending to be Brittany and ask her to meet at this office. Can you fake Brittany's voice?"

J.J. shook her head. "No, but I'll try. I do like your plan. So when Ashley walks in and Brittany has a bird, we confront them both?"

"Exactly."

"I'm trying to think if there's a flaw to this plan. What if Ashley calls Brittany back beforehand trying to change the time or something?"

"That's a good one. I'm not sure how to plan for that. Maybe we just take our chances. If it doesn't work out, we go after Brittany alone."

J.J. shrugged. "I guess that will have to do. So, tomorrow afternoon. I'll be relieved to have this finally settled. I'll call Olivia Barker's assistant and ask for another day's grace."

"I'll be happy when it's finished, too, but I guess I'll then have to start searching for a new employee."

"Maybe we don't need someone. I like your earlier idea. We can surely take care of our own binders and all that other stuff she does. And we can find a computer guru who's off-site and just funnel our requests to him or her. After all, the bookkeeper doesn't have a desk here."

"Agreed. Now, I'm off to discuss some possibilities with the Flynn Center for Performing Arts. I'll probably just head over to Nick's after that, so see you tomorrow, Agent Ninety-nine."

"Oh no, not you, too."

CHAPTER 35

J.J. wasn't sure it would work, but she had her fingers and toes crossed the next afternoon. Brittany sat unaware at the spare computer, her fingers busily inputting the information J.J. had given her. Skye kept looking up at the clock, appearing less than her usual calm, cool persona, which oddly enough made J.J. feel more confident as the minutes ticked by.

Finally, at four o'clock on the nose, the door opened and the person J.J. presumed to be Ashley Rose walked into the office. She looked enough like Brittany to be her twin—the same long wavy blonde hair pulled back into a ponytail, a model's high cheekbones, and a slim build. But Ashley looked to be the shorter of the two.

J.J. heard both girls gasp at the same time, and she moved quickly to shut the door and escort Ashley to a chair. "Ashley Rose, I presume. You may be wondering why we asked you here."

She looked over at Skye, who jumped in. "First of all, I'd like to know why you, Brittany, would jeopardize your job with us by feeding J.J.'s Kirking Manufacturing proposals to Ashley."

Both girls looked to be in shock. Finally, Brittany stammered, "How—how did you find out?"

"It's all my fault," Ashley said, looking like she wanted to sink into the floor.

Brittany stood and looked defiant. "No, it was my idea. Ashley is my sister and she's trying hard to get her business started. You guys are successful. I know you don't need the work, so you could lose out on this one client. You've guessed what happened next?"

"All those plagiarized proposals. That's rather extreme, don't you think?" J.J. asked.

"I guess I'm not too confident about my skills," Ashley jumped in. "I want the job, but I could never have come up with such awesome ideas. You're amazing, you know."

J.J. lost her train of thought. She hadn't expected the flattery. *Nice, but not going to happen.* "And you even changed your last name so we wouldn't guess."

"No, that's my real name. Ashley Rose Stewart. I just dropped my last name."

Ashley had a sheepish look on her face. "I just wish I could have gotten my proposals in first—I mean your proposals. You know, my name in first. First come, first served."

"And what, she'd think that I was using your ideas?"

Ashley shrugged. "I planned to change some of what you'd suggested, but I didn't have time on that last one. You know, I didn't think that one was very upbeat."

J.J. sucked in her breath, and Skye quickly came out from behind her desk. "The bottom line here is you deceived the client and you are now going to withdraw your proposals or we will have to inform Olivia Barker of what you've done."

"No way," Brittany mumbled, glaring at Ashley.

"Yes way," J.J. said. "It won't help Ashley's career to start out with this on her résumé."

J.J. thought she could actually see Brittany's brain changing gears. It was all in the eyes. And then the mouth. A slow smile that was probably meant to be placating but instead seemed sly. "I guess you're right. You could really screw things up for her, couldn't you? Is it okay with you, Ash?"

Ashley nodded and stood. "I guess I wasn't thinking straight. All I really wanted was a break. I didn't mean to do any harm, and I sure didn't want Brittany to get in trouble, too."

Skye shook her head. "You didn't think, period. And I think that Brittany will be a great boost in working with you as you try to build your business. Without any ties to Make It Happen. I'll put your final paycheck in the mail, Brittany."

After a few moments Brittany shrugged then gathered up her things and both girls quickly left without saying anything.

Skye stared at the closed door. "She's either totally naïve or totally deceitful."

"Which one? No need to answer that." J.J. sat down. "It's too bad, but I don't think either will get too far in this or any business with ethics like that."

"You're right. If Ashley had applied for a job here, I might have considered taking her on. We are getting busier, after all."

"We are."

"And we could then take on more clients with someone else in the office."

"We could. But we won't, will we?"

"No." Skye shut down her computer. "I'm bummed out. I think I'll head on over to Nick's and prepare him an after-work cocktail, with one for me, also."

J.J. reached for the phone. "I'd better update the assistant and also make an appointment to see Olivia Barker tomorrow. I think I won't mention what's happened here, just wait for Ashley to withdraw. I've finished the final specs on the event, so I'll go over those and hope she doesn't ask any Ashley questions."

"Good luck. I'll have a drink for you, in that case."

J.J. grinned. "So thoughtful."

J.J. was nursing her own glass of wine after a dinner of leftovers when someone knocked on her apartment door. She looked through the peephole and was surprised to see Alison.

"Welcome," she said, as she opened the door.

"Thank you. I see we're on the same wavelength," Alison said, nodding at the wineglass in J.J.'s hand.

"I take it you're off duty tonight."

"Technically, although I am on call, but Tuesday's are always slow, and since I don't have a hot date, I thought I'd visit with you—if you don't have a hot date, that is." She gave the living room a quick scan.

"Nothing hot going on here. I'll fetch you some wine."

Alison chose the slipper chair and tucked her feet up. "I take it you haven't heard anything lately from Detective Hashtag?"

"No. He's been leaving me alone. Thankfully. But I'd love to hear where he's at with the murder case."

Alison took a sip before continuing. "Well, I can't tell you that because I don't know. But I do know something, and it seems okay to tell you this because you, after all, were involved in the capture of Hank Ransom."

"The capture? What is he, a dangerous escaped felon?" J.J. grinned.

Alison did not return the grin. "Not exactly. But there was an arrest warrant out on him."

"OMG, you've gotta be kidding. What did he do?" J.J. flopped down in a chair.

"It seems he was out on bail while awaiting a manslaughter trial in Rutland. While he was chef at a local restaurant, a customer died of food poisoning."

"Yikes. Someone died?"

Alison nodded. "Hence the manslaughter charge. Ransom swears it was an accident. He says he didn't know the mushrooms he picked and used were poisonous."

"That's pretty lame. Why was he picking them if he didn't know anything about them?"

"I have no idea. That's someone else's problem. Anyway, he's been trying to keep a low profile here in the village, and then you started asking questions about him, so he got nervous."

J.J. thought a moment. "He should have just left town."

"That's why we usually end up catching the bad guys. They're not always the brightest lights when it comes to escaping."

"But he still could be Marcotti's killer. Maybe Marcotti found out and was about to tell the police. After all, he did try to run me down—twice."

"He has a solid alibi, and I mean solid. So, no, he's not our murderer. And he swears, apparently, that all he did was follow you the night he was arrested. He never tried to run you down."

"But that first time. It was the same white van."

Alison shook her head. "He claims not, and besides, there are a lot of white vans in town. So if I were you, I'd just tone down all the snooping you're doing until they find out who that driver is and also lock up the killer. They're probably one and the same."

"Hm. Too bad about Ransom. I mean, I'd like to think it was someone I didn't really know all that well."

"It still could be."

"You do know something." J.J. leaned forward, feeling a frisson of excitement rush through her body.

Alison held up her free hand. "I really don't, and I've told you everything I can. You should be grateful for that."

J.J. smiled and sat back. "I am, and I'm happy you stopped by. We don't often get a chance to just sit and gab."

Alison's phone buzzed. She glanced at it and winced. "The text message I'm always dreading when I'm on call. But it's a fricking Tuesday night! I guess I shouldn't have had that drink." She looked regretfully at the still half-full glass. "Gotta go. Sorry, but thanks for the wine."

J.J. saw her to the door. "Thanks for the info. We'll try again another time."

Alison hesitated. "I can tell you that it's getting down to the crunch in the investigation. I've heard rumors about you popping up throughout it. I really suggest you just back off at this point. It could get dangerous. And not just from Hashtag." She gave J.J. a quick hug and left.

J.J. watched her walk down the hall and then grabbed what remained of the bottle of wine and headed down the hall to Ness's door. He answered her knock almost immediately.

"What have you got there? The end of a hard day?" he asked.

"You could say that."

He opened the door wider and she entered, leaving the bottle on his counter as she passed by on her way to the couch. "I've just run out of suspects. Again."

"It happens." He poured them each a glass and then sat across from her. She thought he looked more tired than usual, and she regretted bothering him with her worries. He needed to book an appointment with his barber sooner than later, and his plaid shirt seemed even more rumpled than usual. Maybe he'd been napping. *Uh-oh.*

"Tell me." It sounded like a command.

J.J. tucked her concerns away and recounted her list of suspects. "To date, the suspects are Candy Fleetwood, Gina Marcotti, Kevin Lonsdale, Hank Ransom, and Don Kelland." Then she went through her list of reasons for crossing each of them off that list.

"You see? Not one of them holds up to scrutiny." She stifled a sigh. No need to get melodramatic.

"Well, I might start by pointing out that it's not your problem. What's more important is who the police have on their list."

"Probably Rocco Gates."

"I notice you still haven't added him to your list. Is that based on anything more than emotion?"

J.J. looked closely at Ness. She was hoping to read his mind. No such luck. She realized as she thought about it that Rocco also had good reasons to be struck off any suspect list.

"Yes, it is. First of all, that feud that seemed so important when the investigation started: they'd each moved on with their lives and were well past the woman they'd fought over. In fact, I've been told by more than one person that the feud was more a habit than anything serious. Secondly, Rocco's affair with Gina— Oops!"

She realized too late she'd let the cat out of the bag.

"Now that sounds promising." Ness leaned forward.

"No, no, it isn't. It's been going on a long time, so there was no need to dispose of the husband. Marcotti had his flings after all, and both Rocco and Gina were happy with the ways things were going. And you did not hear any of that from me."

Ness grinned.

"Okay. And then there's the murder weapon, the knife from Rocco's kitchen," J.J. continued. "How obvious is that? Why would he use his own knife, and worse yet, leave it there? He's not a dumb man. He does run a successful business and that requires him to be smart and clever. Anyone could have taken the knife. The back door is left open for deliveries most of the morning. Anyone who knew that routine—which is probably the same in most restaurants, I might point out, so loads of people might have known—could have snuck in."

She felt a fleeting tickle at the back of her brain but it was just that. Fleeting. Another thought took root, though. "And it just occurred to me: if the murderer did just that, could he have been trying to deliberately frame Rocco? It would make sense, wouldn't it, knowing about their history and all? That's it," she said with a little shriek. "Rather than who would want to kill Marcotti, the question should be: who would want to frame Rocco?"

"That's a very desperate action, killing someone just to get someone else in trouble. That needs rethinking. Of course, it could be a double motive— killing one and framing the other. But you may be onto something."

"Do you think the police might be seeing it that way?"

He shrugged. "I have no idea, but maybe I'll mosey on down to the station tomorrow and have coffee with an old buddy."

"That would be great, Ness."

"No promises, and just remember, you might not like what you hear."

CHAPTER 36

Find out who was trying to frame Rocco. That was the key to the puzzle. J.J. couldn't believe she hadn't thought of that sooner. Why else would someone steal one of his knives? It had to be someone who knew about restaurant routines, the time the staff started arriving, and the fact that the back door would be open for deliveries all morning. Did all restaurants operate that way? Question number one.

J.J. pulled the leopard-print cotton nightgown on over her head and continued her train of thought while she brushed her teeth and finished getting ready for bed.

Who knew specifically about Rocco G's? Hank, of course, but he was off the hook, for the Marcotti murder anyway. What about Zoe? She was there every weekday for a few hours. Could she have a motive? J.J. hoped not because she liked Zoe; that's why she'd never considered her before. Same reason she didn't believe it was Rocco. She'd never make it as a real detective. But she needed to have a chat with Zoe. Maybe she had some ideas.

What about Kevin Lonsdale? He'd been rumored to be leaving Bella Luna, but J.J. had gone along with Gina Marcotti's notion that it wouldn't be a strong enough motive for murder. But what if Marcotti actually found proof that Lonsdale was stealing recipes? They fought and later that night, or rather early the next morning, Lonsdale killed him to keep him from ruining his reputation. That would work. The only problem was how would he have one of Rocco's knives unless it was premeditated? Maybe there was no connection after all.

One thing she did know: it had to be someone who was aware of the ongoing feud between the two. The police had to have a reason to look at Rocco in the first place. And she had to visit Lonsdale again.

She could check in on both Zoe and Lonsdale tomorrow, right after meeting with Olivia Barker to explain a few things while not getting into others and walk away with a signed contract.

Olivia Barker sat back in her chair reading the material J.J. had just handed her. The morning sun shone through the huge window, giving a sparkling sheen to her desktop. The parts not covered with paper, that is.

When she finished, she shoved her purple-framed reading glasses up on her forehead, a move that J.J. was certain she did without thinking many times during the day. With her hair pushed back, her face looked thinner, her coloring an even paler shade of pale. Of course, it could have been the color of her fuchsia blouse that framed her chin. Whatever the reason, J.J. thought Olivia Barker looked poised and every bit the successful businesswoman.

Olivia looked down at the papers again and then focused on J.J. "I like what I'm reading here, J.J. This new idea will work in perfectly, and the costing certainly fits the budget." She sat forward and folded her hands on her desk. "Now, I'd like to know what's going on."

J.J. felt cornered. She had hoped Barker wouldn't want any other details.

"Listen, I got an e-mail from Ms. Rose this morning stating she was pulling out, and I saw your reaction when you heard about the almost-duplicate proposals," Barker continued. "Do you want to fill me in?"

J.J. shook her head. "I'd rather not. It's all been straightened out and I'd like to leave it at that, if you don't mind."

Barker watched her a few moments, then spoke. "In that case, we will. I admire your discretion and I'm very happy with what you've shown me. So I'll sign the contract and have it couriered to your office this afternoon. Right now, I have a board meeting to attend. So if you'll excuse me?"

They shook hands and J.J. left, relieved at the outcome. The assistant looked up at her as she left, right hand hovering above the box of Godiva chocolates that J.J. had brought for her. She smiled and licked her lips. J.J. gave her a quick wave. She couldn't wait to tell Skye.

After she'd finished explaining and they'd both done a little jig of joy, J.J. asked Skye, "Do you need me for the next little while? I have to go check on something."

"Not that I know of. But Nick gave me a couple of names of webmasters, and I think we should take a look at their work when you get back. Or even tonight, if you're not busy. Maybe we can make some decisions. What do you think?" Skye sat down again at her desk and took a sip from her coffee mug.

"Good idea. The sooner the better." J.J. grabbed her jacket but paused before putting it on. "You know, I feel a bit sorry for Brittany, now that it's all worked out."

"I do, too. I've been thinking about her all morning, but I don't believe that giving her another chance is to any of our benefits. She has to learn that once trust is broken, it may not be that easy to rebuild. I know I would not feel comfortable having her work here again."

J.J. shrugged. "Okay. We'll check out those names as soon as I get back, sometime this afternoon."

Skye gave her a salute and then went back to focusing on her computer screen.

J.J. debated about whom to visit first as she made her way to her car parked in the back lot. She could walk to Rocco G's, but maybe she'd drive and start at Bella Luna, and then finish with a light lunch while talking to Zoe. She pulled into the restaurant parking lot and hoped one of the two cars sitting there belonged to Kevin Lonsdale.

The front door to the restaurant was unlocked, even though they wouldn't be serving for another hour. She called out as she went inside and waited at the hostess desk. After a few moments, Lucy came out of the kitchen.

"Ah, Ms. Tanner. Again. You're too early for lunch, you know."

"I know. I was just hoping I might have a quick talk with the chef. I realize he's probably really busy with preparations, but it won't take long."

"I'll ask him." She disappeared back the way she'd come but came back quickly.

"He's far too busy. I'm sorry. He asked instead that you come back when things ease up after the lunch crowd. Mrs. Marcotti has asked that we give you our full cooperation, so he's trying."

"All right. Thanks." J.J. turned to leave but looked back.

Something was nagging at her. It was like walking into a room and forgetting what you'd gone in for. Except she'd had no idea of looking for something when she'd gone to the restaurant. Only of questions to ask.

J.J. went out to her car, her mind racing. What was bothering her? She hoped it would come to her eventually. She started the car and pulled out of the lot, stopping at the four-way stop at the corner. She had a suspicion.

She had to get into Marcotti's office one more time. She knew she couldn't just do it on her own. Or could she? Maybe she'd better give Devine a call. She punched in his number, but the call went to voice mail. She hesitated. What would she tell him? What if her suspicions were wrong? Okay, she'd already been wrong plenty of times. But she couldn't go accusing someone of murder without more than a vague memory. She compromised and left him a message. She told him what she wanted to do and asked him to call.

So, a plan. She already knew the office wasn't locked, and when the restaurant was open, most of the staff were occupied and not likely to walk into the hallway that led to the office. But how to get into the restaurant without being noticed? She didn't have a clue. Maybe she should call Gina Marcotti and, without revealing her suspicions, ask if they could go to the office again.

That would have to do. She turned the corner and pulled over. She'd didn't have the number handy, but she used her smartphone to find it, and called. She sat with fingers crossed while it rang. Finally, when she was just about ready to give up, a breathless Gina answered.

"Yes? This is Gina Marcotti. Who is this?"

After explaining as best she could, J.J. waited for an answer.

"All right. It will have to wait until this evening, though. I'm just on my way to an afternoon appointment that will take several hours. I will be at the restaurant tonight for the evening service. Come when you are ready."

That gave J.J. time to drive over to Rocco G's and talk to Zoe, but she was pretty certain it would be a waste. Even more so when, upon arriving, she found out that Zoe had stayed home to care for a sick child. Rocco asked if he could do anything for her.

"Not really. I was sorry about Hank Ransom, though. What are you going to do for a cook?"

"I already have one. There are a lot of people looking for jobs these days, many of them with excellent credentials. In fact, I hired my first female chef on the weekend. Now, I am not a sexist, so don't look like that. The need for a cook and someone of that persuasion with the right qualifications had never before occurred at the same time." He chuckled. "Come back by the end of the week for lunch on the house. She is creating an entire new menu for me."

He sighed and ran a hand through his hair. "It came as quite a shock, though. The police told me what he'd done." He shook his head. "I had no idea. But when I think, what if it had happened here? Then I really start to shake. What if I had hired a killer?"

J.J. reached out and touched his arm. "Fortunately, that didn't happen. And now that he's in custody, it won't. You can't let yourself dwell on it."

"I know. I know. But it is good to hear someone else say it, too. Thank you, *cara*. Now, let me make you a cappuccino to delight you."

CHAPTER 37

At eight o'clock, J.J. was once again parking in the lot at Bella Luna. She'd hoped to appear when the restaurant was still busy enough so that she didn't attract too much attention but also at a time when Gina would be able to help her. She still hadn't heard from Devine and wondered what that meant, if anything.

"All right. Let's hope whatever you're doing will bring this to a close," Gina said after she'd met J.J. at the door. Fortunately, she'd been standing at the hostess desk flipping through the bookings for the next day.

Lucy spotted them the minute they started walking to the back and hurried over to them.

"I won't be long, Lucy," Gina said. "We just need something out of the office." She continued to walk in that direction with J.J. close behind.

Once inside, Gina asked, "All right. You have my attention. What is it we're here for?"

"That photo that Devine and I came across the other day. We put it back, but I need to take another look at it." She walked over and removed the wooden divider from between two of the shelves and pulled the photo out of its hiding place. She turned on the desk lamp and held it under the light, taking a closer look. Gina approached and looked over her shoulder.

"Tonio was certainly dashing, wouldn't you say?" Her voice sounded wistful. "What are you looking for?"

"Take another look at the woman. Does she remind you of someone?"

Gina took it and peered closely. "No. I don't think so. Well, maybe she does look a little familiar. You know, I think she looks a bit like Lucy, doesn't she? But that's the Italian coloring. Same nose, too."

The door to the office flew open and Lucy slid in, closing it behind her. She held a knife in her left hand, a box of plastic wrap in the other. "I knew it was just a matter of time before that came out. I should have destroyed that when I first found it."

J.J. couldn't take her eyes off the knife. Had Lucy been in the middle of slicing something when she decided to find out what they were up to? Obviously, she'd been listening at the door.

"Who is the woman, Lucy?" J.J. asked, holding the photo out to her. "Is it someone related to you?"

Lucy looked from one to the other, her eyes unreadable. "That picture is of my mama and papa."

Gina gasped. "No, it can't be. Tonio would have told me."

"She's the woman that Marcotti and Rocco Gates had the argument over back in Italy, isn't she?" J.J. asked. "And to the day Mr. Marcotti died, they never fixed it. Nobody apologized. What makes you think he's your father?"

Lucy nodded vigorously. "My mama admitted it just before she died. She said they would have married if it hadn't been for Rocco Gates. He was also in love with her and fought

Antonio for her hand. When neither won, they both agreed to leave the village. Only my mama was pregnant with me. She felt so shamed, she left and went to find work in Florence. She had me and eventually remarried, but it wasn't a happy life for her. I ran away when her husband tried to attack me. I spent many years on the street and then living from job to job, moving around until I finally decided to come here and start a new life."

"Did you come here deliberately looking for Marcotti? How did you know where to find him?"

"He was the talk of the village. Him and Rocco Gates, both. Big men in the restaurant business in Vermont, the United States of America," she spat out. J.J. could see the hatred in her eyes.

"I heard about them when I went back for my mama's funeral."

"Why did you want Rocco to be blamed for the death?" J.J. asked.

"It was his fault that my mama was left all alone. One should die, the other should pay."

J.J. considered what she'd heard. "When did you first see this picture? It took me a couple of tries but I eventually twigged that there was a connection to you. Surely Mr. Marcotti would have realized it when he first saw you. When was that? Just after you started working here? Or maybe he didn't figure it out until sometime more recent?"

Keep her talking. That was J.J.'s only plan at the moment. Maybe Devine was on his way.

Lucy snorted. "He said I looked like someone he once knew, but I played dumb. He even asked if I was from his village and I said no. He left it at that until one day, I was bringing the menu in to him for his approval, and he was sitting there in his chair looking at the picture. He showed it to me and asked if I knew her. I was careful not to show any emotion, but I said to him I didn't know her. Then I left quickly before he could talk more. He never asked me about it again. Men can be so gullible."

Gina straightened her back. "What are you planning to do with us?"

"I haven't had a chance to think about that. I got worried when this one started asking me so many questions the other day. I wondered if she'd found the picture and figured it out. I know she's been busy digging into it all and she wouldn't even be scared off."

J.J. gasped. "Was it you who tried to run me down?"

Lucy sneered. "It was. Kevin had used his wife's van one day, and I borrowed it while he was busy. He didn't even know. It was easy to just take the keys from the pocket of his jacket hanging next to the back door."

"And when you saw us going into the office, what did you think?" J.J. asked, but she knew the answer. Her eyes scanned every surface she could see looking for a weapon without being too obvious about it.

"I knew something was up when you both went into the office, so I got this knife from the kitchen." She pointed it at them and then admired it at different angles. "The knife worked well last time. But it's not a good time to do this, and besides, more deaths by knife might be harder to explain." She raised the roll of plastic wrap in her left hand.

"For now, I will tie you both up and lock you in this room. Have you ever tried to remove this wrap from a sandwich? Not easy to do." She chuckled, sounding quite cold and sane. Not at all a crazed murderer. That scared J.J. even more.

"No one has a need to come in here. I will lock the door just to be sure, and after the restaurant closes later tonight, I will move you into the freezer. Someone will find you eventually. Now, you, Ms. Tanner, sit and put your hands behind you. Mrs. Marcotti will secure your wrists with this plastic wrap. And then I will take care of you. If you try anything, the other will die. That goes for both of you. Do we understand each other?"

They both nodded. J.J. tried holding her wrists a bit apart while Gina wrapped the wrap around them, hoping she could figure a way out eventually. Each ankle was also secured to a chair leg. Then Lucy did the same to Gina.

"You won't get away with it," J.J. said, knowing how lame it sounded. "I'm not the only one who has seen that picture."

Gina added, "They'll know it wasn't an accident. There's a safety release inside the freezer door in case it closes when someone's inside."

"I will attend to that. And, it doesn't really matter anyway. By the time you two are found, I'll be out of the country and there won't be anything to tie me to all of this. Now, to ensure this goes as planned, the final touch: some plastic wrap to the mouth."

Again, J.J. tried for a little space, holding her mouth open slightly while being gagged.

"You have only a few hours to wait. I'll be back to get you later." Lucy turned off the light and closed the door behind her. They could hear the key being turned in the lock. Fortunately, she hadn't thought to turn off the desk lamp.

Gina looked panicked for a moment, and then she closed her eyes and started deep breathing. J.J. thought that looked like a good idea and tried the same. When she felt calmer, she sat looking around the office as best she could, trying to spot something that might give her an idea.

She tried separating her wrists, but the plastic wrap held them securely. Same with her ankles. The only thing she could think of was to keep worrying them, moving her extremities as much as she could to try to loosen the wrap. She noticed that Gina, after watching for a few moments, was doing the same.

She wondered if Devine might come looking for her after

getting her message, but she hadn't told him where she was going tonight. Skye had said she'd call later with some more ideas she had, but J.J. doubted she'd be concerned if there was no answer. And it was unlikely that anyone would just wander into the office and find them tied up. Not with the door locked. She tried making some sounds with her mouth, which she doubted would reach outside the room, and if they did, might just bring Lucy back inside. Not a good plan. The same thing might happen if she tried moving her chair around on the hard-wood floor.

After about fifteen minutes she decided to give it all a rest. Gina had done just that quite some time before. J.J. looked closely at her, suddenly worried about her health. Gina wasn't that young anymore. She had to be in her sixties at least. What if the stress caused a stroke or a heart attack? Another thing to worry about.

The more she thought about it all, the more she hoped Lucy would reconsider her threats. Killing one person and framing another, when you had what you believed was a jus-tifiable motive, was one thing. Killing two innocent bystand-ers was another. Surely no one in her right mind would do that. Couldn't she just leave them in the office overnight and make her getaway?

That was it. J.J. would have to convince Lucy to do just that, if Lucy would remove the wrap that covered her mouth long enough for her to talk. J.J. could live with Lucy getting away, as long as she and Gina kept on breathing.

But who knew? What a powerful hatred Lucy must have been feeling all those years to track these two men down and devise such a plot. It might have worked, too. No one would have suspected her if it weren't for the old photo. How could Lucy possibly think her life would be different with them disposed of? Yet how miserable her life must have been to this point, with revenge as her focus.

J.J. closed her eyes and tried to clear her mind again. *Think. There must be some way out of this.*

She needed some way to get out of the wrap. *Done in by plastic wrap. Not what I want as an epitaph.* And she didn't even claim to be handy in the kitchen. She looked around again, trying to see as much of the office as she could. Was there a sharp edge somewhere within reach? That usually worked in the movies. She couldn't spot anything, but maybe if she looked closely with a more open mind. *Think outside the box, girl.* Aha. There was something. It looked like the end of a box cutter sticking out from under the picture. The one they'd used the other day.

The desk might be a bit too tall for her to get her hands up to, but she had to try. She started by edging the chair over to the desk, stopping after each scraping sound to listen for footsteps in the hall. It seemed to take forever, but once she reached it, J.J. found she could just manage to touch the edge of the box cutter. Grabbing it seemed out of the question, though. She saw that Gina looked alert again and was watching her closely. That was good.

She'd managed to loosen the wrap only slightly, but she found it did allow her to twist her hands so that her fingers were touching. After about ten minutes of concentrated effort, she pulled the box cutter to the edge of the desk and maneuvered it into her hand. She carefully slid it open. *Just don't slice a vein.*

Gina, in the meantime, had managed to get her chair over also and offered her wrists.

J.J. shook her head. At least with trying to cut through the wrap on her own wrists, she knew where her arms and hands were. They heard a noise in the hall and both stared at the door, eyes wide, breathing shallow. When nothing happened, J.J. went back at the slicing.

Finally. She felt one strand of wrap give way, and she

carefully placed the box cutter back on the desk. She worked her hands and wrists until they were eventually free. She held them up to Gina, who had tears in her eyes.

After cutting through the wrap around her ankles and, finally, her mouth, J.J. then totally freed Gina. They hugged each other and then took deep breaths.

"You call the police," J.J. whispered, pointing to the phone. Gina nodded.

J.J. walked to the door and placed her ear against it, listening in case Lucy should come in unexpectedly. She thought she heard footsteps and gestured to Gina to be quiet.

Gina had just hung up the phone, and she whispered, "They're already on their way."

That surprised J.J., but before she had time to think about it, she realized it was definitely footsteps that she heard. She looked at the bookcase and grabbed a bookend in the shape of Italy, which turned out to be solid brass and very heavy. She quickly stepped to the other side of the door, her back against the wall, weapon raised above her head.

The door flew open and J.J. took aim, bumping against the bookcase. Two hands shot up and grabbed her arms in midair.

J.J. shrieked.

"What the . . . ?" Devine shouted.

"Thank goodness," Gina whispered.

When Devine had slowly lowered J.J.'s hand and taken the bookend from her grasp, he said, "Close call, babe. Are you all right?"

She nodded, unable to find her voice.

He flicked on the light and looked over at Gina. "How about you, Gina?"

"I'm fine, thanks to J.J. She was able to get us out of our bindings."

He smiled at J.J. "For some reason that doesn't surprise me."

"What are you doing here?" J.J. asked, finally able to get the words out. She slumped back against the bookcase.

"I got your message and couldn't track you down, so I figured you might be here. I called Hastings and we arrived at the same time. They've taken Lucy into custody."

"But how did you know it was her?"

"Your message said you wanted to check the photo again before confronting her. How many females are there in the restaurant? Not that many, and Lucy was the only one you'd questioned." He grinned at Gina. "I knew it couldn't be Gina."

She smiled back at him a bit shakily.

"What's the story?" he asked J.J. "Is Lucy related to the woman in the photo? Did you find a similarity and that's what brought you back?"

Gina had pulled a bottle of cognac and three glasses out of a desk drawer and poured them each a drink, which she passed over to J.J. and Devine.

J.J. gratefully accepted and took a small sip. The burning as it made its way down her throat felt bracing. "It's funny it didn't click the last time we were here. We actually talked to Lucy after searching the office, remember? I guess I was too focused on the questions and all those other leads. I'd thought the picture reminded me of somebody but then forgot about it. But it came back to me this morning when I stopped by to talk to Kevin Lonsdale. Just the angle of Lucy's face, I guess, tickled at my brain, and after I left, it came to me. Well, it didn't all come to me. I just thought she looked a lot like the woman in the photo."

"And you didn't think it would make her suspicious, your coming back like that?"

"I guess I hadn't really connected her as being the killer, only the fact that she might be tied in some way to the photo. Pretty dumb, I guess."

Devine sighed and put an arm around her shoulder. "No,

not dumb, but you're very lucky. And very ingenious," he added, nodding at the plastic wrap piled on the desk and the box cutter on top of it all.

J.J. suddenly felt totally exhausted. She would have liked nothing better than to curl up on the floor and take a nap. But Detective Hastings entered the room and asked her to go through the entire scenario once again. By this time, Gina had started on a second glass of cognac and wasn't able to add too much to the telling.

"I'll need you both to come down to the station tomorrow and give your statements."

J.J. nodded, as did Gina.

"Why don't you both go home now and get some rest," he added, sounding sympathetic, or so J.J. thought.

Gina stood and reached out to hang on to the edge of the desk. "I should stay here for the closing up."

Devine looked at her. "I'm sure they can handle it on their own. I'll drive you both home and tomorrow you can collect your cars." He walked over to Gina and held out his arm. He grabbed J.J.'s hand as they made their way to the door.

CHAPTER 38

Another Sunday, another gathering of the Culinary Capers, only this time it was for a special luncheon that J.J. had decided to host at the last minute. She had to admit it was a combination of her cooking success earlier in the month that had really boosted her self-confidence, and a celebration of having all the angst and stress of the past month ended with the arrest of the murderer.

The doorbell rang and J.J. glanced at the clock on her way to the door. Right on time. It must be Evan.

"J.J., for you," he said with a quick hug and a flourish of his arm, which held a bottle of red wine.

Alison peeked around him and stuck out her hand, which also held a wine bag. Alison and J.J. hugged, and J.J. hung their jackets while they made their way into the living room.

"I'm glad you were able to come," J.J. said as she joined them.

"How are you, J.J.?" Alison asked. "Life back to normal after your run-in with the murderer?"

"I'll say. I don't think I'll ever get involved in a murder investigation again. Hopefully, never with a murder, either. I've learned my lesson." She quickly crossed her heart and heaved a huge sigh.

"You were really lucky, you know." Alison stood with her hands on her hips. "Detective Hashtag almost had a bird, so I hear, when he found out you'd nailed the case. He has quite an arsenal of descriptive words, although anything said with a Brit accent sounds quite tame, I think. You know, he was equally upset that you'd put yourself in jeopardy. He really is quite a nice guy."

"Yes, I do know that I'm lucky, Alison. And I'm sure Hastings is a nice guy. It just hasn't been the appropriate conditions for me to find that out." She grinned.

The doorbell rang again, followed by the sounds of Beth and Connor letting themselves in. Within minutes, they were all seated in the living room nibbling on plates of buffalo mozzarella with chunks of focaccia that J.J. had set out, and with mimosas in hand, courtesy of Evan, who did the honors and poured.

"Here's to our hostess," Connor said, his glass raised in a toast.

"To Culinary Capers," J.J. countered.

"I am so glad everything is back to normal around here," Beth said, "although I must admit I enjoyed our little tête-à-têtes over coffee as J.J. played investigator."

Evan moaned. "Oh boy. I also hope we never go through anything like that again."

Connor reached over and squeezed J.J.'s hand. Alison noticed and winked at J.J., but she pretended not to notice. Connor's touch felt good—reassuring, but in a companionable way. That thought momentarily depressed J.J. as she realized she was longing for some sparks somewhere in her life. Not here, though.

She smiled at him and then asked Alison what would happen to Lucy.

"There's no hope of her getting out on bail, but I understand Gina Marcotti has hired a top-notch lawyer for her."

"Gina?" That was a surprise, although the more she thought about it, maybe not. Gina was a kind person, and although it was her husband who had been killed, it seemed that Gina could understand what lay at the bottom of it. Of course, perhaps her attachment to Rocco had something to do with it. J.J. had been planning to stop by and talk to him, but she never seemed to get around to it. Maybe because she wasn't really sure what to say.

"Uh-huh," Alison continued. "It surprised everyone."

"I still can't get over how Marcotti didn't see the same resemblance when looking at the photograph," Evan said, shaking his head. "After all, you caught it and you're not even related."

"I don't know. We'll probably never know now that he's dead. Either he was so fixated on the people in that photo—as they had been, and in no way did it intrude into the present—or who knows? He may have had an inkling but didn't want to disturb the status quo, or else he might have been waiting for Lucy to say something." J.J. sighed.

"If she's been hanging around there that long, what was it that caused her to make a move that night?" Connor asked.

"That's something the police asked. Devine said she heard Marcotti in his office speaking on the phone to someone who wasn't his wife. Candy Fleetwood. Lucy got furious that he was again treating a woman so shabbily—namely Gina, whom she likes. She'd taken the knife sometime earlier from Rocco's because it always was her plan to frame him. She went to the Portovino estate, leaving her car outside the gated area, and waited for him to leave. Or in this case, waited for me to leave, and then stabbed him. She was able to walk away without being seen."

Connor let out a low whistle. "She's one very cold-blooded woman."

J.J. nodded. "She was obsessed by the past. It's such a sad story, all of it. I'm just glad it's over. I hope I don't have to give it another thought ever again."

Evan jumped in. "Well then, let's get focused on the matter at hand. J.J., you continue to surprise and delight us. Not one but two culinary pursuits in one month."

J.J. felt her cheeks turning red. "It's my pleasure. After all, you've lived through two of my main meals, and you've all been really supportive and helpful through all this. It's the least I could do. I used *nigellissima* once again. And I have to share my secret." She looked at each of them in turn, ramping up the suspense. "I really enjoyed preparing all of it."

Beth and Evan clapped while Connor whistled. Alison gave her a high five.

"All right, without further ado, the table is waiting. And on the menu: chili crab risotto, cherry tomatoes with olives, and roasted red onions with basil. I have to admit, though, that I caved and the dessert comes from Gelato Heaven. I'm not quite ready to tackle the sweet stuff yet."

Beth patted her arm on the way to the table. "One course at a time."

They all took a seat while Connor poured from the bottle of Soave Classico. After passing all the dishes around, J.J. took a minute to watch her friends enjoying their food.

This is what it's all about.

CHAPTER 39

J.J. took a deep breath and pushed open the door to Rocco G's. She saw him immediately, talking to a customer over in the olive oil section. Zoe was behind the counter and gave her a big smile.

When Rocco had finished, he seemed surprised to see J.J. and his expression turned to a look of pleasure as he gave her a big hug. "It's a so good to see you. I thought you were maybe avoiding Rocco."

Bingo. "Not so. It's been really hectic lately, and then I went home for a visit over Easter, but I couldn't wait any longer. How are you doing?"

He gently took hold of her arm and steered her over to a table in the far corner, holding up two fingers to Zoe at the same time. When they were seated, he looked around the bistro. "You know, I value every day I am able to come here. It has become all the more precious to me after everything that's gone on."

Zoe delivered two espressos with a biscotti tucked onto each saucer. They both took a sip before Rocco continued.

"I feel so heartbroken about Lucy. To think that girl has harbored such pain and hateful thoughts for so long. It has ruined her life. And to think that Antonio and I were to blame. Such foolish young men."

J.J. put her hand on his. "You were not to blame. Nor was Marcotti. Neither of you knew when you left that Lucy's mother was pregnant. You are an honorable man, as was Marcotti, I'll bet—at that time anyway. It's very sad, but that's just the way things worked out."

He nodded. "You are right, but it is still hurtful to think of the role I played." He took a deep breath. "Now, the best thing I can do is to live a good life for however long I have. I will try as much as is in my power to help others."

J.J. smiled. "Sounds like a good plan."

"And for starters, I would be happy if you had a few hours to spare some afternoon, and I will show you all these new vinegars I have imported. I thought it was time to expand the business a little. You will find some of the thicker balsamic a perfect touch for many Italian dishes. I'd be happy to have you do a taste testing."

J.J. laughed. "Sounds like something I should know about."

The bell above the door sounded, and J.J. looked over to see Ty Devine strolling in. He headed straight for the two of them. She felt a bit flustered and tried to calm down without being too obvious about it. She hadn't seen him, either, since that night, and she thought he looked even more dangerous than ever, in a desirable sort of way. His jeans were snug in the right places and the sleeves were rolled up on the light blue shirt he wore. She wondered if he'd left his jacket in the car, because she sure felt it was too chilly to go wandering around without one. *What does it matter?*

Devine pulled over a chair and asked if he could join them. Rocco signaled for another espresso.

"What brings you here today?" Rocco asked, a twinkle in his eye. "I thought you'd stocked up on cooking supplies yesterday."

"I thought I had everything but wanted to be sure." Devine waited until the espresso had been placed in front of him before continuing. "How are you, J.J.?" His deep blue eyes searched her face as if he might not really trust her words.

"I'm just great. Work is busy, I'm actually enjoying my mornings at the fitness center, and I've turned over a new leaf."

Both men looked at her questioningly.

"I vow to never again get involved in a murder investigation."

Devine burst out laughing. "It took you long enough to get to that conclusion."

J.J. tried for a regal facial expression. "Everything in its time."

"That's what I always say." He smiled at her.

Rocco asked, "Would you like another espresso, J.J.?"

She shook her head, still looking at Devine, enjoying the view. *Foolish woman.*

"I'd better get back to doing some work. Sit, enjoy. Thank you both for coming to see me," he added as he left the table, chuckling.

"I have a question for you," J.J. said.

"All right." Devine sounded a bit hesitant.

"How much had you already figured out before I left you the message about going to Bella Luna?"

Devine gave her a slow smile. She felt decidedly unnerved by it.

"I'd eliminated everyone with an obvious motive, namely anyone who hated the guy, so I figured it might be someone trying to kill two birds with one stone. Nail Marcotti and frame Gates. The only thing they had in common—besides their places of business, which really weren't in competition with each other—was that long-standing feud. As soon as you mentioned going back for the photo, it dawned on me, or at least I started wondering if anyone close to Marcotti had ties to the woman they'd fought over."

"Did you think it was Lucy?"

"Does it matter?"

"Well, yes, sort of. I keep wondering why Marcotti didn't realize how much Lucy looked like her mother, and also why it took me so long to click on it."

Devine shrugged. "I'll admit, it didn't come to me right away, either. Probably because there was so much else happening with the case, and that photo, which we'd seen briefly and only once, sort of got lost in it all. As for Marcotti, sometimes we see what we want to see, and sometimes we don't. Does that answer your question?"

"It'll do."

"It is over, you know. Time to put it behind you and focus on other things, like work or play." He grinned as he said it. She tried to ignore the slight flutter she felt. *How silly is this?*

"So, are you hot on the trail of another case?" she asked, redirecting the conversation.

"I'm always working multiple cases. That's the only way this PI thing works as a moneymaker. And I do need money to put food on the table." He smiled again. "It also allows me to take guests out to dinner. Speaking of which, would you like to go out this Saturday night?"

J.J. hesitated. She'd been taken off guard. If she were truthful with herself, she'd admit she had wondered what it would be like to go out on a date with Devine. However, she couldn't quite reconcile that thought with her original image of him, even though it had been changing over the few weeks they'd known each other.

Imperious was one word that came to mind. *Pig-headed*, another. *Egocentric*.

Not her type at all.

She thought of that kiss. She looked at him. He was smiling. Was he thinking of the same thing?

Recipes

Antipasto

J.J.'s motto is, "Keep it simple." This easy-to-assemble menu highlights the delightful flavor of buffalo mozzarella and the fresh Focaccia. Vary amounts according to how many friends will be enjoying it with you.

- Buffalo mozzarella
- Prosciutto slices
- Mortadella slices
- Fresh figs, sliced in half
- Grape tomatoes
- Black olive tapenade
- Greek-style plain yogurt
- Focaccia bread

Slice mozzarella cheese into bite-sized portions. Slice fresh Focaccia to accommodate mozzarella. Place figs and grapes on a serving dish, along with the prosciutto and mortadella. Serve tapenade and yogurt in individual small bowls. Invite guests to combine as desired.

Spaghetti with Chicken, Broccoli, and Sweet Red Pepper

This is one of J.J.'s very few concoctions that she threw together. It's easy to prepare and the amounts can be adjusted according to how many servings are needed. You'll notice she's using one of her flavored olive oil finds from Rocco G's. Feel free to substitute your own choice.

- ½ pound spaghetti
- Himalayan salt—pinch
- Regular olive oil
- 1 large broccoli crown, cut into tiny floret portions
- 1 sweet red pepper, sliced and diced
- 1 garlic clove, slivered
- Mixed dried herbs (or fresh rosemary, basil, oregano)
- Freshly ground pepper
- Half package of frozen chicken strips
- Tuscan herb–flavored virgin olive oil
- Pecorino Romano cheese

Bring large pot of water to boil and add a pinch of sea salt and spaghetti. Cook uncovered, as per instructions on package, usually 10–12 minutes.

Heat skillet on stove and pour in enough regular olive oil to cover the bottom. Add the broccoli bits, sliced red pepper, herbs (either dried or fresh), and garlic. Saute until broccoli look crisp. Remove from pan, add more olive oil and the desired amount of chicken strips. Cook until thoroughly heated (if frozen) or until cooked throughout (if fresh). Add vegetable mixture and toss.

Drain spaghetti when al dente, place in a serving dish, and stir in Tuscan herb–flavored virgin olive oil. Add chicken/vegetable mixture and toss.

Serve with grated fresh Pecorino Romano cheese atop. Adjust cheese and seasoning to taste.

ROASTED PEARS

Beth is always looking for light, healthy desserts to balance the delicious baked goods and pastries she sells in Cups 'n' Roses. Mix and match the ingredients. She's tried many combinations and these are her favorites. Enjoy!

- ∘ 3 ripe pears
- ∘ 1 tablespoon honey or maple syrup
- ∘ Zest from one large lime
- ∘ 1 cup Greek-style plain yogurt or smooth ricotta
- ∘ Seeds from one medium pomegranate
- ∘ Limoncello

Preheat oven to 375° F.

Line baking pan with parchment paper.

Halve pears lengthwise, remove stems and cores. Place pears on baking sheet, cut side up; drizzle with honey or maple syrup and sprinkle with lime zest.

Bake for 18–20 min, depending on size of pears, until softened.

When done, place portions on individual dessert plates, top with yogurt or ricotta, and sprinkle with pomegranate seeds. Drizzle with Limoncello to taste.

Keep reading for a special preview of
Linda Wiken's next Dinner Club Mystery. . .

ROUX THE DAY

Coming soon from Berkley Prime Crime!

"What's the worst that can happen? Another dead body?"

J.J. Tanner stared at her best friend and business partner, Skye, with her mouth hanging open.

Words eluded her.

Skye noticed the look. "Sorry, I guess that was insensitive, given what happened after your last event. Anyway, it couldn't possibly happen again, so what's got you worried?"

"Only the fact that this is my first event for a nonprofit," J.J. answered, finding her voice. "And, I truly believe in their cause, so I'd hate to see it bomb because I forgot to do something, or even worse, made some wrong choices."

Skye flung her hands up in the air. "I hadn't realized you were so uptight about this one. Look, J.J., I've read your proposal and love the idea. You practically forced me to go through your bible for the casino night and I can attest that you've covered all the bases. This is a casino fund-raiser for the People and Causes Foundation, so any monies coming in—no matter how minuscule, if that's the unfortunate case—will make it a success in their book. And in my experience, it's hard not to make money with a casino night. Now, I'm going to take you out for a glass of wine, some free advice, and a lift home. Grab your stuff."

J.J. let out a long sigh, shut down her computer, and stuffed her makeup bag into her purse. "You've already given me a lot of free advice," she said, closing and locking the door of Make It Happen, Skye's event planning business, behind them.

"Did I say the advice is from me? No, I don't think I said who it's from. Do not assume. You know the old saying."

J.J. made a face just as Tansy Paine exited her office across the hall from them.

"Very dignified, J.J.," Tansy commented and strode ahead of them, reaching the bottom of the stairs before they started down.

"Four-inch," J.J. said.

"Uh-uh. At least six, I'd guess. One of these days the stiletto diva is going to do a nosedive down these stairs."

"You are in a morbid mood this afternoon, Skye Drake. I think I'd better buy *you* a drink."

"I was hoping it would work," Skye said as she hooked her arm through J.J.'s. They'd made it to the front door of the two-story historic house where they had their office, along with Tansy Paine's law office, when the door to the right opened.

"Drinks?" Evan Thornton sang out. "Am I invited? I am, aren't I?"

"Of course." J.J. glanced at Skye, who nodded. "Are you ready, or do you want to meet us at . . . Where exactly are we going?"

Skye's eyebrows curved upward and her lips flattened out. "All will soon be revealed."

Evan caught up to them on the sidewalk as they turned left onto Gabor Avenue. He quickly linked up with J.J.'s free arm, and the three of them walked a block toward Lake Champlain and then hurriedly crossed the street at the corner of Claymore.

J.J.'s eyes lit up as they approached the outdoor patio of McCreedy's, Half Moon Bay's newest Irish pub. Beth Brickner and Alison Manovich were already seated at one of the tables and waved them over. J.J. glanced at Skye, who shrugged. "I thought you needed your friends around you at a time like this, so I gave Beth a call and she set it up. There's nothing like talking food to bring back the sanity."

J.J. smiled and squeezed Skye's hand.

"Connor's going to be late," Beth explained. "Something came up at the radio station."

At the mention of his name, J.J. felt her stomach do that flip-flop again. It wasn't that she didn't want to see him, but since she'd signed him on to be one of the emcees at the casino night, Connor Mac's name was now synonymous with her fears of a flop. Skye noticed the look on her face and quickly ordered glasses of Shiraz for them both.

"It might be hard to stay away from talk of the casino night once Connor gets here," J.J. said, "but I really hope we won't be discussing it tonight. I really need to think about something else for a while."

Skye jumped in. "And I hope you don't mind my tagging along. I promised her a drink. Or she promised me one. Anyway, we both need it about now."

"Happy to have you along, Skye." Beth grinned as she plopped a brown paper bag on the table. "Well, I thought I'd take advantage of this opportunity to do the reveal for our next supper-club night." She patted the bag. "It's this baby right here, and you'll have to wait until Connor arrives."

She smiled and tilted her glass of wine toward each of them in turn.

"Yikes. I've totally lost track of time," J.J. admitted. "When's the next dinner?"

"Three weeks from this Sunday. And you'd better remember it's at my house." Beth tapped the top of the bag again. "I think this will be a surprise and we'll have lots of fun with it."

"Are you insinuating we haven't been having fun?" Evan asked, a look of affront on his face. J.J. noticed his blue eyes twinkling and she tried to stifle a grin, waiting to see how this would play out.

Beth looked abashed. "No, of course not. I'd never suggest that." She leaned forward and squinted at Evan across the table. "Nice one, Evan. You really had me going there for a few seconds." She started laughing and they all joined in.

J.J. looked around the table at the four members of the Culinary Capers club. They all took turns hosting the monthly dinner, and that host got to choose a cookbook and the entrée. The others would bring along an accompanying dish, also from that cookbook. Evan had been the one who'd invited her to join, and now, after many months of shared meals and laughter, she considered them all to be close friends. Food could do that.

"Well, while we're waiting for Connor, can't you at least update us on the casino night?" Alison asked. "After all, you know we'll be there for you in spirit."

J.J. thought about it for a moment. *I'm just being silly.* She nodded. "As you know, it's the big fund-raiser for People and Causes, and it's in two weeks on board the *Lady of the Lake*. That's the largest cruise boat in the Crowder Sightseeing Line, so you can just imagine how cool that will be. We cast off at six thirty P.M. and return to the dock at one A.M. Besides the roulette wheel, there'll be blackjack, craps, and three-card poker. We'll serve a buffet dinner at ten P.M., and there'll be a great deejay at the back of the boat for those wanting to dance."

"Aft," Connor said, sinking into the chair beside J.J.

She looked at him.

"Aft. That's the back of the boat. Hi, everyone. Sorry I'm late. Glad you didn't wait for me." He nodded at the drinks.

J.J. took over again. "And our celebrity masters of ceremonies are our very own Connor Mac of radio WHMB morning-show fame, and TV personality Miranda Myers, host of *Tonight's Entertainment* on WBVT." She looked at Connor and noticed a flicker pass over his face, almost so fast that she wondered if she'd really seen it. And what had it meant?

Connor signaled the server and ordered a beer. "No one's ordered any food yet? Are we doing dinner or what?"

"It's my night to cook," Evan explained, "so I'm not eating. Well, maybe an appetizer."

"Okay, then let's get a variety of small dishes on the table." Connor signaled the server again and asked for one of each of the four appetizers on the menu. "I hope that's all right with everyone," he asked.

They all nodded and Alison did the equivalent of a shrug with her eyes.

"Well, I'd like to take over the floor, then, while we're all waiting," Beth said in a louder voice. The patio had filled up quickly, and with the music and conversation from other tables, it was getting hard to hear. She stared at Connor. "I'm doing the cookbook reveal tonight." She pulled a narrow but large book out of the bag. "There's nothing like a good murder to whet the appetite."

Someone gasped. J.J. realized she'd been the culprit, and she suspected that Beth was pleased with the reaction. The others chuckled and gave Beth their full attention.

"So, my choice for the next Culinary Capers dinner is the *Mystery Writers of America Cookbook*." She handed it to Connor, and he started flipping through the pages. "The recipes are contributed by some of the most dangerous crime writers in the country. And I'm hoping they're all safe to use."

She grinned, and J.J. thought it made her look so much younger than her sixty-four years. "I'm really sorry, though, J.J. There are only a few full-page color pictures. I know how much you like those, but I'm hoping you'll bear with me this one time."

J.J. tried to make it look like she was giving her answer a lot of thought. "Okay. But just this once." She smiled to show she was kidding. Sort of. "Have you chosen an entrée yet?"

"I have. I'm going to do the Chicken Gabriella, which is contributed by Sara Paretsky, one of my favorite mystery authors. And I thought it might be fun for us to each talk a bit at the dinner about the authors whose recipes we've chosen. Maybe, if everyone has the time, we could each read a book written by our author and just say a few words about it, too. I think it would be fun and a bit different. What do you all say?" She looked so expectant, and J.J. knew no one would dare to pan the idea.

"Great," Evan chimed in first. "You're right—it will be fun adding another element, and I put dibs on dessert."

"Wow, right in there. We're taking a big leap here, not having a good look at what's offered before claiming a dish, but I'll volunteer for an appetizer," Alison said, moving aside some glasses to allow the first two dishes they'd ordered to be set on the table. "Over to you, J.J."

"Hm. Maybe a side dish."

"Do we need two of those?" Connor asked. "I see they have a soups and salads section, also."

"I trust your judgment," Beth answered. "You can let me know what you think after taking a closer look at what's there."

She glanced around the table. "Thank you. I appreciate you all getting into this. I think it will be memorable and quite delicious."

Evan raised his glass in a toast. "Here's to an evening of mystery!"

ABOUT THE AUTHOR

Linda Wiken is the author of the national bestselling Ashton Corners Book Club Mysteries under the pseudonym Erika Chase, and is the former owner of a mystery bookstore. Visit lindawiken.com.